RESISTING REMOVAL

NOVELS BY COLIN MUSTFUL

Fate of the Dakota: A Novel and Resource on the U.S.
— Dakota War of 1862

Grace at Spirit Lake

Ceding Contempt: Minnesota's Most Significant Historical Event

RESOURCES BY COLIN MUSTFUL

Confronting Minnesota's Past: A Resource to Test Your
Understanding on the U.S. — Dakota War of 1862

The U.S. — Dakota War of 1862 — An online educational
course available at Udemy.com.

RESISTING REMOVAL

The Sandy Lake Tragedy of 1850

COLIN MUSTFUL

ISBN 978-1-7329508-0-1
ISBN 978-1-7329508-1-8 (ebook)

FIC014000 FICTION/Historical/General
FIC059000 FICTION/Native American & Aboriginal

Map on the front cover courtesy of the New York Public Library Digital Collections: Lionel Pincus and Princess Firyal Map Division, The New York Public Library. "Lake Superior, Missabay mountains, Chipeway country, region of rocks and water, Wisconsin Territory; top right" New York Public Library Digital Collections. Accessed October 18, 2018. http://digitalcollections.nypl.org/items/97eed7ac-6e1d-ace9-e040-e00a18061d5d.

Cover Design by Mayfly Design, mayflydesign.com.
Edited by John Haymond.
Proofread by Boyd Koehler.
Published by History Through Fiction Press

To Glenn and Sean Beggin. Two great and selfless educators. Thank you for providing me with so much.

AUTHOR'S NOTE

I am not Ojibwe. I was born at Abbott Northwestern Hospital in Minneapolis, Minnesota in June 1982 to white, working-class residents of St. Paul. My parents both grew up in South Minneapolis and met at Roosevelt High School in the 1960s. Their parents were also working class and lived in South Minneapolis—they were born here, in Minnesota. Their parents before them, my great-grandparents, came to the United States from Turkey, Germany, Ireland, and Norway. They arrived, all of them, in the late nineteenth and early twentieth centuries, long after Minnesota had already established itself as a white majority, English-speaking, agrarian society.

People often ask me "why?" "Why are you so interested in this topic?" My answer, which has become rehearsed, is simple. "I went to school in Mankato," I say. "I was shocked to learn about the hanging of the Dakota and I was surprised that I had never learned about it before. So, I started doing my own research and writing and I found out how complicated and complex it was." That is what I say.

I am not the first nor the last person to be surprised to learn that thirty-eight Dakota men were hanged in Mankato, Minnesota on December 26, 1862. Or that all Dakota and Ho-Chunk people were exiled from the state of Minnesota as a response to what is now called the U.S. - Dakota War of 1862. Or that the land we call Minnesota—the streets we drive on, the lakes we swim in, the farmland we till—was once (not so long ago) inhabited by Indigenous people before a series of treaties, corrupt dealings, death marches, massacres, assimilation policies, and other injustices stripped them of the majority of that land. I am not proud of the way Indigenous peoples have been treated throughout all of North and South American history. Neither am I proud of our history of slavery, war, bigotry, the marginalization of women, and so on. Yet, it is who we were, and it is a part of what we have become today.

Like you, I am curious. I am struck by the series of wrongs that made this country, my home, what it is today, and I am determined to learn more about what happened between white and Indigenous populations. We cannot change the wrongs of the past, but we can come to understand them—why and how they happened—and then someday move beyond such callous, selfish, and primitive thinking. Also, with new understanding, we could be committed to make reparations that deal with the injustice that has been handed down to the Native peoples of Minnesota, Wisconsin, and throughout the country. But first we must become equipped to do so—we must know what happened and why.

What follows in this novel is a literary stab from my perspective and my experience at an important and tragic series of events in American history. This is not a historical record. It is fiction based on real people, real events, and real sources. It is meant to show history through the creativity of my own mind and the knowledge of my own experience and the tools available to me as a historian. It should act as an introduction to a harsh reality that is either unknown, forgotten, or pushed aside. It should provide insight into history while inspiring further research and discussion.

For the writing of this novel, I have relied heavily on the work of Bruce White in his essay *The Regional Context of the Removal Order of 1850*. For anyone interested in learning more about the Sandy Lake Tragedy of 1850, I urge you to read this thoroughly researched, well-documented piece of scholarly work. I have also relied on a scholarly blog called *Chequamegon History* which is produced by historians Leo Filipzcak and Amorin Mello. Their work of publishing and reporting on the history of the Chequamegon region has been invaluable to me. Finally, I have relied a great deal on the memoir of Benjamin Armstrong titled, *Early Life Among the Indians: Reminiscences from the Life of Benj. G. Armstrong*. Although this is an excellent primary source on the history of the Sandy Lake Tragedy and the

Lake Superior Ojibwe at that time, it is also problematic. By his own admission, Armstrong could not correctly recollect the events of his early life. Also, it has been suggested by historians Bruce White and Charles Cleland that Armstrong may have bent the truth to glorify his own role. Nevertheless, whether truthful or not, Armstrong's account has been proliferated to such a degree that it is generally agreed upon as the true and genuine history.

Ultimately, with the writing of this novel, I encourage readers to find out more about this history. I urge readers to think critically and understand that Armstrong's account may not be exactly what happened. It is influenced by his own perspective, background, and personal motivations. It is singular, as is, unfortunately, much of our history. Although it is a cliché, history is written by the victors. It is written and perpetuated by those in authority, those with power, and those with a voice. Therefore, whether Ojibwe, white, man, or woman, I wish to empower all readers to open themselves to multiple perspectives. Read and understand history, but take it one step, two steps, or even three steps further. Who was involved and why and what were their circumstances—what was their perspective?

History is more than what we can read in documents or commemorate with stones and plaques. Rather, history is a representation of real events that have consequences that echo through the years—in politics, economics, culture, religion, etc. It influences how we relate to one another and impacts everything we are and see and do. The important thing, whether studying historical documents or considering the impact of historical events, is to be open-minded while challenging our own assumptions and prejudice.

To know history is to understand who we are today—a diverse, multicultural world all vying for fulfillment and well-being. It is no different now than it was in centuries past. Only today, we know more than we did yesterday. With our new knowledge and new perspectives, we can move toward acceptance and reconciliation—acceptance of our past and reconciliation with each other. That reconciliation might look different for each person, group, or society, but it cannot be achieved without an understanding of what brought us to where we are. This novel, along with your own personal path to discovery, will help you reach that understanding. As we move forward, together, we can create a world filled with less tragedy, strife, and injustice. We can create a culture of enrichment that values everyone's story no matter what their history.

CHAPTER 1

Tourism season had just begun and the town of Ashland, Wisconsin, was buzzing with activity. Outside, the rising sun shone brightly off the still waters of Chequamegon Bay as tourists lined the docks to board the steam-powered ferries headed for Madeline Island. Downtown, Thomas Wentworth sat quietly in his office, sipping his morning coffee and trying to ignore the increasing clamor from the horse drawn carriages and buggies on the street. A visitor walked in unexpectedly, startling Wentworth and causing him to burn his upper lip with hot coffee.

"Pardon me," the man said, removing his hat. He had a long gray and white beard and a face worn with age, but in a handsome sort of way. "Are you Thomas Wentworth of the A.W. Bowron Press?"

"Indeed I am." Wentworth put down his coffee and stood to greet the man.

"My name is Benjamin Green Armstrong and I am in need of your …" he paused, "journalistic talent."

"Armstrong? The well-known interpreter and trader from the early days?"

The old man smiled revealing his gray teeth which matched his gray beard. "That I am."

"You are a legend in this region," Wentworth said with enthusiasm. "It is an honor to meet you. How can I be of assistance?"

Armstrong motioned to the chair beside him and Wentworth nodded, inviting him to sit down.

"I believe I have a story to tell," Armstrong said. "I have seen many decades and experienced many unique and sometimes troubling events. I think it is time to share my story with the world, but I don't know how. I would like to dictate it to you, that you might write it down and distribute it."

Wentworth did not need to think on the proposal. Very little happened in Ashland in 1890 that was worth reporting and he saw this as a grand opportunity to make something extraordinary—something memorable. "Of course, Mr. Armstrong. Of course. Your story would be most compelling, and it would be my great pleasure to help you share it."

Armstrong did not immediately react. He tilted his head and eyes toward the floor and sat deep in thought. "You will write it exactly as I tell it?" he said finally.

"Exactly."

"And you can distribute it throughout the country?"

"Throughout the world," Wentworth said, followed by a large grin. "I can assure you, your story will enter the annals of history."

CHAPTER 2

The sky was a cloudless, deep blue that Benjamin had come to expect on his father's Alabama plantation. It was an ordinary day. Awake with the sun, then immediately to his chores feeding the pigs, chickens, sheep and horses. Having fed the animals, he watered the vegetable garden and raked the stables of manure, a dirty, but not altogether unsavory task.

It was the same routine every morning since he was old enough to lift a bucket of feed or drag a rake. By this time his friends were already attending school, some for many years. Benjamin longed to join them, but his father forbade it. "Your life is in the fields," his father said. "You will work this plantation as long as you live. You have no use for school."

Benjamin resented his father for this. He was a curious and smart boy with a penchant for adventure. The thought of a long life of hard, manual labor while remaining in one small corner of an ever-expanding young country seemed unbearable to him. He sought a life beyond the daily routine.

Having completed his morning chores, Benjamin set about to work Hector, his family's enormous shire, who was being trained to plow the fields. Ordinarily, his father assisted him in training the stubborn horse, but he had not yet vacated the house and Benjamin did not dare go in and wake him. So, he hitched the plow to Hector and took his spot at his rear, whip in one hand and plow handle in the other.

"Yah! Yah!" Benjamin commanded Hector to push forward, but the horse would not budge. "Yah! Yah!" he repeated, this time adding several strikes of the whip. Again and again, he urged the horse forward until his voice became raw and his shoulder began to ache. Exhausted and desperate, Benjamin decided to mount the horse. Perhaps if he could kick the great animal and pull at his mane, it might incite movement. But no matter how he kicked and pulled and shouted, the horse remained still. It wasn't easy for a ten-year-old boy to motivate a stubborn plow horse.

Overcome, Benjamin lowered his head in failure when a gust of wind swept across the farmyard kicking up dirt and debris. Benjamin raised his arm to protect his face as Hector neighed in discomfort. Behind him a decaying tree snapped. Frightened by the abrupt noise, Hector sparked to life. The horse bolted forward in panic and fear, oblivious to the small boy on his back or the plow hitched around his neck. Benjamin nearly slipped off onto the plow but managed to grab the horse's mane as he clung for dear life.

The frightened horse galloped headlong across the field, blind to any obstacles. The plow at his rear bounced and bounded off the dry, hard dirt. Benjamin watched as the wooden plow frame broke and then shattered like glass hitting the floor. He knew that if he had lost his grip, he, too, would be shattered.

Benjamin nearly panicked, but he quickly pushed aside his fear and let his experience take over. He had spent many afternoons teaching horses to trot, canter, and gallop, even training some of the wilder ones. He pulled himself upright, loosened his grip, and slowed his breathing. He knew that if he relaxed, the horse might too. But Hector continued to gallop toward no certain point, bucking and kicking. Benjamin nearly fell off and might have been crushed by the twelve-hundred-pound animal. He kept his grip with his right hand on the mane while placing his left hand on the horse's withers just above the shoulders. He then applied pressure with his fingertips letting Hector know he was there—letting Hector know there was no threat. Then he changed his rhythm to equal Hector's, moving up and down in the same pattern as the horse. He felt the horse begin to calm, but then Hector bucked aggressively, nearly tossing Benjamin's small body aside. In one final effort, Benjamin yanked back at the mane with all of his strength, acting like reigns that were not there. This distracted poor Hector, who suddenly forgot what had spooked him and he slowed to a stop.

Though relieved, Benjamin's heart was racing with both panic and exhilaration. He felt invigorated. In those few tense moments, he realized, he had never felt more alive and more free, more in control of his own destiny.

"Are you all right, son?"

Benjamin was startled by the voice of a man from just behind him. The man had come from the road, but because of Benjamin's frantic state of mind, he had not noticed his approach.

"I believe so." Benjamin looked at his arms and legs and saw no cause for alarm, then lowered himself from the horse. "I can't say the same for the plow."

The man laughed while looking back at the broken pieces of wood strewn in Hector's wake. "That was a tremendous feat the way you handled that horse. I am amazed you didn't get hurt."

"Thank you, Mister . . ."

"Thompson."

"Mister Thompson. I have grown up with horses. I know how to ride."

It was obvious to Benjamin that his new acquaintance was not from Alabama. He wore a top hat and a long, dark frock coat that cinched at the waist and extended to his calves. His boots were polished, and his pants were pressed. Benjamin looked over his shoulder to see that Thompson had been traveling in a coach pulled by several horses and driven by a chauffeur. He was a man of the city, Benjamin concluded.

"I am the owner of a horse show," Thompson said bluntly. "I'd like to employ you and your skills in my show. I can already tell that you will be one of my finest riders."

"But I have my farm work," Benjamin said. "I have to stay here and tend my duties."

"Nonsense." Thompson smiled like an undeterred salesman. "I will pay you $50 per month plus expenses. You will travel the entire country doing shows for live audiences. You will ride well-trained horses while providing joy and entertainment. Can your farm work provide that for you?"

Benjamin was intrigued. This is exactly what he'd been longing for. He hated being stuck on the farm and felt used and unappreciated. His only reluctance came from knowing he would miss his mother, but he wanted his freedom more. He wanted adventure.

"You will be a star," Thompson said. "And you will be well taken care of."

Benjamin was at a crossroads. Could he really leave his life and his family behind based on the promise of a stranger? His brother had. His brother left years ago and hadn't come back. Benjamin detested his father, the wretched man. And, in hindsight, the ride on Hector wasn't frightful; it was exhilarating. It was thrilling unlike anything he had ever experienced, and he wanted more of it.

"Come with me." Thompson paused while trying to recall the boy's name.

"Benjamin. My name is Benjamin Armstrong."

"Well then, Benjamin. What do you say? Do you want a better, more exciting life?"

Benjamin looked back at the farmhouse and the broken plow. His father had finally made his way to the porch, but he was so droopy from the night before he could barely lift his head, let alone assist with the farm duties.

"Perhaps you would like to talk it over with your father," Thompson suggested.

"No," Benjamin answered, "no I don't. I will join your show."

He decided then and there to run away with the showman. Without saying good-bye, without even packing a bag, he left to join the traveling horse show and he never looked back.

Three and a half years passed. Benjamin had become the best rider in Thompson's show, just as Thompson predicted. And Benjamin loved it. He loved his freedom, he loved the challenge and reward of skillful riding, and he loved the accolades of adoring crowds. But one day he found that he could not ride anymore. He had taken ill—very ill. He began coughing continuously, he had chills at night and he could hardly hold himself steady atop a horse. The doctors said that he had consumption and no medicine they provided could improve his condition.

"I am very sorry that you cannot ride anymore," Thompson said. "You were the most successful rider I ever had and if you are ever able to ride again, come see me and you shall have a place as long as I have a place to give anybody."

Thompson then paid Benjamin's salary, which was quite a large sum of money, and politely suggested Benjamin return home. Benjamin thanked Thompson, being truly grateful, and boarded a train for Huntsville, Alabama, barely a young man yet.

When Benjamin arrived in Huntsville, he noticed a young man on the platform who looked strangely familiar. Stepping off the train, he realized it was his long-lost brother.

"Alfred! Alfred is that you?" Benjamin called out.

The young man turned, and, seeing Benjamin, a huge smile came across his face. "Benjamin!"

The two hugged. It was a long, heartfelt embrace.

"Look at you! You have grown so big," Alfred said.

"I didn't think I would ever see you again," Benjamin said. "How did you know where to find me?"

"The Showman, Mr. Thomas tracked me down. He wrote me a letter and told me about my famous brother!"

Benjamin's smile was suddenly replaced by a fit of coughing. He leaned over and placed his hand over his mouth and could barely breath.

"Relax," Alfred said as he patted Benjamin softly on the back. "This is too much excitement in your condition. Let's get you some rest."

The two of them left the train station that day ready to start anew, but Benjamin never quite overcame his illness. Over time it grew worse. Eventually the physicians determined that it would be better for Benjamin to leave the southern climate and go either west or north if he hoped to survive his sickness.

All of this seemed so unfortunate and stressful to young Benjamin at the time. He had taken a huge risk to run away from home. But his risk worked out as he had earned notoriety and fortune as an accomplished rider. He traveled the country and loved what he did. Suddenly all of that was taken away, stripped like bark from a tree. He was sad and depressed, which only worsened his condition. But there was purpose in his adversity. Although he could not foresee it, Benjamin had embarked on a profound path.

At the advice of the physicians, Benjamin and Alfred set out west as soon as he was healthy enough to travel. They decided to make their home in St. Louis, Missouri. Benjamin's health returned slowly, though not fully. For several years they lived in St. Louis which was a burgeoning frontier town—a booming place filled with rivermen, speculators, and westward pioneers. It was a new kind of place for Benjamin without the refinements of an eastern city and without the rural hospitality of the South. St. Louis mixed a longing for exploration with a sense of chaos and Benjamin enjoyed it. But eventually, Benjamin's symptoms returned, this time worse than ever. Physicians declared that he was in the last stages of consumption and if he hoped to survive, he must go further north.

During all this time, Benjamin had heard many talks about the great Northwest country which lay up the Mississippi River several hundred miles. Army officers had often returned from this region after meeting with and negotiating treaties and boundaries with the native Indian peoples. Benjamin found this intriguing and it sparked his sense of adventure. In 1837, he learned of a great treaty, the Treaty of St. Peters they called it, which opened up millions of acres of land for settlement and timbering on the east side of the Mississippi River.

With consideration for his condition and his dire need for a change of climate, Benjamin decided that he should head for this new and wild frontier. So, he bid farewell to Alfred and his friends, unsure if he would ever see them again and boarded a steamer headed upriver for a place called Prairie du Chien.

Benjamin did not know what to expect. As far as he knew, he was headed into an endless and untamed territory. He had heard tales of wild Indians, French fur traders, Canadian voyageurs, but never met any himself. What he found when he arrived at Prairie du Chien was a busy and bustling city. Everywhere, business was being conducted, canoes and boats moved in and out of the port, and carriages crowded the streets. The city was alive. Although he had traveled much of the country, this was new—this was different. It was a foreign place marked by foreign languages and inescapable beauty. The river in that region was characterized by rocky bluffs rising straight out of the water, lined with trees of silver maple and green ash. The combination of beauty and bustle, of strange and familiar, mesmerized Benjamin. It was a place destined to thrive.

As Benjamin stepped off the boat, filled with wonder, he was also filled with uncertainty—he didn't have a plan. He looked around his new setting, and he observed trades happening between whites and Indians, between Americans and French, and people of mixed races as well. He heard languages of all sorts, several of which he could not identify. As he watched the busyness of the world around him, he stopped at the sight of a girl. She was an Indian girl. Her hair was long and dark, and it shone brilliantly in the sunlight. He tried not to stare but couldn't help himself. The girl turned and looked, and their eyes met. She smiled.

What beauty is this? he thought, as his heart jumped from within. Her radiant smile gleamed like the sun before it sets, inviting to the eye, pleasing in its brilliance. Her skin a tawny brown, flawless and inviting. Her eyes dark and piercing but filled with life.

Benjamin followed the young woman seeking to get her attention. She continued down the street, not knowing he pursued her.

"Miss. Miss," Benjamin called out. But she did not recognize his call.

"Miss. Miss," he called again, not knowing his intentions.

Suddenly she turned and there they were, face to face.

Benjamin was speechless, stunned to silence by her beauty.

"Boozhoo," Benjamin heard her say though he had no idea its meaning.

"Ah—," he stuttered like the nervous young man he was. "Hello."

She laughed, her smile shining brilliantly once more, her eyes glinting with a sparkle.

"Benjamin," he finally said, pointing to himself.

"Charlotte," she replied.

Benjamin just stared at her, not knowing what to say, hypnotized by her natural grace. It had a numbing effect upon him.

"You live here, in Prairie du Chien?" he asked after the long, awkward silence.

She did not answer but tilted her head and lowered her eyebrows quizzically. She did not speak English.

Benjamin waited, both in nervousness and thought, when suddenly she began to speak. She spoke quickly in her native language and he could not understand a single word. She was indicating that she had to go. "La Pointe" Benjamin heard her say in between the native words. But then she turned and walked away into the crowd of the market. Benjamin reached out in a futile effort to get her to reconsider, but it was too late, and she was gone.

La Pointe. Benjamin repeated this over and over in his head. This must have been the place she had come from, he thought. The place she lived.

Benjamin did not stay long at Prairie du Chien. Rather, he continued upriver to Lake St. Croix and a place called Page's Landing. The city's namesake, Mr. Page himself, was on board the boat.

"I am a lumberman," he told Benjamin in a booming, enthusiastic manner. "I was in Prairie du Chien to purchase supplies for my camp of workers."

Benjamin nodded with interest but didn't know what to say.

"You are quite a young man to be traveling alone on the frontier," Page said. "Are you looking for work in a lumber camp?"

"I don't know, exactly," Benjamin said. "I have been ill for some time now and I have come north for the fresh air."

"Is that right?" Page replied. "Well I can't have you out here alone. The frontier can be a harsh and lonely place."

Benjamin nodded again. He was not seeking charity, but he was wise enough to accept it.

"Tell you what," Page continued. "I will provide you with lumber to build a place for yourself back of Willow River, the next trading post upriver. In exchange you can work in my lumber camp. How does that sound?"

Though Benjamin still had money remaining from his days in the horse show, he knew he would need help in this new and foreign place. Reaching out to shake Page's hand he accepted the offer.

With the help of Page and a few of the lumbermen, Benjamin built a small but cozy cabin in the woods outside of town. It was secluded and comfortable and offered Benjamin a certain peace he never had before.

Though lonely out in the wilderness as he was, Benjamin's health improved rapidly. Every day he was able to run through the woods, to hunt, swim, and exercise. The air felt good in his lungs and the wilderness was invigorating. The change in climate had a tremendous effect on Benjamin's health and well-being. Still, his new life was hard. Working to cut down lumber was exhausting and dangerous work. His hands became calloused from the saw handle and his back ached from continual labor. Meanwhile, he struggled to care for himself. Hunting and fishing was difficult, and he often went without meals. But as time went on, he learned. He learned to set traps, he learned which bait was most effective to catch fish, and he planted a vegetable garden filled with potatoes, carrots, peppers, and squash.

All the while he never forgot his encounter with the young Indian woman named Charlotte. He learned from Page that La Pointe was an Indian village and trading post where the native Ojibwe lived. The Ojibwe, as he learned, were a huge Indian nation who lived along all shores of Lake Superior stretching as far as one could imagine to the north, west, and south. Although Benjamin would admit it to no one he had his sights set on La Pointe and the Ojibwe girl who consumed his mind. Toward such an endeavor he met a young man of mixed race, Ojibwe and French, and in exchange for ten muskrat pelts a week, the young man assisted Benjamin in learning the Ojibwe language.

Benjamin worked hard and practiced nearly every day. In just six months' time he was able to converse quite freely in the Ojibwe tongue. So impressed was his tutor that he began teaching Benjamin for free. Day after day passed while Benjamin's loneliness grew and his fixation with Charlotte continued. Having become fluent in her language, Benjamin decided it was time to leave. He bade farewell to Mr. Page and his lonely shanty. With only one change of clothes and a few supplies he headed north toward the great Lake Superior, toward La Pointe.

Living at Willow River had been wonderful. He learned to care for himself, to hunt and fish and work hard like he had on the farm in Alabama. But now, after conquering the fear of the frontier, he faced a new fear. He headed into the wilderness beyond the trading posts and lumber camps. He headed into an untamed world and he wasn't sure what he would find. But he was determined to do so because his heart was unsettled and unfulfilled.

––––––––––

It was a long and tedious journey. He followed an old Indian trade route, but days passed and then weeks and he saw no signs of another human being. He was in the deep woods. He had not lost his sense of direction and he knew, after so many days of traveling, that he was nearing his destination of La Pointe. But he grew tired and weak. The journey was more difficult than he expected. He ran short on supplies and he could find no wild game. Many days passed that he went without food and he hoped to fall upon the ancient Ojibwe village soon.

But then another day passed. Then another and he was still alone in the woods. He began to wonder if he was not lost. For the first time, he began to fear for his life. Benjamin grew sick and weary, often stumbling over rocks and roots. At night, he covered himself with a thick blanket but could not avoid feeling chilled. He hardly slept, and he was constantly hungry.

Then, after a month in the forest, Benjamin came upon a barn. It was the first sign of a community he had come across since leaving his shanty. Much to his dismay the barn was dilapidated—it was abandoned. The windows were broken, the wood rotting, and the paint chipped and dirty. It had not seen occupants in years. The sight of this barn, which at first gave him great hope, instead caused him a feeling of intense depression. Its rotting wood and decrepit form stood hauntingly before him, a loathsome edifice, a relic of life lived and long gone by. It was not his salvation as he had hoped. It was nothing more than a blot on the landscape.

Being too weak to continue, Benjamin sat down inside the old barn and wrapped himself in his blanket. He listened to the wind blow, the leaves rustle, and the birds chirp. It was a peaceful place—a restful place. He had accepted his circumstances, his fate. Slowly, he closed his eyes, never expecting to open them again.

Confused and quite near death, Benjamin was startled by the morning sun which pierced through the open window of the barn causing him to shield his eyes. He heard a rustling and the voices of two people speaking Ojibwe. A man knelt at his side and gave him a moist cloth to suck on. Then he forced a thick, sweet liquid, like sap, into Benjamin's mouth. In that moment of desperation, its sweetness tasted like salvation and its texture like savory comfort.

The man continued to provide him with water and food aiding Benjamin in his critical condition. After a short time, the sun lifted from within the window which allowed him to see once more. The man helping Benjamin was Ojibwe, dark-skinned and dressed in a breech cloth and leggings. Benjamin turned to view the other person who appeared only as a figure, a silhouette inside the shaded barn. But then the figure stepped forward, revealing itself like a star at twilight.

Was it her? he thought. *It can't be. My poor health has deceived me.*

They made eye contact. At first she looked concerned, worried about Benjamin's condition. But, as if recognizing him, she smiled.

It was her! Benjamin realized. Bright, beautiful, radiant smile. A smile he recognized so clearly. Suddenly, Benjamin's feelings of depression began to lift, his weariness inconsequential, his health ready to be restored. In that moment, he determined that he was motivated to live.

"I believe this man will survive." The man at Benjamin's side spoke to Charlotte, not knowing Benjamin could understand him. "His situation is urgent, but he can be nursed back to health."

"Miigwech," Benjamin muttered, having just enough energy to speak. *Thank you.*

"You speak the way of the Ojibwe?"

Benjamin nodded.

"My name is Giizhigoon and this is my sister, Charlotte."

She is not his wife!

"We are niece and nephew to the great Kechewaishke, known to the whites as Chief Buffalo. Kechewaishke is gracious and kind and he would expect us to care for you. We will nurse you back to health and once you are strong enough to walk, we will take you to our island village."

"Your island village?"

"La Pointe."

CHAPTER 3

The Speaker of the House, Joseph Furber, stood before the twenty-seven men of the Minnesota Territorial Legislature. The room was small and crowded and sunlight poured in from the dusty streets of St. Paul, Minnesota's Territorial Capital.

"Gentlemen," Speaker Furber said. "As it has been discussed, a Resolution has been prepared pertaining to the Ojibwe Indians living upon the ceded territories. I will read it for you now and a vote shall follow."

The speaker cleared his throat, looked over the assembly, and unfolded a document on the desk in front of him.

"Be it resolved by the Legislative Assembly of the Territory of Minnesota: That to ensure the security and tranquility of the white settlements in an extensive and valuable district of this Territory, the Ojibwe Indians should be removed from all lands within the Territory to which the Indian title has been extinguished; and that the privileges given to them by Article Fifth of the Treaty of July twenty ninth one thousand, eight hundred and thirty seven, with the Ojibwe Indians and Article Second of the Treaty with the Ojibwe of the Mississippi October fourth one thousand, eight hundred and forty two, be revoked."

Speaker Furber turned his eyes back to the assembly of pioneers, farmers, fur traders, missionaries, and businessmen. "All in favor say 'Ay.'"

"Ay." The entire assembly spoke in perfect unison.

"All opposed say 'Nay.'"

The speaker waited a moment, but all that could be heard was the sound of hammers and saws caused by the construction in the streets.

"The Resolution passes," Speaker Furber said. "One copy shall be transmitted by the Territorial Governor Alexander Ramsey to the Honorable Henry H. Sibley, our delegate to Congress, who will transmit it to Washington."

With that, Speaker Furber banged his gavel to initiate the next order of business.

CHAPTER 4

Beneath a makeshift tent, above a hole in the ice, Benjamin and Giizhigoon lay on their bellies peering into the dark hole. The wind howled intermittently, but the two companions were shielded from its bite. At La Pointe, and throughout the northern region, winter was a season to be survived. Survival meant food. And food meant fishing, in any season, in all seasons.

"The hard moon has just passed," Benjamin said to Giizhigoon, as he examined which wooden lure to use.

It had been five years since Giizhigoon found Benjamin in the barn and saved his life. Since that time, the two had become inseparable. Benjamin quickly learned to love and respect Giizhigoon who had nursed him back to health and took him under his wing, teaching Benjamin much about the Ojibwe culture and ways of life.

"I have barely any provisions remaining. I need to catch some fish today," Benjamin said. "I am beginning to fear I will not have enough to last until spring."

Giizhigoon was concentrating on the piece of whittled driftwood he was using as a bobber. "You are a rich trader," Giizhigoon said playfully. "You have all the food you need."

"I am not rich, nor a trader. Not yet, anyhow." Benjamin did not wish to be associated as a trader because of the reputation they had: a reputation of exploitation and wealth-seeking at the expense of the Ojibwe. "I work in the employ of a trader and I must gather and farm and fish all the same as you," Benjamin said, shimmying back and forth along the snow and ice trying to get more comfortable as he prepared to throw his line down the dark hole.

Benjamin had a good life at La Pointe. Once he had regained his health, he found work at the trading post. Quickly, he was integrated into the community as if he had been there all along. He enjoyed the changing of the seasons and the flow and pace of life. He looked forward to winter hunts and fall harvests. He relished summer dances and the spring trade. He loved the secluded nature of his island home that was also the hub and center of Ojibwe life and trade.

"There!" Giizhigoon pointed at a long, spotted fish, most likely a sturgeon. It maneuvered slowly toward the light created by the hole in the ice.

Benjamin stiffened with nervous anxiety. The sturgeon was the most prized and sacred fish. The abundance of the sturgeon meant wealth, while its scarcity meant poverty. To catch one was the ultimate goal and prize.

Giizhigoon handed his jigging stick to Benjamin as he reached for the spear. He leaned forward over the hole, left hand along the perimeter, right hand cocked and ready to strike. His thick, bearskin robe hung at his sides grazing against the compacted snow beneath him. But his eyes, his eyes told the story. They were fixed on the water below. The deep, dark hole where light danced casually down its icy edges but was quickly enveloped by the mysterious watery depths.

Giizhigoon's eyes shifted back and forth ever so slightly as he searched for some glint of the willowy, scaly fish. Closer and closer he leaned, arm taut like a band ready to snap.

Breathless, Benjamin watched.

Without even a splash Giizhigoon's spear entered the water. His left hand rose off the ice; his right hand, still clutching the spear, entered the water, but his eyes were fixed and steady. He began to lift his submerged hand slowly from the water as he shifted his feet from behind him to beneath him, counterbalancing the weight at the end of the spear.

"Oninasabii! Oninasabii!" he shouted. *Prepare the net! Prepare the net!*

Shaken from his trance, Benjamin grabbed the woven string of nettles that lay beside him. As Benjamin lowered it into the water he could see the giant fish convulsing violently but wrapped inescapably around the sharp copper tip of the spear.

"Quickly!" Giizhigoon urged, perhaps growing tired from struggling with the powerful fish.

Benjamin lowered the net in place, and together they lifted, barely able to fit their prey through the two-foot hole. Displaced lake water came bubbling out spilling at the sides of the hole, but so too did their catch—the large and ugly monster-like fish, with barbels below its mouth and boney scutes across its back—the life-giving sturgeon. No matter what happened the rest of the day, this fishing trip was a success.

Giizhigoon was more than a friend to Benjamin—more than a mentor. Giizhigoon was his brother-in-law. Two years after arriving at La Pointe, Benjamin and Charlotte were married and started a family together. It didn't happen right away. Benjamin tried onerously to gain Charlotte's attention, but his efforts went ignored. It wasn't until Giizhigoon explained that he must garner the attention of Charlotte's father if he wished to marry the young woman. And so he did. He brought baskets filled with fruits and vegetables to Charlotte's father. He brought fish and furs, he brought tools and blankets, he brought beads and moccasins, he brought everything he could think of and almost gave up hope. But one day Charlotte's father agreed that Benjamin could marry his daughter, and Charlotte agreed, too.

Benjamin and Charlotte were happy together and before long they had two young children. A girl named Marie and a boy named Samuel. A few years before, Benjamin never imagined he could be so happy and content as he was at La Pointe. But that happiness came with skepticism. He could see that life was changing—that the ways of the community were being challenged. Businessmen made their way to the island more frequently as lumber and mining companies began to spring up in nearby areas. With the businessmen arrived rumors that the government would ask the Ojibwe to remove from their island home. Every year the rumors became louder and more frequent until it seemed inevitable that the Ojibwe would be forced to give up their homes and move west.

As Benjamin and Giizhigoon returned from their fishing trip, the thought of removal weighed heavily on their minds. That day, the government agent had called a council and everyone at La Pointe was invited to attend.

"Are you nervous about the council?" Benjamin asked Giizhigoon as the two of them trudged slowly and steadily along the snow-covered path back toward the village.

Giizhigoon was silent as if he had not heard the question. He was a reflective man and Benjamin felt sympathy knowing what this council might represent for him and the La Pointe Ojibwe. Bad news was expected. The news was important to Benjamin too, since he lived there and since he had become a part of the community, but he also knew that it was all the more meaningful for those native Ojibwe who had called La Pointe home for centuries.

"Of course I am nervous," Giizhigoon finally answered. He did not change his pace nor his expression but continued to walk slowly, his head low and his shoulders slumped. "I cannot bear to leave this place. It should remain our home now and for many generations to come."

Rumors had spread that removal was imminent. They had actually been spreading for years. Promises had been made to the Ojibwe that they would not be asked to remove from La Pointe for fifty to one hundred years, but already, just a few years later it seemed that promise was about to be broken. The United States government, Benjamin concluded, was set on moving the Ojibwe west into the newly created Minnesota Territory. If that were true, it would mean heartbreak for the native Ojibwe. For Benjamin, La Pointe was not his homeland, not in the same manner it was for the Ojibwe, for Giizhigoon and for Charlotte. Its rocky shores did not welcome Benjamin's ancestors, its abundant forests, vibrant streams, and the life-giving lakes that surrounded it did not encompass Benjamin's childhood, did not fill his memory, did not live in his bloodline.

"Do you know what this island represents to me? What it represents to the Ojibwe people?" Giizhigoon asked.

"I'm trying to understand. Having lived among you for five years, I know how important and valuable it is. I know it is sacred."

Giizhigoon sighed, then began to explain to Benjamin the deep meaning behind his homeland. "This island is called Madeline Island. Named for the wife of a mixed-race fur trader named Michel Cadotte. But before then it had another name. Our ancestors called this place Moningwunakauning, the home of the golden-breasted woodpecker."

"I have never been told this."

"Very few white men know this," Giizhigoon said as they continued their slow march. "Let me tell you a story, brother. Let me tell you our history."

Giizhigoon took a deep breath, inhaling the natural beauty and essence of his homeland.

"A place where the food grows on water." Giizhigoon began, his tone changing to that of storyteller, filled with deference. "That is what Gitche Manitou, the Great Spirit, said to our people. No one remembers how long ago. Ten, fifteen generations. The migration itself lasted nine hundred years. It began from the Great Salt Water Sea, known today as the Atlantic. Westward they forged, generation by generation, making just enough progress to distance themselves from the clans at their heels.

"Eventually they found the place, the place where the food grows on water, the place that would sustain them, the place they would call home. It was here, this island," Giizhigoon pointed to the ground, "that became their central location. From here they expanded and prospered, spreading throughout the region, exploring its trees and lakes, its prairies and valleys, its ecosystems filled with life. Fish of all kinds, bear and mink, fox and wolf, deer and rabbit, beaver and muskrat, even the trees bled sugar to feed them. All things conspired in their favor."

Benjamin tussled with the heavy fish hanging over his shoulder, switching from right to left, trying not to lose focus on the story.

"But a threat was on the horizon. New tribes, new clans. Not those with native skin, but those with much paler skin. Not those with bows and arrows. The new clans, the new tribes, they came with exploding fire sticks. But they sought not war. They sought not land nor water, nor food, nor anything useful. They sought pelts. They did not want the beaver; they wanted the skin of the beaver. They did not want the bear;

they wanted the skin of the bear. In exchange they offered tools and weapons unlike any ever created before. The fire stick that could kill an animal at a distance no man could ever hope to run. A knife that cut through wood as if it were water. A thing they called metal that never broke, never chipped, never changed its shape, never melted over hot fire. Soon an alliance was made with these pale faces. They called themselves the French. And after the French came another tribe of pale faces called the British. Our ancestors decided it was logical to take things of use from the French and British and to give nothing useful in return, just the scraps of a hunt. It was the beginning of a new age.

"Before long, the foreign talkers wanted more. They wanted more than pelts. They wanted more than an alliance. They wanted the hearts and souls of men. They wanted tradition. They came wearing robes and hats and crosses. They spoke of a man named Jesus and a God named the great *I Am*. But they did not stop there, these men in robes. They brought with them their language, their manner of dress, and their way of life. They cut furrows into the land and dropped seeds into the soil. They hurt the mother earth by plowing her fields and cutting her timber. They put up shelters that could not be moved and they built schools where they spoke their language and taught their knowledge of the world. They never asked, they only did.

"But these white men did not change the world. They did not destroy the place where the food grows on water. AMERICANS," Giizhigoon emphasized the word. "That is what arrived next. That is what they were called. They arrived as friends, not as foes. Trade, prosperity, friendship; this is what they offered. But they did not shake hands or smoke the peace pipe like the strangers before them—like the French, like the British. They came with words on paper. Letters that combined to make sounds that combined to make meaning. Symbols. They gave out names to the people. They assigned positions. Some they called chiefs, some they called warriors. They spoke to the chiefs and made them sign their papers. They talked about the promises of the Great Father who lived in a place called Washington City. They promised gifts and money and power. They wanted only a little, not much, but only a little."

Only an Ojibwe, Benjamin thought as he listened intently, could give such an eloquent oral account.

"The Americans, though, they wanted more—more than what they said. They wanted more than pelts. They wanted more than the hearts of men. They wanted more than an alliance. They wanted the land and everything in the land and everything on the land. They wanted the lifeblood of the earth itself.

"They came slowly. First, it was men in uniform. Then more men in robes with books in their hands and crosses hanging from their necks. Then came the men with fire water. Alcohol!" Giizhigoon raised his voice in anger. "Putrid, noxious liquid that made men and women stupid and lazy and caused them to throw away their earnings. Then—then came the farmer and his family. The men who built permanent log dwellings and cleared the earth of its natural growth. Move west they said, we want only a little. Move west again, they said, we want only a little. They sectioned and parceled the land. They assigned ownership. They promised that the sections were in place forever. We want only this section, they said. But forever was not forever. Their words had no meaning. Their promises had no value. They wanted bigger sections. They wanted all the sections.

"Get out of the way," they said.

"The place where the food grows on water, where our animal brothers live, where all trees and plants, grasses and flowers grow, was gone, was taken, was destroyed. Razed to build roads and homes, to harvest metal and wood, to grow corn and wheat. All at the hands of the so-called Great Father. All at the pleasure of the president.

"So you see, my friend. I am very anxious today. Very sad. I know why the agent is here and I know what he wishes to take from us."

Benjamin was silent, his heart beating just a little harder, a little louder for his friend. There were no words for the sympathy he felt. Instead, he remained silent and the two marched on, slow but steady, snow crunching loudly beneath their feet, their steady breathing visible in the crisp winter air.

———

That afternoon the La Pointe community gathered for council outside of the American Fur Company fort which consisted of two large stores painted red, a long storehouse for fish at the wharf, and a row of neat frame buildings painted white. This was the commercial center of the island and a place where much business took place. About a half-mile distant were the Catholic and Protestant missions along with a school, storehouse, several agency buildings and several log frame homes. By the year 1850, La Pointe had become a relatively large village with an equal array of movable, birch-bark wigwams and permanent log-frame dwellings. It was really quite lovely to behold the alluring mixture of indigenous and frontier cultures and architecture.

The population at La Pointe varied at any given time during the year, depending largely on the season. There were about five hundred permanent white and mixed-race residents and anywhere from several hundred to more than a thousand native inhabitants. To the south, past the bay and beyond Chequamegon Point was Odanah, a small settlement of Protestant Ojibwe established and led by the missionaries Leonard and Harriet Wheeler.

As the Ojibwe gathered for council with the agent they were noticeably apprehensive and frustrated. There was great concern among them that they would be asked to move from their homes, just as Giizhigoon had expressed. This feeling of apprehension about their future had loomed over the people for the past several years.

"Hello, Mr. Armstrong!" came the vibrant young voice of Julia Wheeler.

"Well, hello there, little darling," Benjamin said joyfully as the child ran into his arms. "Where is your mother?"

"She's coming," Julia said with a brimming smile. "The new baby has her attention and made her slow."

"Well, there is no stopping you, is there!" Benjamin chuckled as he teased the energetic and happy child.

Julia laughed but quickly her smile turned.

"Are they going to tell us we have to move, Mr. Armstrong?" Julia asked with a genuine look of remorse. Though she was only five years old, Benjamin could see she, too, sensed the atmosphere of displeasure.

Benjamin thought hard, not wanting to disappoint the young girl. She was such a little sunbeam and a joy to be around. Benjamin wanted to calm her fears and assure her that they would not be asked to move, but he also did not want to lie.

"It's best for you not to worry about such things. Leave that to the grown-ups."

"But I don't want to move. Our house and school and friends are here. I like it here."

"I know you do." Benjamin patted her shoulder, while looking around for her mother, Harriet.

"Oh, thank you!" Mrs. Harriet Wheeler said gratefully, almost out of breath as she pushed through the ever-increasing crowd. In her arms was one baby; in her carriage was another, and alongside her was Leonard Jr., Julia's older brother. "These days it is impossible to keep up with that little girl."

"Don't run off like that!" she scolded, turning her attention toward Julia.

"Yes, mum," Julia said with a soft look of guilt.

Harriet was a kind-looking woman with a narrow face and soft blue eyes. Her curly hair was wrapped in wool and she wore a long winter coat to shield her from the cold. She was tall and thin, but what Benjamin noticed most was her sense of duty to her calling. She was always busy, always occupied, caring for her children, tending the gardens, or giving lessons to the Ojibwe at Odanah.

"We made it just in time," Harriet said giving her attention back to Benjamin. "These trips to the island can be difficult, especially during winter. The last thing we need is to be moved two hundred miles west. Quite honestly, I'd rather be going home to Massachusetts."

Harriet's face drooped below her eyes, and her posture slacked. She was visibly worn and tired. During Benjamin's brief time in the region he came to discover that missionary life was hard on a family. It was indeed a life of sacrifice and privation.

"No one is enthusiastic about the prospects of removal," Benjamin said, trying to shield his voice from the children. "It has been weighing on this community for too long."

"Leonard says he will not let it happen, though I don't know how he intends to accomplish that," Harriet said while rocking her baby gently and at the same time bouncing her carriage softly.

"If anyone can do it, he can."

As Benjamin and Harriet continued their conversation the crowd around them grew rapidly. Attendance was actually somewhat light, due to the fact that it was winter, and many Ojibwe families were dispersed on winter hunts. Nevertheless, the council was of great interest. Everyone who could come, did.

"Ojibwe of La Pointe, Bad River, and the vicinity," the agent declared as the council was finally ready to start. "I have an important announcement sent down to me from the Commissioner of Indian Affairs in Washington."

The La Pointe community gathered tightly around the agent, eager but worried to hear what he had to say. Even those traders and merchants that would not be required to remove had something to lose if the Lake Superior Ojibwe were forced west into Minnesota Territory.

The agent, John Livermore, was a Democrat who had been appointed just a year prior. His role was as an intermediary between the Ojibwe bands at La Pointe and the United States government. He was just one of several agents who had been appointed to La Pointe over the years. The Ojibwe had grown accustomed to these changes and the varying methods of each agent. They knew that no matter who represented the government, it was important to take his orders into account.

"The commissioner has asked me to inform you that the time to remove has come," Agent Livermore announced.

The crowd, Ojibwe and others, let out a unified groan followed by scattered commotion and audible shouts of dissatisfaction. Agent Livermore was prepared for such a reaction and waited while the crowd expressed its anger.

"This is for your benefit," he shouted as the commotion began to die down. "The location selected for you has not yet been determined but will be on or near the Upper Mississippi. Your land will be plenty. The lakes are filled with fish. Your kinsmen will be near and the white settlers will be far away. There, in this new region, you will be able to continue your ways of living for many years to come. Your annuities will be paid there. The traders will meet you there. And your Great Father will continue to provide for you. I tell you again, this will be for your benefit."

The commotion rose once again. As Julia stood beside Benjamin he could see a look of confusion and dismay on her face. He placed his hand on her head, trying to comfort her, while thinking of his wife, Charlotte, and his two young children.

Then, as the commotion reached its climax, the great Buffalo, Kechewaishke, chief elder among the La Pointe band, raised his walking staff to calm the crowd.

"You see the people be excited," the elder statesmen said in imperfect English. "This is not what we been told just some years ago. The man who came here to make the treaty told us we did not have to remove for many years. He say our children and our grandchildren could stay here for many years. I was an old man then. Even my fire has not yet gone out, and now you say we must remove."

The treaty Kechewaishke spoke of was signed in 1842 between the Lake Superior Ojibwe and the United States government. This treaty was often the topic of conversation among the Ojibwe at La Pointe. According to the treaty, the Lake Superior Ojibwe sold their lands in Wisconsin, but they maintained the right to live upon and use the land. They were told by the agent at the time that they would not be required to remove for fifty to one hundred years. Now, eight years later, that promise was being broken.

"These were not my words," Livermore said. "I merely communicate to you the orders of your Great Father."

"He is not our father and we are not his children. We speak now with you. If you tell us to remove, you break our treaty agreement. You destroy our alliance."

"I have destroyed nothing," Agent Livermore replied while taking a step back, perhaps feeling under siege. He had two armed guards behind him and an interpreter at his side. "You signed the agreement. You sold this land. Now you must accept those terms and move west. This is the pleasure of the president."

Undeterred, Kechewaishke took a step forward. "This is not what was said to us. We were told we could stay here until our annuities had ceased. We were told that our young men could grow old here."

The agent took a deep breath, his face almost hidden beneath his muskrat fur cap and behind his wool scarf. "You should not be governed by any conversation you had, only by the words of the treaty itself."

"This is a great wrong," shouted Oshoga, one of the chief elders like Kechewaishke. Though middle-aged, he was a fit, robust looking man. "The words that come from the mouth mean the same as yours on paper. The Great Father, as you call him, cannot say one thing and do another. We do not agree to move from here. We never did."

The crowd became excited once more. Shouts of derision flowed from the mass of people toward the agent. Benjamin, though no more pleased than the crowd, stood in quiet observation and apprehension with concern for his friends, family, and community.

The agent replied calmly. "I would advise you to heed the wishes of the United States government. Believe me when I say that it is the intention of your Great Father to do you justice. Submit yourselves to whatever your Great Father should in his wisdom think best to do in this matter."

"And if we refuse?" Oshoga said.

"To refuse would be a great folly. If you remain here, your annuities will not be paid to you and your families will grow cold and hungry. If you remain, your Great Father will no longer bestow his gifts upon you or upon your people. It would be a grave mistake."

With the support of the crowd at his back, Oshoga answered the agent. "We lived many years before the Great Father came to this land. We survived the British who are now gone. We survived the French who are now gone. This was and will remain our home. Our children were born here, and the graves of our fathers lie here. We gave you the pelts of our animals, we gave you lumber from our trees, we even gave you the minerals from beneath the rocks on our shores, but we did not sell our own graves; we did not sell the ground upon which we lie. This you cannot have at any cost unless you wish to take our lives as well."

"Ho, ho!" the crowd cheered in agreement. Even those non-natives, such as the missionaries, clerks, traders, and miners, applauded in acquiescence. If the Ojibwe were forced to remove, their lives would be changed, too.

"Very well," Agent Livermore answered, his voice echoing off the long storehouse. "I have told you what you need to know and have completed my obligation. I will tell my superiors of your objections. The specifics of removal will be brought to you at a later date. What you choose to do will be up to you."

The agent quickly turned to leave, determined to move beyond the uncomfortable circumstances. He was ushered out by continuous yelps and moans of a community in defiance.

"So, we must leave our homes?" Julia asked, tugging Benjamin by the hand.

"No, Julia. It will be okay." Benjamin looked softly into her eyes, and with a sense of pity, he wondered if she was old enough to know the truth from a lie. As Benjamin looked up, Harriet pursed her lips in acknowledgment of his kind words.

"Come on, Julia," she said, reaching out her free hand. "It's time to go."

CHAPTER 5

Indian Agent John Livermore entered the office of the Territorial Governor Alexander Ramsey. It was late afternoon and Ramsey busied himself with his pen and paper, writing one correspondence after another.

"Excuse me, sir," Livermore said as he approached the former lawyer. "I have just returned from La Pointe and I wish to express my concerns."

"Concerns?" Ramsey said as he looked up from his letter. "What concerns?"

Livermore removed his hat and sat down. "I understand my instructions regarding the Ojibwe Removal, but if it is to be done this year I must protest."

Ramsey straightened his posture and tilted his head, the light fading behind him as the sun fell lower in the horizon. "Go on."

"Removal will be problematic for several reasons," Livermore said. "To begin, there need to be provisions to feed them upon arrival. Also, there had better be plenty of canoes to carry them there and those cannot be built until June when the bark can be peeled. Also, the lands to which they will be removed are already inhabited by other bands, who themselves receive no annuities. Perhaps we should send a delegation of chiefs from each band in Wisconsin to select new locations?"

Ramsey looked down toward the side as he thought for a moment. "Is that all?"

"Yes. I just—I strongly recommend that removal be delayed one year until we are more prepared. If the Indians arrive in large numbers in Minnesota Territory before there are adequate provisions, it could result in a great calamity."

Ramsey leaned forward, placed his elbows on his desk and crossed his hands. "I understand your concerns, Agent Livermore, but my hands are tied," he said. "Commissioner Brown has instructed me to fulfill the removal order that was signed by the president earlier this year. Until we hear otherwise, we must fulfill those orders."

Livermore lowered his head, unsatisfied with the governor's response.

"I will set aside funds for you to hire a superintendent of removal to assist you in the process. You may hire whomever pleases you. I suggest you implement removal policies as early in the season as practicable."

Livermore nodded reluctantly. "Very well."

CHAPTER 6

The store wasn't very busy in the winter. Annuities had been used up, pelts had been brought in, and the Ojibwe were dispersed throughout the vast region. An occasional villager sought supplies on credit, or business negotiations took place within the store's comfortable confines, but little else.

Benjamin worked as the store's clerk. He kept the books, managed the inventory, collected supplies, swept the floors, maintained the grounds, and even acted as interpreter. There was very little that a clerk didn't do. Benjamin enjoyed his role in the store, being a central figure to all that went on, and he aspired to have his own trading post one day.

The store at La Pointe was owned and operated by Mr. Julius Austrian. Austrian, originally named Oesterreicher, was a German immigrant who had years ago bought the store from the American Fur Company. Once a small trading post, Austrian had turned it into a center for all types of commerce and business. In particular, the store sold dry goods, but was also engaged in the fish business, furnishing nets as well as salt and barrels to the fisherman who caught and packed the fish. It was a departure from the old way of doing business when the trading post was managed by a large company or nation and deals were made with entire bands of native peoples. By 1850, it was done on a one-on-one basis and involved much more than the trading of furs for goods.

For many years prior to 1850, furs had been diminishing in value and growing in scarcity. This scarcity was not only caused by over-hunting, but by the development of land which destroyed and separated habitats relied upon by the native Ojibwe. Traders, voyageurs, and Ojibwe alike had to look for new sources of income and unique ways of creating profit. For the store owners, like Austrian, this came in the form of fishing, mining, lumbering, and land speculation. For the Ojibwe, their most valued commodity was no longer their pelts, but their land and their labor.

———————

"This is completely unjust!" Austrian pounded his fist against the counter.

Benjamin turned, pausing from one of his many tasks dusting and cleaning the shelves.

"There are no settlers in this northern region. No one is clamoring for farmsteads upon this land. They remain south, around Prairie du Chien and St. Paul. There is no reason for removing the Ojibwe from here!"

Austrian had good reason to be upset. The Ojibwe were his main source of income. Every spring they bought supplies on credit, every fall they brought in pelts and used their annuity cash for goods such as blankets, firearms, and whiskey. Without the Ojibwe, the store would not be a viable enterprise.

"You know who is doing this—it's the governor of the new Minnesota Territory."

"How do you mean?" Benjamin knew that Minnesota had become a territory just one year earlier, but he could not make the connection between its governor and the Lake Superior Ojibwe.

"He sees this as a business opportunity," Austrian said. "It is a chance to grow the population and economy of his territory."

"I don't understand. How?"

"You see—ah," he said stuttering, still somewhat uncomfortable with the English language. "If the Ojibwe are moved from La Pointe to some place in Minnesota, the payment will be moved too. And if the payment is made in Minnesota, the economic benefit will go to Minnesotans. Once payment is made, it will be followed up by traders, contractors, and businessmen all competing for a portion of the Ojibwe money. Entire communities will spring up around the payment creating even more business opportunity and economic benefit. Meanwhile, it leaves us with nothing."

"An economic incentive," Benjamin inferred, beginning to understand Austrian's explanation.

"Exactly! Thankfully, it would not be the end for me. I might just have to expand into other ventures such as land speculation. I can see this place being a destination that is richly sought after in the near future. If I can use my profits to buy the land, it will be worth a great deal of money in a few years."

"I've seen the changes," Benjamin said with a nod. "Prairie du Chien is a bustling frontier town and I think La Pointe will be too."

Before Benjamin could continue, Makadebineshii, also known as Blackbird, entered the store. Blackbird was a part of the warrior class and a prominent member of the La Pointe Ojibwe. He held strongly to the traditional Ojibwe way of life and did not readily negotiate with the United States government on any issue. Blackbird moved purposefully and had a stern look on his face.

"I need supplies," Blackbird said in his native tongue, forgoing all niceties. Not fully understanding the Ojibwe language, Austrian looked toward Benjamin for a translation.

"He needs supplies," Benjamin said.

"What, exactly? For a journey?" Austrian asked in his thick German accent.

Blackbird turned toward Benjamin, also needing the words interpreted. Again, Benjamin translated, then listened carefully for Blackbird's response. Ojibwe was a complicated language and though Benjamin could communicate in the language, he had not yet mastered it.

"St. Paul, he says," Benjamin explained to Austrian. "He plans to meet with the governor to plead his case against removal."

"That won't do any good. The politicians in this country are only after their own benefit. He will simply turn them away."

Benjamin translated the words to Blackbird who was undeterred by Austrian's pessimism.

Blackbird began to speak, explaining in detail what he planned to say to the governor. His dark, determined eyes showed the seriousness of his request.

"He says there are many problems with the removal request. He says canoes for the journey cannot be made until June when the birch bark is ready to peel. If he waits until then, he will arrive too late in the season to prepare for winter. He also says that the lands in Minnesota are already occupied and that there is no room for his people."

"I agree," Austrian said. "There are many problems with the removal request. I just have my doubts in the political process of this country."

"But will you supply me?" Blackbird asked as Benjamin continued to translate back and forth.

"Yes, I'll supply you," Austrian said. Then, turning to Benjamin, "Mr. Armstrong, get a wagon ready. Have it supplied for a two-week journey and record everything in the ledger."

"Of course." Being very curious, Benjamin turned toward Blackbird. "What else did you discuss with the elders in council?"

"We are upset, we are scared," Blackbird said with a look of concern. "I will travel to St. Paul to argue our position with the father of this place called Minnesota. Runners will be sent out to our various bands to determine if anyone among us has committed even a single wrong. We remember when they told us that if we commit no wrongs we will never be asked to move. We will not be removed from our homes. I will tell the governor this."

Blackbird shook hands with Austrian, finalizing the deal. He vowed to return in an hour for his wagon of supplies, then departed quickly. His beads clattered with each step and could still be heard as he moved toward the distance.

Austrian said nothing and reached for his ledger.

As Benjamin gathered supplies and loaded them into the wagon, he fixated on the words of Blackbird, remembering his mission to send runners to the various Ojibwe bands. This in itself was remarkable, exemplifying just how determined the Ojibwe were not to move. Their peoples covered a vast territory making communication difficult at times. To travel over such a huge expanse in the heart of winter was no easy task. But, if anyone could do it, it was the Ojibwe who were adept at winter travel and survival.

La Pointe was the center of the Ojibwe people—geographically, spiritually, culturally, politically—spreading out in all directions. They lived throughout the upper peninsula of Michigan as far as Sault St. Marie. From there they spread south, east, and north along the shores of Lake Huron, Lake Erie, and Lake Ontario. In the north, across the British line, their people stretched over a thousand miles from Quebec to Lake Winnipeg. In Wisconsin, they spanned south and west toward the Mississippi and St. Croix rivers. In Minnesota, they extended across the territory north of their boundary with the Dakota from Lake Superior to Lake of the Woods, to the Red River Valley. Their territory was so vast, it would take weeks to travel from one end to the other.

But the runners Blackbird promised to send out did not need to reach the farthest corners of Ojibwe territory. They were not interested in determining the behavior of the entire Ojibwe nation. They were interested in those bands that had agreed to the terms of the treaty in 1842. Only these bands would have an effect on the agreement if they had broken any terms. This included several bands, still very far reaching from La Pointe. To the east there were the L'Anse at Keweenaw Bay and Lac Vieux Desert. To the south were the Lac Courte Oreilles bands and to the west were the St. Croix bands. In Minnesota Territory were the bands of Fond du Lac, Sandy Lake, Mille Lacs, Grand Portage, Bois Forte, and Leech Lake. The more western bands were known as the Mississippi Ojibwe. There were also any number of smaller communities, such as those along the Wisconsin, Snake, and Chippewa rivers. And, there were those at Gull and Red Cedar Lake. Their entire population was probably around 15,000, being about 9,000 within the boundaries of the United States. The fact was, communication among the Ojibwe was not a fast or easy task, yet it was vital in dealing and negotiating with the United States government.

Blackbird returned just as he said he would. He was joined by five other Ojibwe, all on horseback and all of them young and eager to make for the Minnesota capital.

"The wagon is ready," Benjamin said as he laid down the last bag of flour. "You have enough for twelve days. Six days to St. Paul and six days back."

"Miigwech Chi-miigwech," Blackbird said as Benjamin moved to hitch up the oxen. *Thank you.* "The Loon Clan is a clan of leaders. Accepting our role, we go to speak with the Father of this region."

Benjamin turned back with a look of curiosity.

"Are you not familiar with the Loon Clan?" Blackbird asked, recognizing Benjamin's curious look.

"Giizhigoon, my brother-in-law, has mentioned the clans, but I never fully understood."

As Benjamin laid the yoke, Blackbird began to explain the Ojibwe clan system, proud, it seemed, to have the opportunity to do so.

"We are all related," Blackbird said. "All Anishinaabe people are tied together by blood. What separates us is our clan or dodem. The whites call it totem."

"Yes," Benjamin acknowledged, "I have heard this."

"For the Ojibwe, the clan is more important than place of birth or where we set down our wigwam. Clan is family, no matter where we live or what tribe we hunt with."

"Why do you call yourself the Loon Clan?" Benjamin asked as he finished hitching the wagon.

Blackbird moved to the seat of the wagon, his comrades ready to follow as their horses snorted impatiently. "Every clan is associated with a symbol from nature. We are the Loons, but there are many others, like the Bear, Marten, Catfish, Crane and Wolf. These are the six principal families."

"And the Loon is the leadership clan?"

"Royal clan," Blackbird said, correcting Benjamin. "Nature placed a collar around the neck of the loon representing the royal wampum around the neck of a chief or leader. This is our badge of honor, a badge respected by all of our people."

"Then I can see why you are called to go," Benjamin said, stepping aside and offering a slight wave of his hand.

Blackbird nodded, then gave the reigns a heavy tug, setting the oxen in motion.

"Travel safe," Benjamin said, as he watched the six determined men move with purpose toward the frozen ice crossing. "Good luck!"

Returning home that evening, Benjamin thought about his wife, Charlotte, and his two young children, Marie and Samuel. He wanted so badly to give them the life he didn't have. He wanted to be a good father and husband, always providing and ensuring his family was safe and healthy. Benjamin learned quickly that this wasn't easy. Disease, hunger, and privation of all kinds stalked them from year to year. Now, adding to their troubles, was the threat of forced removal. Benjamin wanted more than anything to keep his family in one place, but he doubted whether he could fight removal while also providing for his wife and children. Both were full-time responsibilities. Choosing one, meant giving up on another. But how could he give anything less? How could he expect anything more?

"Any news of the removal?" Charlotte asked as Benjamin entered their small wood-frame home.

Charlotte sat near the fire with Samuel, who was just two years old, at her feet while she stitched baskets made of birch bark to prepare for the approaching maple harvest.

"Yes," Benjamin said softly, the hearty smell of pemmican stew filling his nose. "Blackbird and five others have departed for St. Paul. They wish to meet with the governor and plead our case against removal."

"I suppose that might help," Charlotte said, concentrating on her basket in hand. "But this whole thing is madness. How can they just decide to uproot an entire community?"

Marie, who was three years old, ran over to greet her father, moving quickly across the creaky wooden floor. The little cabin consisted of just one room with only a flax curtain to separate the sleeping and living quarters. But it was comfortable and had all the necessities Benjamin and his family required to survive.

"I know, Charlotte. No one is pleased." And no one was. Benjamin had yet to meet with anyone happy about removal.

"I've heard that the reverends Wheeler and Hall are preparing to travel to Minnesota," Charlotte said, still concentrating on her basket. "Does this mean..."

"It means this is real," Charlotte said, finally looking up from her task. "I think they are traveling there to explore land suitable for us to settle upon."

"When? I mean, when will the reverends depart?"

"As soon as the weather warms, I presume." Charlotte paused, trying to stitch the corner of her basket very carefully. "I want you to talk with Leonard," she said referring to Reverend Wheeler. "Find out if he is really going. Find out if we will certainly be moved from here."

Benjamin paused, worried by the thought that removal might be inevitable. He did not want to make his worry known, but he wasn't sure he could hide it. "I can do that, but I doubt if he can provide certainty one way or another."

"Look." Little Marie grabbed Benjamin's attention. She pointed to a drawing of her and her friends. They were dancing in the Ojibwe style. The little stick figures had smiles on their faces. It reminded Benjamin of the great community they had at La Pointe. The community that was being threatened.

"I will speak to the reverend first thing tomorrow," Benjamin said as he sat down at the table and let out a tired sigh.

"Good," Charlotte said, putting down her basket. "I will get the table ready for supper."

The next day Benjamin headed south across the frozen bay to visit the reverend. The winds howled briskly as they often did over the barren surface of the lake. But rather than deter Benjamin, it gave him something else to focus on, something rather than his constant stress and doubts.

The Wheelers lived in a small settlement called Odanah which was the Ojibwe word for village. It was a small farming community founded by Reverend Wheeler himself in 1845. Reverend Wheeler and his wife Harriet had come to La Pointe in 1841 as members of the American Board of Commissioners for Foreign Missions. They were Protestants and staunch followers of the Christian religion. They had a deep-seated compassion and love for the Ojibwe people whom they viewed as destitute and much in need. With this compassion, the Wheelers offered many services to the Ojibwe people. Mrs. Wheeler often met with the women, teaching them to read and sing, while Mr. Wheeler filled many roles such as that of doctor, carpenter, farmer, teacher, and intermediary between the Ojibwe and the United States government. His passion and zeal were indeed unmatched.

It was this passion and zeal that led him to Odanah. He believed that he was not accomplishing enough at La Pointe. He found it difficult to influence the Ojibwe toward the teachings of Christianity while they were constantly on the move, hunting, fishing, or gathering. Farming, Wheeler believed, was the key. If he could teach the Ojibwe to farm, then they could live a more settled, permanent life. This way and only this way, according to Reverend Wheeler, the Christian word could begin to take effect. In addition, farming created a more permanent presence that allowed the Ojibwe to attend school more often. The Wheelers taught classes in reading, spelling, arithmetic, bookkeeping, English grammar, geography and composition. But attendance was often low or inconsistent, due mostly to the roaming habits of the Ojibwe who still maintained a traditional way of living.

So, Reverend Wheeler and his wife Harriet established Odanah as a farming community of Protestant Ojibwe, across the bay and away from the many and various influences of La Pointe. The location was quite pleasant, being at a point where the river branched off in two separate streams. Their home was large and always occupied by various visitors. And their summer garden was extraordinarily grand and beautiful—second to none in the region.

"It is nice to see you again," Reverend Wheeler said as Benjamin arrived at his large, wood-frame home. "We don't see so much of you in the winter. This separation from the island sometimes feels bigger than it is."

"It is big enough."

Both men laughed.

"But that is precisely the reason I established this place here," Reverend Wheeler said. "It is far enough from La Pointe to avoid its influence but close enough to enjoy its benefits. We have nothing particularly to trouble us here except the mosquitoes later on in the season."

"The mosquitoes, indeed," Benjamin said, then quickly turned to the matter that weighed upon him. "You, too, must be displeased with the removal request."

"Oh, of course," Reverend Wheeler said with a change of tone. "If the Ojibwe are removed there will be nothing left for the missionary to do here. Plus, we have worked so hard to create a more permanent community where the Ojibwe can remain and be always attached to learning and the gospel—where they do not have to continue their ways of idolatry and nomadism. All of that might be lost."

"I see." Benjamin nodded his head. He thought for a moment, wondering if this was the right time to ask the Reverend Wheeler about his beliefs toward the Ojibwe. He decided it was. "The injustice of removal aside, do you ever question your reasoning for attempting to alter the Ojibwe way of life?"

This was a foreign notion for the devout missionary and not something many people even considered. After all, it was Reverend Wheeler's life work to save the Ojibwe, not to hinder them.

"Certainly not. We are rescuing these poor people from squalor. We are providing them a better life both now and beyond. We find that Christianity and civilization go hand in hand. They are inseparable."

Inseparable, Benjamin thought. The reverend's mind was so convinced that Benjamin decided not to push the subject further. Though Reverend Wheeler was well-meaning, he could not see the error of his ways. He could not see the long-term effects of his cultural persuasions. Benjamin considered himself fortunate to have a wife like Charlotte and a brother-in-law like Giizhigoon to show him the richness of Ojibwe culture.

"Then why travel to Minnesota?" Benjamin asked, pushing his thoughts aside. "Doesn't it show some form of agreement to the removal order?"

Tilting his head upward, the reverend thought for a moment. "In a way, yes. But we have to be prepared for all possibilities. Sherman and I," he said, referring to Reverend Hall, "will explore the potential regions and decide upon the best, most livable region. If no region is suitable, it further supports our argument against removal. And, if removal is unavoidable, at least we will know the place where we can find the best living conditions."

"It does make sense when you put it that way," Benjamin said. "How long before you depart?"

"Soon. In a few weeks, when the weather warms above freezing in the day but below freezing at night. That is when the Ojibwe will depart for their sugar bushes. At that time, we will discontinue the school and head for Minnesota. I am actually quite excited to do some travel. I have been locked up here far too long and could use a change of scenery."

"And Harriet?"

Reverend Wheeler took a long, strained breath. "Harriet will stay and care for the young ones. She is anxious for a break from missionary life, but that may have to wait until next fall."

"And the removal efforts?" Benjamin prodded, trying to get as much information as possible. "Do you think it will really happen?"

The reverend placed his hand on Benjamin's shoulder as a friendly gesture. "I can't make any promises, but make no mistake, we will fight against the removal order with every tool we've got."

CHAPTER 7

Clement Beaulieu stared across the table at his brother-in-law, Charles Borup. Spring had finally arrived and outside the air was pleasant, the flowers bloomed, and the rivers were swift. Inside the feeling was tense.

"Removing the Ojibwe to Gull or Sandy Lake would surely wrong the poor Indians," Beaulieu argued. "The lakes are too small and can only support thirty or thirty-five families. They would have to spend part of the year at Mille Lacs or Leech Lake."

Borup stared back, dragging his hand through his thinning hair. "You are looking at this all wrong," he said in a thick Danish accent. "This is good business. Oakes has been hired as the removal agent and Livermore will be removed soon."

Beaulieu took a long sip from his cup of tea, a look of skepticism across his face.

"Trust me," Borup said. "With Oakes in charge of removal all provisions and money will flow through St. Paul. We have Sibley's backing too. And, once Livermore is removed, there will be no obstacles in the way of our company. We will control the entire region."

"And the Ojibwe?"

"Never mind the Ojibwe. Their removal is sure to come sooner or later. We might as well profit from it."

CHAPTER 8

In the early days of spring, the Ojibwe gathered in the sugarbush which was any forest filled with maple trees. Here they met with friends and relatives they had not seen since departing for their winter camps while they tapped the trees in order to gather sap. This was an important part of the seasonal Ojibwe living because it represented the end of the dark, hungry days of winter and the beginning of new life and sustenance. The Ojibwe drilled holes in the trees and gathered the sap in birch bark buckets. This could only be done in spring because the sap rose up the trunk during the warm days and went back down during the cold nights. Once it was gathered, it was boiled for several hours until it became thick and turned into sugar. Spring was also a good time for trapping furs because the furs were often thick and glossy after a long winter. Nets were spread to catch wild flocks of pigeons while men often speared fish through holes in the melting ice.

Though spring was an enjoyable time of new life, nothing compared with summer in Ojibwe country. La Pointe was a stunningly beautiful place to be in the summer. The days were warm and pleasant while the nights were cool and comfortable. Summer was a social time of gathering and visiting with friends. It was a time of relaxation and enjoyment filled with storytelling, dances, and games. With the spring sugarbush passed, the fall rice harvest to come, and the long, hard winter far off, summer seemed almost carefree.

Yet, with so many reasons to relax and enjoy life during the summer, the Ojibwe still worked hard. They knew the summers were short and they understood that the abundance of the season would not last all year. And so, the men hunted and fished and labored while the women and children planted gardens filled with corn, pumpkins, and squash. They also dug wild onions, and picked grapes, butternuts, hazelnuts, and berries of all kinds. They built large, deep pits lined with rocks where the berries could be dried and stored. They also made large fishing nets by linking together nettles they picked off the ground. Summer truly exhibited the resourcefulness of the Ojibwe.

———————

One warm, serene evening in the month of June as Benjamin was turning over the store's canoes to dry, he noticed a plume of smoke coming from the eastern shore of the mainland. This was often used as a signal that someone was seeking a ferry to the island. Having completed his chores for the day, Benjamin decided to investigate. Pushing a canoe into the water he rowed to the other side. On the opposite shore, next to a smoky pit, stood Giizhigoon and his twelve-year-old son Makwa, meaning *bear* in English.

"Boozhoo, friend!" Benjamin exclaimed with pleasure as Giizhigoon and his son grabbed the front end of the canoe and pulled it ashore.

"Good evening, brother. Thank you for answering our signal."

"My pleasure," Benjamin said, just happy to see his friend. "The waters are tranquil, and I enjoyed the trip."

Giizhigoon and Makwa were each dressed in trousers and a smock which were dirty and well-worn. Their hands and faces were covered with dirt and smut.

"Were you working the mines today?" Benjamin asked, though the answer was clear.

Giizhigoon answered with a silent and tired glare, narrowing his eyes.

"Since dawn," Makwa said in plain English.

Giizhigoon said something quickly to his son in Ojibwe, so quickly that Benjamin did not understand. The boy lowered his head in a manner of shame and pushed the boat out into the water as he climbed in after his father.

"Was it a productive day?" Benjamin asked, trying to change the mood while gently dropping his paddle into the water.

"No," Giizhigoon said looking out over the tranquil waters. "All day we hammered with our picks, striking the earth and all we found were rocks."

This disheartened Benjamin who had so much respect for his friend.

"But I must work," Giizhigoon said. "My son, too."

"I'm sorry, Giizhigoon," Benjamin said as he paddled steadily.

"Life was not always like this. When I was a boy we were carefree and happy. There was no one here to take our timber. There was no one here to harvest our copper. But now we cannot keep them away. Now we must do their work for them or we will starve."

"I have seen many changes too," Benjamin said. "During my five years on the island I have seen the value of the fur decline and I have seen the newcomers increase year after year."

Giizhigoon cradled Makwa affectionately at his side. "Greed has swept across our land. Everything that is given is taken away and everything that is promised is revoked. The rivers have been tamed, the forests have been broken, and the ground has been uprooted. The more they take, the more they want. Not later, but like hungry vermin they want it now."

Benjamin appreciated Giizhigoon's honesty and understood the deep sense of loss he expressed.

"In the earlier days, we could protect ourselves and our land. We stood on equal footing with our foes, like two great bears vying for the same caribou. But that power was lost along the way. Now my people can only take what is given like dogs licking bones after their masters' feast. That is what I feel like. Like a dog licking some bones."

Benjamin stared back, empathetic but speechless.

Giizhigoon continued, "Now there is a looming darkness. Anxiety has taken hold of our community, no one knowing if we should stay or if we should go. Councils are held nightly as the elders try to determine a course of action." He leaned over, placing his hand in the cold lake water as the canoe skittered forward. "This lake has supported us for hundreds of years," he said, bringing the water from his hand to his mouth. "But some of us have given up hope. The anxiety, the fear—they have caused some of my brothers and sisters to stop hunting, stop planting."

Benjamin knew this. The agent promised to provide food and other provisions once the Ojibwe were moved. This caused some of the Ojibwe on the island to stop supporting themselves, expecting the government would follow through on its promises.

"I'm sorry," Benjamin said, "we can't give up hope."

"Just look at me and my son." Giizhigoon gestured toward Makwa's tattered, dirty clothes. "We are reduced to servants, laborers in a place we were once free. But now, we may not even be able to be laborers in our own home. We may be sent to another."

Benjamin's heart sank, like it had many times in the previous months. What could he say after that? How could he possibly console his brother? Instead, Benjamin turned his attention to his nephew, Makwa.

"Have you been attending school, Makwa?"

"Yes, I attend two times a week if my chores are done." Makwa straightened his posture and grinned. "I'm learning to read and write!"

"That's great! I didn't learn to read or write until I was much older than you."

"Father says I will be a storyteller. He says it's in my blood. He says the Ojibwe are natural storytellers."

"I don't doubt it," Benjamin said. "You will be a great storyteller. Perhaps you could tell me a story now."

"Now?" The boy seemed surprised and he looked toward his father. Giizhigoon nodded, giving his permission.

Makwa's young eyes lit up. "I know just the story."

Benjamin smiled, encouraged by his nephew's enthusiasm.

Makwa, with the sun at his back and the wind streaming through his hair, began his story.

One day Loon asked Beaver for a favor. "Will you build a dam to create a pool where my family can live?" he asked.

The animal replied, "I am not Beaver, I am Muskrat."

"I'm sorry," Loon said, then he went to find Beaver.

"Beaver," he said, "will you build a dam to create a pool where my family can live?"

The animal replied, "I am not Beaver, I am Otter."

"I'm sorry," Loon said, then he went to find Beaver.

"Beaver," he said, "will you build a dam to create a pool where my family can live?"

The animal replied, "I cannot build you a dam, I am not Beaver, I am Mink."

Loon became very upset. He could not recognize Beaver from Muskrat, Otter, or Mink. I know, he thought, I will give each a new tail—ones that are different from each other. Then I will know who to ask when I need a favor.

So Loon gave them each a new tail. To Otter he gave a tail that was long, flat, and furry. To Mink he gave a tail that was long, narrow, and dark. To Muskrat he gave a tail that was skinny, furless, and pointed. And to Beaver he gave a tail that was wide, flat, and strong.

This is good, Loon thought. Now, they could accomplish more because they could recognize each other by their skills and talents. Now, when they came together, they could help each other better.

Benjamin's heart was filled with warmth. "That is a lovely story. Makwa, you are a wonderful storyteller."

Makwa grinned and his face reddened as he blushed with pride.

A silence fell over them. As Benjamin continued to paddle the sun dipped and the air cooled. He felt the breeze cut gently around his head and neck and listened to the repeated melody provided by the splash, pull, and drip of the paddle, squinting toward the sun as it set.

————

A few weeks later, one warm summer evening, a stranger arrived at Benjamin's home. The unexpected knock at the door startled Charlotte, who was busy weaving a fishing net, while the children played with little wooden dolls. Benjamin stood to answer the door, curious to know who it was.

"Good evening," a sharply dressed young man said just as soon as the door opened. The man wore a dark brown suit with a thick bow tie and a high collar. He had a dark, thin-brimmed hat that was just slightly off tilt. Benjamin looked down to see the man carrying a leather portfolio of some kind.

"Evening, sir," Benjamin said. "What might I help you with?"

"My name is Cyrus Mendenhall," he said. "I am associated with the Methodist Episcopal Mission Society. I am also a mining entrepreneur, and I am currently conducting an inspection trip along the Lake Superior shore. As I travel, I am gathering signatures of those who wish the government to withdraw removal efforts."

"Very good, that's very good."

Mendenhall nodded and furled his brow as if asking to come in. Benjamin recognized the cue.

"Please, do come in," Benjamin said as he turned and ushered Mendenhall inside.

Mendenhall took one long stride inside where he politely removed his hat and looked about the cabin.

"This is my wife, Charlotte."

"Pleased to make your acquaintance, Mr. Mendenhall," Charlotte said.

"These are my children." Benjamin pointed to Marie and Samuel who quickly got up off the floor as if unleashed and hugged Mendenhall by the leg.

"They are not shy," Charlotte laughed.

"I see that," Mendenhall said looking down to the floor as if he were tiptoeing on broken egg shells.

"Please, have a seat," Benjamin instructed his guest. "Would you like any coffee or tea?"

"No, thank you. I appreciate your hospitality, but I should not stay long. I have many more homes to visit."

Mendenhall sat down and unlatched his portfolio, revealing an enormous stack of papers.

"Is there something you wish for us to read?" Benjamin asked as he pulled up a chair next to Mendenhall.

"A memorial, yes. But I can read aloud for you to hear." He proceeded to look through the documents, trying to locate the proper one. Finally, he pulled out what appeared to be a thick piece of stationery with a formal correspondence upon it and many signatures below. He began to read.

"Memorial to the President and Congress of the United States, relative to the Ojibwe Indians of Lake Superior. That the inhabitants of La Pointe county have nearly unanimously signed a petition showing to your memorialists, that the Ojibwe Indians in the region of Lake Superior are peaceable, quiet and inoffensive people, rapidly improving in the arts and sciences; that they acquire their living by hunting, fishing, manufacturing maple sugar, and agricultural pursuits ..."

Mendenhall continued reading the memorial. It went on, in a direct manner to request that the orders for removal be rescinded. Furthermore, it requested that annuity payments be made at La Pointe as they had been previously done.

Benjamin listened carefully, feeling pleased with the wording and its intent. "Well stated," he said as Mendenhall finished reading the memorial.

"Yes, but it is just one of many memorials and petitions that have already been signed and sent," Charlotte added. "Do you really think this will help?"

"I understand your concern, but if enough people sign and enough petitions are sent, surely the government will be forced to consider our request."

"My wife and I would be happy to sign."

Mendenhall laid the memorial on the table as Benjamin dipped a pen in ink to sign. Charlotte sighed as she walked over to the table to sign, still frustrated by the potential futility of the document.

As Benjamin signed he looked across the names of the petitioners. Some he did not recognize, but many he did. They were traders, miners, and businessmen from across the region. This encouraged Benjamin to see reputable men and women of all backgrounds, all of them in unison against the government's removal request. Clearly, the citizens of the region wanted the Ojibwe to stay and that should mean something.

"I am deeply grateful," Mendenhall said as he gathered the memorial and placed it back into his portfolio. "This will help combat the intentions of the new agent."

"New agent?" Benjamin asked, having not heard about any recent changes.

"Yes. The role has been handed over to the former trader, Mr. John Watrous."

"Ah!" Benjamin let out an audible grunt of disgust. "This can't be true."

"Then you know what we are up against?"

"Yes, Mr. Watrous spent a number of years here. He sought only his own interests, like any good businessman I suppose, but he did it in such a vile manner. In trade he was incorrigible and in dealings he was a scamp."

"Is that what caused his exit from here?" Mendenhall asked.

"He tried to undercut the other traders," Charlotte said. "Competition was great, and he began extending more credit than he could afford. Once he realized the error of his dealings he sold his business to George Nettleton. Also," Charlotte said as she changed to a more somber tone, "his wife died in the epidemic of '47."

"That's truly sad, but his exit from the trade was probably for the best," Mendenhall said. "He came from Ohio with the idea of making a fortune in the Indian trade."

"But now he's back," Benjamin added derisively. "This time as a political appointee."

"Yes," Mendenhall said, "after leaving La Pointe he became a member of the Wisconsin Territorial Legislature. Now, no doubt with the help of some political friends, he has managed to oust Agent Livermore and have himself named to the position. I suspect he has new plans for making his fortune."

"This is troubling news," Benjamin said shaking his head and looking toward Charlotte and his children with worry. With the political motivation of a new agent, Benjamin knew the fight against removal would become even more challenging.

"We certainly appreciate what you're doing Mr. Mendenhall," Charlotte said, giving up her earlier pessimism. "My people have called this place home for many centuries. It isn't right that we should be forced to move. We are grateful for what you are doing."

"It affects not only the Ojibwe, but all of us living in the Lake Superior region," Mendenhall said as he collected his things and moved toward the door.

Benjamin then thanked Mendenhall, handing him his hat.

The stranger, now friend, nodded his head, put on his hat and stepped through the doorway.

"Have a good evening," Mendenhall said with one last look toward the home. "If we can help it, the removal order will be revoked."

Rushing toward the doorway, Marie and Samuel waved goodbye, a look of youthful innocence on their faces. Benjamin sighed, placing his hands on their heads.

As Benjamin went to work the day after Mendenhall's visit, he found Austrian in his office hunched over his ledgers examining the debts and credits. "I heard you were visited by Mr. Mendenhall," he said looking over his bifocals.

"Yes, he was a straightforward gentleman with a suitable purpose."

"He is good at business, too," Austrian said. "He relies on the labor the Ojibwe provide."

Benjamin stiffened at the thought, remembering Giizhigoon's lament. "But I think he has a heart for the people as well," Benjamin added.

Austrian pushed his ledger aside. "I agree, he does. Terminating the removal order is not just in his best interests, but in the best interests of all of us in this region. For that he is willing to stick his neck out."

The entrance door slowly creaked open, interrupting their conversation.

"Better attend to that individual," Austrian said, returning to his papers.

Benjamin entered the long corridor between the office and the store's entrance. As he moved he identified the person who entered as an Ojibwe. He was covered by a blanket—which was common no matter what the season—his back was arched, and he carried a long wooden staff in his right hand. He appeared to be an old man, probably a beggar seeking food.

As Benjamin grew closer he realized that it was not just any old man, it was the chief elder Kechewaishke, the most revered and respected Ojibwe of La Pointe, perhaps of the entire Ojibwe tribe.

"Kechewaishke, it is an honor," Benjamin said in Ojibwe while giving him a slight bow. Although Benjamin had married his niece, he had never met the chief. Kechewaishke was always occupied, concerned with important matters of the tribe.

"You speak English to me," Kechewaishke said using his imperfect, but understandable vocabulary. "Take this offering," he said as he reached out and dropped a fistful of tobacco into Benjamin's hands.

Kechewaishke was short with a round and somewhat plain face, but with expressive eyes. He was somewhere close to ninety years of age but did not appear so in countenance or abilities. He was spry for an old man and was still filled with awareness and perception.

"To what do I owe this offering?" Benjamin asked.

"I have a request," the elder replied. "I request that you join our council."

Benjamin was surprised and felt nervous. "To what purpose—wh-why me?"

"We see the written letters passed around," the chief explained, speaking of the petitions like that of Mendenhall. "Ojibwe elders want your help to write a letter. We want help to tell the Great Father that we wish to remain in this place, our home. You are wise, you can help. You are good."

The elder's praise demonstrated that Benjamin had earned the trust of community. He was flattered by the invitation but did not feel worthy of the request.

"I am not well educated," Benjamin said, remembering his days as a boy when he longed to attend school rather than work his father's plantation. "I'm not sure I am the right man for the job."

Kechewaishke smiled, revealing his toothless grin. "You know more than you think. You been many places. You seen many things. You are the right man. You will write our letter."

Benjamin could see that he was not going to win this argument. "Yes," Benjamin said ignoring his nervous anxiety. "I will."

Kechewaishke smiled so large it was not just an expression of his face, but of his entire being. "Good," he said. "That is all I have to say. I am glad that you will help." The elder turned to leave. "Tomorrow, after the meal. This is when we will council."

"I shall be there," Benjamin said.

As he watched the elder depart, Benjamin felt a strange joy, a fulfillment he had not felt since arriving at La Pointe some years ago. He felt validated as if he was finally fully integrated into the community.

―――――

The council gathered shortly before dusk while the sun was low in the sky and the air was warm and comfortable. A large circle was formed, and the pipe was passed, as was customary before any important gathering. The elders, like Kechewaishke and Oshoga, were seated at the head of the circle while the other leaders and people of influence filled out the rest of the circle. Behind them stood warriors and men and women of all kinds who were interested in what would be said. Benjamin was seated near the head of the circle at a small table with pen and paper, to serve as the scribe.

"Ojibwe men, women, and children," Oshoga said from his seated position at the head of the circle. "We gather for council to petition the Great Father in order to tell him that we do not want to leave our homes. We do not want to leave our ancestors' home. We do not want to leave the graves of our fathers. We have spoken before, but the Great Father does not hear us. We must be louder. We live away off, more than one moon, farther than the east is from the west. The Great Father forgets what we need. He promises to give us many things, but it gets lost along the way. We went to St. Paul, but his representative did not recognize us. We must remind him of our needs. We must remind him of our children's needs. We gather now to put our words on paper. We gather to remind the Great Father that we are still here, and we should remain here. That is all I have to say."

Oshoga bowed his head. The crowd was silent, not even a hush could be heard.

From behind the elders, White Thunder stepped forward. "The agent has a forked tongue. They say we can stay but then force us to leave. Do their words have no meaning?"

The crowd responded with shouts of agreement.

"My father is buried here," another Ojibwe voice shouted from within the crowd. "If we leave here and I enter the spirit world he will not be able to find me."

Again, there were audible grunts and shouts of agreement. Men pounded the ground while others yelped.

As Benjamin watched the scene unfold, he was unsure if he should start recording. There was so much emotion coming forward that it was difficult for him to capture it in a professional, persuasive tone. As the Ojibwe continued expressing their grievances he felt more and more anxious, wanting desperately to record the right words, while using the most influential tone. After all, he was writing a letter meant for the eyes of the President of the United States.

"There are many reasons to be upset," Kechewaishke said in a low and steady voice. "Let us only focus on those reasons that will convince the Great Father that we are right and just. We must not speak like children or we will be treated like children."

The Little Current stood and raised his voice. "The land is not needed or wanted by the pale-face. They do not like the northern climate. Their farms are a great distance from us and so we should not be removed."

"Very good," Kechewaishke said, speaking Ojibwe, "this will be included in our petition." Kechewaishke looked toward Benjamin to indicate that he should begin recording.

"We have committed no wrongs, or *depredations* as the pale-face calls it," Blackbird said as he stood to make his voice heard. "We have asked our neighbors and they came back and said they, too, committed no wrongs."

"Yes," Kechewaishke said. "This is true."

Benjamin wrote these reasons down in note form, knowing he could formalize them later.

"And we are advancing," another voice said.

Benjamin was surprised to look up and see that it was his friend and brother-in-law, Giizhigoon.

"We have, many of us, taken up the plow," Giizhigoon continued. "We have worked in their mines and lumber mills. We have entered their schools and spoken their language. We have sung their hymns and practiced their religion. We have done everything they have asked us to do and in return we should be allowed to stay."

Shouts, applause, and utterances of '*ho, ho*' followed as everyone at the council showed support for Giizhigoon's statement.

Kechewaishke raised his hands to silence the crowd. "Record these things for the Great Father to hear," Kechewaishke said as he looked once more in Benjamin's direction. "Tell him that the removal order is wholly uncalled for. Tell him that the land is not needed or wanted for his white farmers. Tell him we are living the way he has instructed us to. Most of all, with your words, capture our pain, our sorrow and our deep regret. Tell him that this removal will only make things worse for his red children."

The Ojibwe applauded, showing their support for Kechewaishke's request. As they did, Benjamin's doubt and anxiety began to grow. His words would be laid before the President of the United States. His words and perhaps his alone would have the power to save or condemn these people—the power to save or condemn his own family.

With this new, daunting responsibility Benjamin concentrated long and hard throughout the night, writing and rewriting every line of the petition. It had to be perfect. And so, he penned the words of the Ojibwe petition as best he knew how, making one draft after another. Though he knew he could never be completely satisfied with his wording, he finished it with a strong tone arguing that the Ojibwe of La Pointe and all surrounding neighbors were against a measure fraught with so many evil consequences as the proposed removal. With that he laid down his pen. Satisfied with his work, Benjamin fell asleep at his desk.

Weeks passed and there was no formal word about the potential removal. The new agent, Mr. Watrous, was almost always absent and
gave no indication that a new home had been selected for the Ojibwe.
People at La Pointe began to feel hopeful that, at the very least, removal would be put off for another year. As fall approached and winter
became more than an afterthought, the Ojibwe resumed their normal
traditions in preparation for the changing of the seasons.

"It's a good harvest this year," Benjamin said as he struck the wild
rice stalks with his ricing stick. Giizhigoon stood behind him pushing
the canoe with a pole slowly through the lake creating a well-defined
path behind them through the reeds, rice, and lily pads.

"Yes," Giizhigoon agreed as he paused to wipe the sweat from his
brow. "The Creator has been good to us. Now we must work hard
to gather, process, and store the food that has been so abundantly
provided."

Benjamin continued to whack the stalks, pulling them over the
canoe with one rice stick and striking the bent stalks with the other.
With each strike the stalks gave up their rice which fell harmlessly into
the canoe. The sound was soothing and repetitive, like wheat swaying
in the wind. Giizhigoon pushed and Benjamin whacked, filling the canoe to the brim with rice. For many hours they continued, filling one
canoe after another. It was hard, but necessary work. With enough
rice, the Ojibwe could be confident that they would have the food they
needed to survive another long winter. It was a tradition and a source
of much pride.

But, by 1850, the payment of government annuities often inter-
fered with traditional Ojibwe living. Many of the Ojibwe bands were
forced to travel a great distance to receive payment and often had to
spend many weeks waiting upon the agent. This interrupted their
traditional tasks and often threatened their survival during the long,
hard winter despite the assistance monied annuities could provide.

Late in the month of September, the agent called a gathering at
La Pointe. It was much like the gathering in February and everyone
knew that an important announcement was coming. As many people

as possible, whites, those of mixed races, and Ojibwes, came to the gathering place, but many others were absent because they were tending to their fall survival activities. Benjamin and Giizhigoon worked hard and gathered as much rice as they could before returning to La Pointe for the meeting.

Standing before them was Charles Oakes, a trader living at La Pointe. "Thank you for making time to gather. I will be brief today," he said.

"Where is the agent?" Oshoga asked before Oakes could make his announcement.

"I have been instructed by the agent to pass along an announcement," Oakes said.

Charles Oakes represented the last vestiges of the American Fur Company at La Pointe, the rest having been bought by Julius Austrian, Benjamin's employer. A few months back Oakes had been named the Superintendent of Removal. This came as a concern to many La Pointe residents because Oakes was business-oriented and had little knowledge of the Ojibwe people or way of life. It was feared, and more than likely true, that he would use his position as removal agent as a source of profit for himself and his company.

"The payment will not be made at La Pointe as it has in the past," Oakes announced. "It will be made at Sandy Lake near the Upper Mississippi."

A dejected cry of protest rose from the crowd.

Oakes ignored the objections and continued. "Payment will be made on October twenty-fifth. Payment will be made to the elders and heads of family. If you do not travel to Sandy Lake, you will not receive your payment at any time. You must also bring your families. If you do not bring your families, you will not receive payment."

Loud shouts of protest were raised by all who were gathered, including Benjamin who normally kept his discontent to himself. But, as a white man married to an Ojibwe, he was entitled to part of the Ojibwe annuity. It affected him as much as it did anyone.

One man cried out in protest. "Why is the payment being made so late?"

"Are we being asked to remove, or only forced to travel for payment?" another shouted. "I cannot be expected to bring my family."

Oakes raised his voice to speak over the crowd. "Ladies and gentlemen! Ladies and gentlemen! This is not a council. It is not open for discussion. I am giving you the instructions of your agent as passed down from government officials. You have no choice in the matter. If you wish to receive your annuities, you must come to Sandy Lake. That's final."

Oakes made his exit while the small crowd continued to bemoan the announcement. No one was really sure what it meant or what the intentions were. Was this a part of the removal effort, or would they be allowed to stay living upon their homeland? All that the Ojibwe knew now, all that Benjamin knew, was that if they wished to receive their promised annuity payment, they had to travel to Sandy Lake.

CHAPTER 9

Governor Ramsey stood patiently on the deck of a sixty-foot keel-
boat as the crewman tossed ropes ashore which were gathered by
other crewmen and tied to the sturdy wooden poles on the side of the
dock. Stepping off the boat he was met by John Watrous, the newly
appointed Indian Agent of the La Pointe sub-agency.

"Congratulations on your new appointment," Ramsey said as the
two men shook hands and smiled. "I have heard many positive things
about you. Except from Livermore, he considers you a scamp!"

Both men laughed. "Having just lost his job I suppose he would,"
Watrous said.

"You're an Ohio man, right?"

Watrous nodded. "Ashtabula County. Then I moved on to the Wisconsin Territorial Legislature before becoming a trader at La Pointe."

"A trader? That can be big business. Why did you move on from
the trade?"

Watrous shook his head with regret. "Competition was fierce the
year I began, and the companies extended too much credit. I'm embarrassed to say it, but I fell into debt and could not get out."

"Never mind that. You work for me now." Ramsey cut to the business at hand. "Are we prepared for the trip upriver? I only wish to
remain in Indian country long enough to give an adequate report to
Washington."

"Yes," Watrous said. "We are prepared. But speaking of Washington, have the removal funds been appropriated by Congress yet? That
stands in the way of our efforts."

"I have received no word from Washington yet. Brown has resigned and will be replaced by Luke Lea which has caused a delay in

communications. And Congress is occupied with the debate of slave versus free states. Indian annuities are last on their list."

"If that is the case, how shall we proceed?" Watrous asked.

Ramsey leaned in toward Watrous and spoke softly. "Whether the money is appropriated or not, you must convey them to Sandy Lake, and there time the payment in such a way as to interpose obstacles to a return to the country they left."

Watrous took a step back contemplating the governor's plan. "Very good," he said with a nod as if it were as plain and ordinary as his morning coffee.

CHAPTER 10

"We are departing in a week's time."

"Departing!" Charlotte repeated, her eyes narrow, her shoulders raised. She was visibly upset. "And I will travel with you? Along with the children?"

"No," Benjamin said. He did not want an argument, but he knew he must be honest and straightforward. Charlotte was uniquely capable and determined. She often challenged Benjamin and took an active role in the family's decision-making. She was independent, not always conforming to traditional gender roles. Benjamin loved this about her, but it also made it difficult for him when trying to make important decisions that extended beyond his own family.

"No?" Charlotte repeated. "I thought the agent instructed the men to bring their families if they wished to receive payment?"

"He did. But the elders met in council and decided it was too dangerous."

"Dangerous?"

"Yes," Benjamin said, maintaining a calm demeanor. "This decision by the government has come very late in the season. By the time we receive payment, it may already be winter. If entire families travel to Sandy Lake and winter sets in, it will be too cold to safely return home."

Charlotte turned her back to Benjamin, alone in thought.

Benjamin didn't know what to expect next from his wife. Would she forbid him from going? Would she encourage him to be safe and return quickly? He waited nervously.

"How will we be taken care of in your absence?" Charlotte asked, finally turning back to Benjamin and pointing toward Marie and Samuel.

"I have spoken with Mr. Austrian. He has agreed to my leave and said that he would provide all that you and the children need while I am away. It shouldn't be more than a few weeks that I'm gone."

Charlotte rested her hands on her hips and sighed. "I still don't understand," she said. "Are we being removed to Sandy Lake or just being asked to receive payment there? Why don't they continue the payment here, where we live, where we have always lived?"

Benjamin hated to see his wife in distress. He loved her dearly and he was eternally grateful for that pivotal moment when he met her, often wondering what life would be like if he hadn't chased after her at Prairie du Chien. Now, years later, he owed her so much.

"We all agree that there is no justice in these circumstances," Benjamin said. "No, we are not being asked to remove, but after meeting in council the elders believe it is more complicated than that."

Charlotte nodded but wasn't satisfied. "What do you mean?" she said in Ojibwe.

"The elders believe that the government wishes to force our removal by making us travel west for the necessary payment in the hopes that once we arrive we will be forced to stay because of the onset of winter."

"They wish to trap us at Sandy Lake?"

"Yes," Benjamin said solemnly. "It is horrible, I know. That is why we shall not take our families. Instead we are sending only the men and we will travel light so we can carry annuity goods home. We will not allow them to keep us there."

Charlotte countered. "Still, it is an unnecessary risk and I'd rather you stay home with the children and me."

"I know. But we have so little. I fear that our family will spend the winter in great discomfort without the provisions of the annuity payment. These annuity goods will get us through the winter. According to the agent, payment will be made at the end of October. If all goes well I will be back before December, having endured some difficult travel but nothing worse. The supplies will be worth it."

Charlotte sighed heavily as she came to accept the circumstances. "Very well," she said. "But you must return as soon as possible."

Benjamin did not want to put Charlotte and his family in this situation. Life in that region was truly one of risk and sacrifice. Illness and hunger and deprivation were ever-real and ever-present. It was a fact of life.

Benjamin sat down beside his wife and took her by the hand. "You have nothing to worry about. The days will pass quickly, and we will be better off upon my return. The Ojibwe—our community—we will all be better off. And by next year we will have the payment moved back to La Pointe."

Benjamin, Giizhigoon, and nearly one hundred Ojibwe men departed La Pointe in mid-October. Along with them were a dozen or so women, a few mixed-race voyageurs and several white traders. As a group, they traveled by canoe along the southern shore of Lake Superior. Traveling light, they carried only what they needed to get there and little else.

Staying within close proximity to one another and to the shore, travel was somewhat safe and easy. The days were still warm, though the daylight was short and getting shorter. Fortunately, the weather remained calm. The evenings were spent fishing or hunting small game for supper. Every evening while the meal was prepared the men smoked the pipe around the fire and every night, being that shelter was too cumbersome to carry, everyone rested easy under the light of the stars.

One night, while the group slept, Benjamin stayed awake to stir the fire and keep a general watch. The fire was important because it kept the wolves away. Wolves are cunning animals who rely on their excellent senses to outwit and capture their prey. At night they moved quietly under cover of darkness and had been known to steal away with supplies and sometimes even young children.

But on that night, Benjamin struggled to stay alert. He was tired from several days of travel and he felt so warm and comfortable next to the fire that eventually he gave in to his desire for sleep.

He awoke some hours later to see that the fire had burned out to nothing more than an orange glow of branches and sticks. Startled by the sudden realization that he had slept while on watch, Benjamin leaned forward to see if he could rekindle the fire. As he moved forward, he noticed movement.

Instinctively, Benjamin held his breath, stayed absolutely still and looked carefully into the darkness of the camp. As he focused, he began to see an object moving slowly toward him, its silhouette dark and unclear. Fear began to surge through Benjamin's body. Something was coming.

Then, moving into the light of the glowing fire, it growled. A low, guttural, persistent growl. It was a grey wolf.

The wolf was on the opposite side of the dying fire no more than fifteen feet from Benjamin. Its hair stood on end, its head was low, its fangs exposed, and its dark, determined eyes were fixed on Benjamin. It continued to move slowly forward, poised to attack.

Frozen by fear, Benjamin stared back uncertain what to do and incapable of moving. In mere moments the wolf would be upon him.

Just then Giizhigoon stepped forward from behind Benjamin. His arms were wide, his feet were spread, and his robe cloaked his body like an outstretched cape. Giizhigoon approached the wolf speaking in soft, steady tones. Still gripped by fear, Benjamin just watched as Giizhigoon moved slowly, calmly forward. The wolf stopped growling and took a few steps back, its fangs still exposed but its posture less threatening. Then, Giizhigoon bolted forward with one quick step and the wolf turned and ran.

Benjamin was amazed by what he had witnessed. Giizhigoon had taken on the wolf fearlessly, confidently, and came out victorious.

The threat being dismissed Giizhigoon turned toward Benjamin. "Sometimes even your brother needs discipline."

This was all he said as he slipped back into the darkness of the camp. As Benjamin regained his presence of mind he proceeded to stir the fire, having no more trouble keeping his eyes open.

———

The final leg of the journey to Sandy Lake was the most difficult. Known as the Savanna Portage, it took the group from the St. Louis River to the marshy area surrounding Sandy Lake. Brimming with tamarack peat bogs and forests of aspen and birch, the old trail was beautiful but difficult to travel. Requiring more than determination, the Savanna Portage required experience and grit, something frontier living provided.

Used for centuries by the Ojibwe and by the Dakota before that, the Savanna Portage provided an important link between the waterways of the Mississippi River and the waterways of the Great Lakes. In order to use the portage, travelers had to pick up their canoes and supplies and make a difficult six-mile hike through marshy and wet terrain. But, for the natives, traders, and missionaries that used the portage, the journey was worth it. The portage gave travelers access to huge water systems that could take them almost anywhere. For that reason, the Savanna Portage was used frequently.

Finally arriving at Sandy Lake, the group from La Pointe encountered a disappointing setting. First of all, neither the agent nor any government official was there to welcome them or hand out rations. The rations they did find were few, were mostly spoiled, and were quickly being used up.

"The Great Mississippi overflowed with water," explained Flat Mouth, a leader from the Leech Lake band of Ojibwe. "It has made the rice unusable and has caused the storage areas to collapse. We don't have time to wait upon the agent."

Another disappointing fact was that many of the Ojibwe bands had chosen not to come at all. These included the L'Anse, Pelican Lake, and La Vieux Desert bands. The Wisconsin River Band sent only two representatives. This, in and of itself was not bad, but it brought into question the risk incurred by Benjamin and the La Pointe Band. Nevertheless, by November there were about four thousand gathered at the lake. This encouraged Benjamin until he noticed people starting to get sick.

"I have not eaten in days," Giizhigoon admitted to Benjamin one evening while those gathered continued to wait for the agent's arrival. "I am in great pain and cannot eat."

"What kind of pain?" Benjamin asked.

"In the stomach and bowels. A sharp, agonizing pain. It is persistent and getting worse."

It sounded as though it might be dysentery, Benjamin thought. An all too common affliction.

"You need water and rest," Benjamin said as he went to fetch a fresh pitcher of water. "You should not go out to hunt until you feel stronger and can eat."

Giizhigoon drank the water and nodded his head. He did not look well. His face was flushed, beads of sweat covered his forehead, and his eyes were red. Benjamin was deeply concerned but did not wish to worry his friend by growing anxious.

Over the next several days many others fell ill, and then they began to die. It was one or two at first, but then more, many more. Two and three began dying daily, then four and five. All experienced the same symptoms. Stomach cramps, abdominal pain, and severe diarrhea. Some recovered but many did not. They took on fevers, became nauseated, some even hallucinated from time to time. They had little or no food to nourish them and could not replace the water they had lost fast enough to avoid dehydration.

Benjamin, too, began to feel ill. No one was spared at least some level of discomfort.

As more and more died, the scene at Sandy Lake became grim, even grotesque. The bodies could not properly be disposed of as there were not enough strong and healthy men to dig holes for burial. Traditionally, the Ojibwe wrapped the bodies of their deceased in birch bark and brought offerings of tobacco, food, and water for four days while the spirit of the deceased journeyed to the other world, a land called Gaagige Minawaanigozigiwining—the land of everlasting happiness. But at Sandy Lake this wasn't possible. Too many died, too quickly. It saddened the people, it overwhelmed them with grief.

Giizhigoon held on for weeks, making slight recoveries but then experiencing major setbacks.

"I am not well," he said to Benjamin as he lay under his temporary shelter along with several other of the sick and infirm. "I do not see myself recovering from this sickness."

"Do not speak in such terms," Benjamin said. He adjusted Giizhigoon's pillow, tightened his blanket, and patted his forehead with a cold towel.

"No, no, no," Giizhigoon muttered, going in and out of coherence. "I need you to care for my son. Take care of Makwa."

Benjamin tried to maintain his composure, but he was shaking with sadness and fear as he looked into Giizhigoon's dying eyes. "Your son will be taken care of."

Giizhigoon, with what little strength he had, begged Benjamin closer. "I will tell you a story now," he whispered.

"I am listening."

Though Giizhigoon was near death, he suddenly appeared composed and determined.

"This is a tragedy," Giizhigoon said softly. "What has befallen the Ojibwe—the Anishinaabe—the original people. Not just what is happening here today but what has happened for countless seasons before. We are wronged, we are hungry, we are dying. Our people and our traditions."

Benjamin grasped Giizhigoon's hand.

"But, I am reminded of the Creator and what he told us. I am reminded of what he showed us."

Giizhigoon coughed violently, barely able to breathe and having trouble speaking. Benjamin waited, knowing his friend had something important to say.

"What?" Benjamin asked. "What did he remind you?"

"Ma'iingan," he uttered. "Our brother, the wolf. The Creator put the wolf upon this earth to show us the way. The wolves are our educators, teaching us about hunting and working together in large family units. Wolves are an example of perseverance, guardianship, intelligence, and wisdom. Long ago the Anishinaabe and the Ma'iingan walked the earth and came to know all of her. In this journey, they became very close to each other. They became like brothers. In their closeness, they realized they were brothers to all creation. But one day the Creator said, 'You are to separate your paths. You must go different ways. What shall happen to the one of you will also happen to the other. Each of you will be feared, respected and misunderstood by the people who will later join you on this earth.'"

Giizhigoon went into a fit of coughing once again, this one more violent than the one before. Benjamin laid his hand on Giizhigoon's forehead, leaning him back gently.

"We are misunderstood," Giizhigoon continued though barely intelligible. "Just like our brother the Ma'iingan."

Giizhigoon paused, turning from side to side in agony. Benjamin could only sit and watch, feeling his own type of agony.

"I never wanted to cut my hair and replace my breech-cloth with a calico shirt. I never wanted to break the soil or harvest metal from the womb of the mother earth."

"I know," Benjamin said.

Giizhigoon looked deeply into Benjamin's eyes. "You must care for our people. You must care for our homes. What befalls the Ma'iingan will befall us as well. If there is no one to protect our land, or the land where the Ma'iingan roam, there is no one to protect us. You must do this, brother, or the Ojibwe will not survive. Protect us."

"Yes," Benjamin said grasping Giizhigoon's hand tightly. "Yes, I will."

"Now, brother, we too must separate," Giizhigoon said. "We must take separate paths."

"Hold strong, nisayenh," Benjamin said, trying to keep the tears from his eyes. *Hold strong, brother.* But Giizhigoon closed his eyes and fell into a deep sleep. Benjamin could only look at him, helplessly.

Giizhigoon survived another few days, but he was unable to speak, unable to eat, and barely able to breathe. When he passed away he was placed in a mass grave along with countless other Ojibwe. He died on November 24, the same day the agent, Mr. John Watrous finally arrived at Sandy Lake.

———

That evening, Flat Mouth, known as Eshkibagikoonzhe by his people, stood before the agent in confrontation. Flat Mouth was the leader of the Leech Lake band of Ojibwe and he closely rivaled Kechewaishke in status and influence.

"Look around you at the tragedy that has struck my people," Flat Mouth said through the help of an interpreter. The agent leaned against a tree and examined his fingernails, apparently disinterested in what the Ojibwe had to say.

"This was caused by the spoiled pork and flour your government provided. And now you come with no money and no supplies! The very reason you asked us here was to provide our annual payment, the payment promised us for this year and many years to come, the payment upon which we have come to depend for survival."

"I cannot be blamed for the stubbornness of the facts," Agent Watrous said. "I could not predict the flooding of the Mississippi or the poor harvest of fish. I could not know that your money wouldn't be appropriated until it was too late in the season. I am not the cause of your predicament."

"Yet you stand to profit while my people die."

The elder stood firm, dressed head to toe in traditional Ojibwe regalia. Beads hung from his sash and ears while quail feathers extended from his ornate headdress. His age-lined face hardened in anger as he shouted his grievance.

"We've learned of your ambitions. You wish the Lake Superior bands to be moved here permanently so that your small agency will become a large agency and your salary will increase. We know your ways and the ways of others like you. You have caused us to die."

Agent Watrous casually examined his coat as if he had no interest in the conversation. Seeing dust or dirt, he calmly brushed it off. "I admit that your situation is dire," he said, "but I admit to nothing else."

Flat Mouth paused and looked in all directions. He breathed deeply and heavily. As Benjamin looked on he could see the elder's eyes and heart filling with torment.

"Someone. Must. Be held to blame." Flat Mouth spoke slowly biting off each word. "The facts alone cannot account for our pain and suffering." Flat Mouth paused. No one spoke or moved, not even the agent. "We have been called here and made to suffer by sickness, by death, by hunger and cold." Flat Mouth's eyes and countenance went from torment and burden to anger and energy. Flat Mouth wanted retribution for the deaths of his people.

"I lay it all on him," Flat Mouth continued, impassioned. "I charge it all to our Great Father the governor. It is because we listened to his words that we have now suffered so much. We were poor before, but we are poorer now. We have been taken from our country at the most valuable season of the year for hunting and fishing, and if we had remained at home we should have been better off."

Those gathered were quiet and still, knowing Flat Mouth spoke from the heart. Even the agent looked up recognizing the desperation and passion coming from the great elder.

"Tell him I blame him for the children we have lost, for the sickness we have suffered, and for the hunger we have endured. The governor promised to feed us while here. He has not done it. It makes our hearts sore to look at what we have sustained while at Sandy Lake. You call us your children, but I do not think we are your children. You are not our father, and I think you call us your children only in mockery. The earth is our father and I will never call you so. We did not sell the ground to our Great Father. We gave it to him in order that he might follow our example and be liberal to us. But he only grows greedier, forcing us onto smaller and smaller plots of land. Now he extinguishes us and turns our rice beds into graveyards."

There was complete silence as Flat Mouth finished his speech. A chill filled the air, cold enough to make breath visible, dissipating slowly above the heads of the attentive crowd. All present turned their eyes to Agent Watrous and his interpreter for a response.

"The circumstances are indeed unfortunate, and your Great Father is not without compassion," Agent Watrous said in a slightly softer tone than before. "Your Great Father does not want you to experience grief and sorrow. What hurts the Ojibwe hurts your Great Father as well. What is done is done, but I assure you that I will gather all possible resources and I will give them unto you. It is not without sadness that I look upon your situation. I promise supplies as soon as possible and that you will leave here better off than you are today."

Flat Mouth, though still fuming, appeared satisfied with the agent's response as the two of them nodded, not out of respect or gratitude, but as a sign of mutual duty for the roles they were assigned.

Those gathered quickly dispersed, no less angry and no more relieved, but with few options. Survival had become the priority. Poverty and hunger were felt by every individual at Sandy Lake. But now, desperate as they were, they had to wait. If the Ojibwe were to return to their homes, they required food and supplies to get them there.

———————

The chiefs and elders gathered in the presence of several traders. One such chief was Bagonegiizhig, called Hole-in-the-Day the Younger by the whites. Bagonegiizhig was a young and ambitious leader from the Gull Lake band of Ojibwe. Bagonegiizhig assumed a leadership role only just recently, following the death of his father. He was intelligent and brave, and it was clear to everyone he met that Bagonegiizhig would play a major role in the future of his people, especially during these times of turmoil.

Once again, Benjamin looked on, hoping for the best but fearing the worst.

Agent Watrous stood before the traders. "I am joined by the chief officials of the Ojibwe in order to acquire much-needed supplies."

"How much is required?" asked George Nettleton, a trader from La Pointe who had been contracted to assist with the removal efforts.

"As much as possible," Watrous said. "We have some four thousand Ojibwe gathered here, and you are no doubt aware of their plight. They need enough food, blankets, and hunting materials to get them home safely."

"We are aware," said Clement Beaulieu, a trader from Crow Wing whose family was well known throughout Ojibwe country. "But we must protect our own interests. You have no money for the Ojibwe which means you have no money for us. Our credit has already been extended too far."

"I have been authorized by the governor," Watrous said, "to make a purchase on credit. When funds arrive, I assure you that the debt will be paid."

"I cannot provide goods based on assurances," said Charles Borup, a St. Paul merchant and trader. "Competition in Ojibwe country is fierce and if we provide all our goods now, we have nothing left to barter and may never recover our losses. You of all people know that, John."

The traders were shrewd. They traveled to Sandy Lake like vultures, presuming payment would be made and that they could then get money from the Ojibwe. But now the circumstances had changed. The Ojibwe were in dire need and the government was responsible. All leverage was on the side of the traders and they knew it. Being familiar with the trade, Benjamin knew it, too.

"I will supply ammunition," Beaulieu said. "So that they may hunt on their return trip. But I must ask an inflated price under the circumstances. Say, ten beaver pelts for one cartridge."

"That is outrageous," Benjamin yelled, bursting forward. "That is five times the standard cost. A man should be able to obtain an entire rifle for that price."

"Who are you to say?" the trader shot back.

"I am a clerk for Mr. Julius Austrian at La Pointe. I know the standard prices."

Beaulieu smiled nefariously. "Well, my offer stands as stated."

"I, too, must increase my prices," Nettleton said. "When demand is high and repayment is uncertain, prices rise. Fifty beaver pelts for a firearm."

"You thieves," said the brash and confident Bagonegiizhig, with the young mixed-race politician William Warren acting as his interpreter. "You strip our land of everything and then offer it back to us at a price we cannot pay. It is as if you reach into our very own medicine bag and take out its contents and say we owe you to get it back. We are not birds feeding from the mouths of our mothers. Neither are we fish unaware of the hook dangling behind your bait."

The young, handsome leader spoke without fear in front of the white traders. He stood straight, spoke with eloquence and passion, and was determined to protect the rights of the Ojibwe.

"My people have suffered a great loss, and you circle us like a coyote over a pile of bones. What you offer now will be offered back to you. Greed for greed. Suffering for suffering. Death for death. We see through your tricks, and we recognize your motivations. Be certain, the Ojibwe are a kind and open people. We care for our brothers like a mother bear cares for her cubs. But to ignore a wrong is the act of a coward. To turn away from the suffering wrought upon us would be shameful, like a dog tucking his tail between his legs. We will not ignore your injustice."

The traders shook their heads and muttered groans of disapproval. They scoffed at Bagonegiizhig's impassioned speech.

Agent Watrous finally spoke up, hoping to avoid violence. "We can negotiate," he said. "Let's just relax and settle on a negotiated price."

After a long and tedious negotiation, Watrous managed to talk the prices down, but they remained at three to six times the standard price. Making matters worse, the money to pay for it was to come out of the Ojibwe annuity funds.

Grief stricken and tired, Benjamin and what remained of the La Pointe group departed Sandy Lake in the first week of December. They were among the last to go because they were among the last to receive provisions purchased from the traders. The provisions were limited, not enough to supply them for the entire trek back to La Pointe. But there were no more forthcoming and they could not afford to wait longer.

Kechewaishke, who had remained silent throughout the ordeal, approached Benjamin as they began their walk along the Savanna Portage.

"Miigwech, Benjamin." *Thank you, Benjamin.* "For your bravery in the face of the agent. For your courage before the heartless traders."

The old man held out his hand which was filled with tobacco leaves, an offering of compassion and comfort.

"What has happened here is unthinkable," Benjamin said, politely accepting the tobacco. "I only did what was right."

Kechewaishke nodded in agreement. "An Ojibwe cannot have too many allies."

As they walked, Benjamin's heart was heavy. But so too were the hearts of all Ojibwe. Looking back at Sandy Lake was a burden too sorrowful to bear. Those who survived pressed on, but as the snow fell and the waterways became thick with ice, they knew their suffering was not yet over.

CHAPTER 11

A light snow fell over the city of St. Paul brightening the darkness of the late evening and creating a picturesque view of the snow-covered buildings and street lamps. For a city that had grown so rapidly, it was in that rare moment serene and peaceful. Inside the home of Governor Alexander Ramsey, a small party gathered to celebrate the holiday season and to give thanks for the prosperity of the previous year.

Seated in the parlor around a large polished oak table and warmed by a crackling fire were Ramsey and his wife Anna, Charles Oakes and his wife Julia, Charles Borup and his wife Elizabeth, and John Watrous. As they exchanged pleasantries, Watrous revealed a gift he had wrapped and brought. He handed it to Ramsey.

"Open it," Watrous said, his face brimming.

"You didn't have to..."

"Nonsense," Watrous said. "I owe you this and much more."

Ramsey slowly unwrapped the gift as his guests watched expectantly. "Beautiful," he said as he pulled out two fur gloves and held them in front of his face. "These are absolutely lovely!"

"They are made of mink—the very finest fur."

"And there's more," Ramsey said as he pulled out a hand-crafted cigar box. "This is too much."

The guests gasped as they admired the fine artwork of the carved and painted box.

"This is so lovely," Anna said with twinkling blue eyes as she looked across the table at Watrous. "Mr. Watrous, thank you so much."

"It is my pleasure," Watrous said.

"We have so much to celebrate this year," Anna said. "A new home, a new job, and a new Territory that is growing every day. It's just a shame your wife can't be here to join us."

A palpable silence fell over the room as everyone turned toward Anna with looks of uneasiness. Startled, Anna put her hand to her chest and pulled her head back. "I'm sorry…"

"She died in the smallpox epidemic of '47," Watrous said. "It struck the Ojibwe at La Pointe hard and my wife couldn't escape it."

"My apologies," Anna said, "I didn't know."

A few moments of awkward silence passed.

"Is it true what Alex and I have read in the papers?" Anna asked, trying to change the subject but making a poor choice of topic. "There are sad accounts of the Indians suffering due to want of provisions and disease."

"Anna, please," Ramsey said. "Now is not the time to discuss such matters."

"No, no," Watrous said. "It's quite alright."

"The papers do tend to embellish," Elizabeth said as she leaned forward with curiosity.

"I've heard the same rumors and it seems impossible," Julia said as she too leaned in with curiosity. The men, Oakes, Borup, and Ramsey, just looked at each other, acknowledging that they knew the sad truth of the matter.

Watrous sat back and crossed his leg over his knee. "They do tend to embellish, but unfortunately I can tell you that most of what they've reported is true. Many Ojibwe died at Sandy Lake and it can be assumed that many more suffered on their way home."

"That is terrible," Anna said with a gasp. "How did this happen? Was there something you could have done?"

"Unfortunately, the circumstances were beyond our control. But we have learned much that will allow us to continue our efforts next year."

"Next year? Will there be more suffering?"

Ramsey sat up and put his hand on his wife's knee. "No, darling. As John said, we have learned much from this year's attempt. Next year it will go smoothly."

CHAPTER 12

After enduring weeks of hunger and sickness the Ojibwe were anxious to leave Sandy Lake behind. But not everyone could just walk away. Many were still too sick, while others stayed behind to care for the sick. This led to many tearful goodbyes between those who remained and those who departed. The greatest fear and heartache came in not knowing if loved ones would ever see each other again. By this time survival had become precarious at best.

As the men and women from La Pointe began their journey home it was clear right away that their canoes would be of no use because a foot of snow had fallen and the waterways had frozen over. This created a tremendous obstacle. Canoes were a huge asset to the Ojibwe people and they represented much hard work and labor. Also, to be unable to use them on the waterways meant that all goods and provisions had to be carried upon their backs. This left each man with a pack weighing anywhere from sixty to one hundred pounds. And so there they were, hungry and cold, grief stricken, trudging hopelessly through the snow.

"I cannot eat the bark of the trees anymore," Kechewaishke said as the men sat together in camp. "It has been three days since I have tasted meat and it was five days before that."

Benjamin silently commiserated with the Ojibwe leader. The group still had many days' travel before they would reach La Pointe and people were dying. Looking around at the gaunt faces, Benjamin began to fear that he would not see his wife and children again. He feared that he would not be able to care for Makwa. He sat silently next to Kechewaishke, meditating on his fear.

"Our men die," continued the elder. "Young men. Strong men. They have left and gone to the spirit world. Their children are orphaned. Their wives are widowed. The time of plenty is long past."

"I am sorry, Kechewaishke," Benjamin said, breaking out of his rumination. "There is no justice in this. There is no fair explanation. Now I fear that we, too, may die."

Kechewaishke turned to Benjamin and looked at him gently, like a father to a son. "I had a vision," he said. "In my vision, I have seen you fight a great warrior alone behind the trees."

"Me?" Benjamin said with surprise pointing toward himself. "I am no warrior."

Kechewaishke did not pause to give Benjamin his assurance; he just continued speaking. "I thought the warrior defeated you, but you did not give in. The warrior laid down his bow and you returned in victory holding the bow high above your head. There was great celebration when you returned, and everyone was happy."

It was not uncommon for the elders to explain the world through visions, but Benjamin could not interpret Kechewaishke's meaning.

"What does this mean?"

"Go into the woods and find this warrior." Kechewaishke pointed, holding his arm out steady. "The Mooz. Find him. Defeat him. Return to great celebration."

"But I am not a great hunter. The moose will be too difficult to kill. In the winter, the air is too cold and still. He will hear me from far away and will be alerted of my presence. It is impossible for me."

"I can make a wind," Kechewaishke said as if it were simple and easy. "Though it is now still and cold the warm wind shall come before night."

Sitting around the fire, no one refuted Kechewaishke. They merely looked on, desperately, waiting for Benjamin to act. Benjamin, believing the task was futile, decided it was best to trust the wise elder. "I will go."

Hunting was a rigorous discipline that took many years to master. Benjamin was still learning and he pondered how he might possibly find and kill a moose. The Ojibwe consider the moose to be shier and more difficult to take than any other animal. But, being starving and sick, it was worth a try to capture the elusive animal. If nothing else, Benjamin was inspired by Kechewaishke's strange and unexplainable vision.

Benjamin started north against a cold and brisk wind, hoping to hide his scent from the perceptive animal he hunted. Moving cautiously, he had just enough powder and ball to load his musket a few times. He also carried some tobacco and a knife. The snow was deeper now, perhaps about two feet. It was smooth and flawless with heavy drifts and shallow voids, almost like sand in a desert. Benjamin zigzagged slowly through the forest looking for any signs of an animal presence. But the branches were unbroken, the bark unstripped, and the snow was free of prints or droppings. For several hours Benjamin continued this way, his hands and feet becoming numb, his face stiff and red. Only through constant motion did he remain the least bit warm.

While Benjamin rested against a birch tree, he heard a strange and long drawn-out bellow. Startled, he turned his head so his ear faced in the direction of the sound. This was his chance, he realized. What he heard was the unmistakable call of a bull moose.

Moving slowly, much slower than before, Benjamin went in the direction of the call. He hunched and stayed low while holding his rifle at the ready. He had never killed a moose before, only being party to those who had. Cautiously, he passed through a grove of trees and up a small knoll. Suddenly, he saw it. There, at the edge of a small, snow-covered meadow was the bull moose, nipping at some bark.

The large, brown, antlered animal was easily visible among the crisp, clean white of winter and birch. He was a beautiful creature. Powerful yet graceful, with a huge, muscular physique, long pointed ears, and large, concave antlers atop his oblong head. The bull moose seemed a mystery out there alone in the northern forest.

His heart racing, Benjamin carefully calculated every movement now, being certain not to create any unnecessary noise. Even his breaths were patterned out in a slow, methodical manner. Having the moose in his sights, Benjamin raised his rifle. The moose appeared completely unaware of his presence. Benjamin steadied his rifle and aimed for the ribs, hoping to strike the animal through the heart and lungs. He took a long, deep breath...

Just then the wind changed and came from the south, from behind Benjamin. The moose turned his head and became aware of his presence. In a moment of panic, Benjamin fired, hitting the animal in the back as it tried to dart away. The moose staggered, desperate to get away but incapable of running. Benjamin stood up from his kneeling position and sprang forward to make sure he kept the moose in sight. It bellowed in agony but still managed to increase its distance from Benjamin. Following the trail of blood in the snow, Benjamin moved as quickly as he could while trying to reload his musket. He stopped to open the flintlock of his musket and then quickly retrieved a paper cartridge from his pocket. He looked up to tear the cartridge open with his teeth and realized he had lost sight of the moose! Frantic, Benjamin ran forward, musket in his left hand and open cartridge in his right. He could not lose the animal—it may have been the difference between life and death.

Benjamin leaped over a felled tree and almost lost his cartridge, but with a steady hand he continued forward. The moose let out an agonizing cry, revealing its location. It stood, fifty or so yards distant peering back in search of its pursuer. Benjamin took the opportunity to finally empty the powder into the pan of the open flintlock. With great haste he lowered the butt of the musket, pulled out the ramrod, and drove the ball down the barrel. As he reloaded the moose began to move again, just as determined to get away as Benjamin was to kill it. Moving forward, Benjamin closed the distance between himself and the injured animal. Finally, he stopped, dropped to a knee and aimed at his moving target. Calmly, Benjamin inhaled, looked down the sight of the barrel, pulled back the hammer and fired.

The thud of the great animal crashing to the ground created an echo that reverberated off the frozen trees. The bull moose bellowed and moaned and let out one final snort and was dead. Relieved, Benjamin let his musket hang loosely around his shoulder as he moved forward to examine his prey. As he leaned next to the animal he watched steam rise from the wound. Still exhilarated from the pursuit he noticed the pounding of his heart and trickles of sweat falling from his brow. Sitting there in silence, he dropped some tobacco in the snow as an offering of thanks to the brother animal who had given its life to spare his own.

Benjamin made camp in the woods that night. Filled with pride, he enjoyed a great feast of moose meat. It was a satisfaction unlike any other before, a victory among so much loss. In the morning, he built a sledge of evergreen branches and loaded it with as much meat as he could pull. The rest he buried in a cache, intending to return for it later. As he headed south, back to the main party, a southerly breeze continued. Though he traveled against it, this time it was mild and welcoming. Arriving back at camp, Benjamin received much praise and adulation. Those suffering from hunger would have relief, albeit temporary.

"You have defeated a great warrior," Kechewaishke said to Benjamin. "You have returned with your bow held high."

The elder's prophesy was right, and Benjamin could only smile in return. It was good to feel joy again.

———————

The next day Benjamin went out to retrieve his cache, with instructions to meet the party in camp that night as they would proceed forward. This time Benjamin did not go out alone but was accompanied by the Reverend Sherman Hall. Reverend Hall was a devout Protestant minister who had lived at La Pointe many years. He and his family came from Vermont in 1831. At the time, coming from Vermont to La Pointe must have seemed like traveling to the end of the world. But, as a member of the American Board of Commissioners for Foreign Missions, it was Reverend Hall's duty to travel to far-off places for the purpose of rescuing souls for Christianity. Benjamin didn't have a deep relationship with Reverend Hall, but he knew him to be a good and decent man.

"It is seldom noted," Reverend Hall said after more than an hour of silent walking, "that strength and athleticism are necessary characteristics of a frontier missionary."

The comment was unexpected but not unwelcomed after such a long silence. "Is that right?" Benjamin said.

"Undoubtedly. I have set out many times through the deep and endless wilderness going from station to station to do good work for the cause of humanity. Over the years I have tirelessly endured many hardships."

"That would be hard work," Benjamin said, trying to be polite.

"But, I admit that the hardship we have encountered at Sandy Lake has been more trying than any before."

"The grief is overwhelming," Benjamin said as he lowered his head and sighed. "I did not think it would come to this."

"Neither did I," Reverend Hall said quickly.

There was a pause in the conversation. Both men breathed heavily as they worked hard to walk through the snow.

"Can I make a confession?" The reverend spoke with uneasiness in his voice as he looked at Benjamin, his brown eyes piercing and innocent.

"Of course," Benjamin shrugged, "though a preacher making a confession seems out of character."

The reverend smiled. "I suppose it does, but after what happened I cannot hold this in."

"I am listening."

"It is a sin of omission," he admitted cautiously. "When we learned of the effort to remove the Lake Superior Ojibwe, I did little to organize against it. I did nothing to stand in its way."

"You did not promote it, though," Benjamin said, sensing the guilt the reverend felt inside.

"No, I did not. But I went along with it, though I knew it was wrong."

"There was nothing you could do."

"Perhaps." The reverend paused. He was deep in thought as he tried to reconcile himself. "I think about what has happened. Such an immense tragedy. Such an unjust punishment. In hindsight, I should have done everything I could to prevent it."

"We could all say the same thing."

Reverend Hall kept his eyes on the snowy path in front of him.

"The truth is, this has caused me to reflect on these past nineteen years and rethink about what to do next."

"How do you mean?"

"When I arrived, I was so young and ambitious," he said, speaking freely now. "I thought I could save souls and greatly improve the lives of the Ojibwe people. My first few months church attendance averaged twenty-five. Now," he stuttered, "now it is just sixteen. Nineteen years and nothing to show for it."

"That is not true," Benjamin said, knowing the reverend had a large impact on the island community. "You translated the gospels. You educated the community. And you make a positive impact in the lives of the people."

"That is kind of you to say, but I am not so certain," said the reverend, a tone of shame in his voice. "At first the La Pointe Ojibwe welcomed me and allied with me. But they have since clung stubbornly to their way of life and rejected many of my teachings. They have refused the benefits I provide."

Benjamin contemplated this, not sure how to soothe the Christian missionary. "I understand your sacrifice," Benjamin said. "But I think you fail to recognize their contributions. I have learned this from my wife and men like Giizhigoon. The Ojibwe culture may be different, but it is not lacking. They cling to it for its value, not its ignorance or insufficiencies."

There was another pause. Benjamin worried that he might have offended the reverend.

"That is a progressive notion," he finally said, "but I understand your perspective. I think I still have much thinking to do after all this. And I am not ready to give up. I do not feel that the time has yet come when the churches ought to close their efforts. I still wish to save these people."

"We have a long way to go," Benjamin said, offering his sympathy.

Eventually, the two men recovered the cache and reunited with the larger party that evening. On their way, Benjamin spent a lot of time talking with the reverend. Somehow it was soothing and healing. Throughout the conversation Benjamin put aside his stress and grief, and he was proud to see that Reverend Hall was gaining a new perspective.

————

The surviving members of the La Pointe group arrived back at the island in late December, two and one-half months after they departed. The village, the agency, and the island were quiet. La Pointe appeared untouched by the reality of what just happened. Many loved ones reunited, but many did not. Sadness and grief spread throughout the community. Suddenly the pristine, snowy whiteness of the landscape turned to darkness as people mourned.

Benjamin, his heart heavy, found young Makwa and told him about the death of his father.

"He was brave and strong," Benjamin said. "He held on as long as he could."

Makwa was silent. His head dropped, and his heart did too. Without a word, Makwa took off running, seeking somehow to dull his pain.

"Makwa!" Benjamin yelled. "Makwa!" he yelled again in a futile effort. Makwa did not turn around.

Finally returning home, Benjamin embraced his children and kissed Charlotte.

"I am sorry," he said, filled with guilt and grief. "I was wrong to go, and I was wrong to expect things to be better off after my return. I should not have left you."

"We are just glad you are home," Charlotte said as her eyes welled with tears. She did not turn from him or scold him; she didn't even wipe the tears as they rolled down her cheeks.

For Benjamin, it was a moment of complete, unguarded relief.

As Benjamin watched his children play, oblivious to the tragedy that occurred, he thought about the lasting relevance of what had happened. During his years as a part of the Ojibwe community, despite many challenges nothing this devastating had ever befallen them. Looking further back the Ojibwe had endured wars, and famines, and disease, but never anything quite like the death and suffering at Sandy

Lake. They were lured where they did not want to go. They were fed spoiled food and denied their promised payment. They were made to return in the heart of the cold, barren, and harsh winter. About one hundred seventy died at Sandy Lake and another two hundred thirty, from various bands, died trying to return to their homes.

The tragedy was public and, in many ways, calculated. At La Pointe, for those that survived, the tragedy provided a small sense of hope that it might result in a definitive end to removal efforts. Surely the government would not repeat such a debacle, nor could the community endure it. As winter dragged on in early 1851, life resumed but the future remained uncertain.

CHAPTER 13

Hole-in-the-Day the Younger, head man of the Gull Lake band of Ojibwe and burgeoning leader of the Mississippi Ojibwe, stood before a white audience at the Presbyterian Church in St. Paul. At his side was his friend and interpreter William Whipple Warren, a mixed-race Ojibwe and government-appointed farmer at Gull Lake. Together, the two men had a remarkable and influential presence. Hole-in-the-Day was confident, with a stern, determined face, jet black hair tied back with fancy and colorful beads, and a black suit that contrasted his Indian-style moccasins. Warren was young and intelligent with a pensive face, and he was dressed in a tailored suit with a silk neck tie.

"The more treaties we make the more we become miserable," Hole-in-the-Day said in Ojibwe as Warren translated. "Each treaty takes more land and gives us less money. Then, when we come for our money, we are given spoiled provisions and made sick and left to die. I arrived late at Sandy Lake, but when I did, four, five, and six people died every night and day."

The audience gasped in unison.

"The provisions that were not spoiled were not enough to sustain us. The portion for an adult was not enough to fill my two hands." Hole-in-the-Day held out his hands like a cup. Another gasp from the audience followed. "Why?" he said adamantly. "Why does the Great Father not send someone who will report to him our grievances and sufferings. Why does the Great Father not care for his red children?"

CHAPTER 14

"Marie. Samuel. This is Makwa, he will be staying with us from now on."

The children smiled as they looked up at Makwa. Marie first, and then Samuel mimicking his older sister.

"Makwa is going to help your mother and me around the house. He will also join me hunting and fishing. I think he is old enough for that now."

Marie raised her arms toward Makwa and said hello. Makwa stood politely a few feet back and gave no response.

It had been a few months since the death of Makwa's father, Giizhigoon. Benjamin had promised to care for him, and he intended to make good on that promise. But Makwa mourned deeply over the loss of his father. He had been silent, never saying a word or cracking a smile since the tragic news had been delivered.

"Do you think he will be all right?" Charlotte asked later in the evening.

"Give him time," Benjamin said. "The boy lost his father and I know what that is like. Let him grieve and just give him time to adjust."

Charlotte grimaced. "I feel so helpless. So many have experienced loss in the wake of Sandy Lake and there remains so much grief, anger, and uncertainty."

"We have to stay together. The community is strong."

"What are they saying?" Charlotte asked. "The Ojibwe leaders, I mean. You've overheard them in council."

"They're angry. They refuse, under any circumstances to return to Sandy Lake. They say it is a graveyard."

"I can't blame them for that."

"Some of the younger, more resolute members wish to retaliate with violence. The elder members still seek diplomacy and negotiation. They all have come to realize that they were coaxed into signing treaties that they did not understand and that have been used against them."

"This has been going on now so long," Charlotte said as she took Benjamin by the hand, "it is hard to envision a peaceful outcome."

Benjamin squeezed Charlotte's hand in return. "Some have said that if they are to die, they might as well do it here, at Moningwunakauning, where they can be buried alongside their relatives."

Charlotte gasped, startled by the sentiment. "Will there be fighting?"

"I am not sure what is to be done, but I do fear that anger may lead to violence."

"Has the agent or the government given any sort of response or further instructions? They couldn't have just ignored what happened. Hundreds died."

Benjamin nodded. "Yes, they have responded. The agent has called a meeting with the Lake Superior Ojibwe here at La Pointe in June."

"Will he make last year's payment? Will he announce an end to these painful removal efforts? Will he apologize for the suffering he has caused?"

Charlotte's emotions were turning toward frustration. Like everyone living at La Pointe, she was tired of uncertainty and mistreatment.

Benjamin took Charlotte's other hand, now face to face clutching both hands. "No one knows, Charlotte. We just have to keep fighting for what is right. For Makwa and for the entire community."

Charlotte looked deeply into Benjamin's eyes, her face gentle and compassionate. "I know," she said. "We need to stay strong."

———

As winter turned to spring the days at La Pointe passed with relative monotony. People hungered because of the missed payment, but they survived. Then, like it had every spring, the sight of the first steamer brought great relief with the knowledge that supplies could once again be replenished. People emerged from their homes and wigwams ending the confinement of a cold, dark winter.

But the heaviness and uncertainty brought about by the removal efforts were far from over. The La Pointe Ojibwe continued their councils trying to decide what action to take to avoid permanent removal and to have their payment made to them on the island. News of the recent tragedy reached the white populations of Minnesota and Wisconsin and this garnered much support in favor of the Ojibwe. It also provoked anger toward Watrous, the agent. In the matter of removal, it seemed that everyone was on the side of the Ojibwe. This was at least one reason for encouragement.

But whatever good fortune there might have been, it disappeared with the arrival of William Boutwell in the spring. Boutwell was a missionary from the interior who had been hired by Watrous to act as the Assistant Superintendent of Removal.

"He is disgraceful," Harriet Wheeler told Benjamin shortly after Boutwell's arrival to La Pointe. "He accepted a bribe from Governor Ramsey of four dollars per day to assent to removal."

Benjamin was saddened but not shocked by this bit of information. He was learning that the only ones who favored removal were those who stood to gain from it economically.

Boutwell's first order of business was to inform the Ojibwe that Agent Watrous called a general meeting for June 10, 1851. Watrous was at the time absent from La Pointe as was often the case. So Boutwell relayed the message and also sent out messengers informing all the Ojibwe located in the ceded territory to assemble on that date. All Lake Superior and Wisconsin bands were called to gather on the island.

After a short time, Ojibwe warriors and elders began arriving from all directions, some with their families. No one was sure what the agent had in mind, but all were resolute against removal.

"Where is the agent?" Oshoga asked, speaking to William Boutwell on the day of the meeting.

"Agent Watrous is disposed at the moment, making proper arrangements for your new home," Boutwell answered, standing confidently before about five hundred Ojibwe. The removal agent had a stern, sour looking face with a full head of hair and gray sideburns. He was dressed neatly with a vest, suit coat, and neck tie looking more like a banker than a missionary.

"He tells us not to grow crops," Oshoga said, who looked quite the opposite of Boutwell, dressed in deer skin leggings, moccasins, and a feathered headdress. "He says his farmers are preparing crops for us. But we say we will not go."

"If you do not go, you will not receive your payment." Boutwell spoke matter-of-factly, much like Watrous had the year before.

Were there no repercussions for the death caused at Sandy Lake? Benjamin wondered. *How could they use the same plan as before? Had they no conscience?*

"We have discussed this already," Oshoga said, speaking of the many councils that had been held among them. "In the previous season you took us from our homes during the rice harvest, and you kept us away until the hard moon arrived. We were starved and made sick and died. We have lost confidence in your words and would rather die here, where our fathers are buried. You have given us no reason to do as you wish."

Boutwell was undeterred and replied calmly through the help of an interpreter. "I will express your concerns to Agent Watrous. But rest assured the agent will not change his mind. Besides, he is more diligent than before and will not let there be a repeated tragedy."

The faces of the Ojibwe were filled with anger and resentment, skeptical of Boutwell's words.

"How can we trust the words of the agent when he is not even here to give them to us?" said an Ojibwe leader from a more eastern band. "In the time since Watrous became agent we have found not a single promise kept."

The crowd responded with agreement, chiding the government official in front of them.

Oshoga continued his lament. "Even now we were promised provisions and there are none. Look around you. We have little money and what we have we have used in coming here. Now, we will return home never again to return at the call of a government official."

"I understand that you are disappointed," Boutwell said, "but you must allow the agent time."

As Boutwell spoke the Ojibwe began to disassemble, very disappointed that they had been lied to once again.

"The agent will arrive in a short while," Boutwell shouted over the commotion, "and you should be ready to speak with him at that time."

Kechewaishke stepped forward. "Tell the agent, we demand to be paid here or Fond du Lac. Beyond there we will not go."

With that the meeting ended, having accomplished nothing but the flaring of tempers and the renewal of dissatisfaction.

––––––––––

Over the next few weeks some of the Ojibwe who had gathered at La Pointe departed for their homes, no longer willing to wait on empty promises. Others, however, continued to arrive in hopes of meeting with the agent. In the meantime, Benjamin and Charlotte decided to officially adopt Makwa in a public ceremony. The ceremony was not necessary, but Benjamin saw it as an opportunity to take people's minds off the tensions at La Pointe and, hopefully, to help Makwa overcome his grieving.

"In ceremony we represent the four orders," announced the elder who was officiating the ceremony. He was dressed in full native regalia with moccasins, deerskin leggings, a colorful wampum sash, and had long braided hair decorated with beads. A large crowd of supporters gathered, encircling Makwa. "The rock," the elder said, pointing to a large boulder at the center of the ceremonial grounds. "That upon which we walk and run and hunt, and sleep. The fire. That which keeps us warm, gives us light, and turns meat into nourishing food. The air. That which fills our lungs, carries our songs, and fills our sky. The water. That which quenches our thirst, carries our boats, and harbors our fish. These are all represented here, because without them we cease to exist. The four orders are a part of us and we a part of them."

The elder bowed his head as several long, ornamented pipes were lit. The pipes were passed slowly among the elders and witnesses who were seated in a circular fashion. Benjamin and Charlotte received the pipe last while Makwa stood near the official in the middle. He was silent, though observant. He was also dressed in traditional native regalia.

"We now call upon the Great Spirit and all our ancestors traveling along the spirit road," the official said.

One prayer after another was recited by the elders and Ojibwe witnesses. Even Reverend Wheeler took a moment to recite a Christian prayer. With each one several Ojibwe youth sang in elongated, low, repeating tones. The music they created was enchanting and filled with emotion.

"Let the drummers now honor this new and growing family with your songs of praise." The official slowly lifted his arm, pointing to the drummers whose sticks were held high above their heads.

Boom, ba, boom.

All at once the young Ojibwe warriors began beating their drums.

Boom, ba, boom, ba, boom.

Over and over they hammered at their large, painted drums creating a loud, rhythmic, and captivating beat.

Then the chanting began in unison with the beat of the drum. Beautiful sounds of low, long, staccato tones that filled the air and reverberated through the crowd. Sensing the mystique of the event Benjamin closed his eyes, lost in the music, lost in the ceremony.

"Makwa, Samuel, Marie, Charlotte, Benjamin." The official called each name as the music finally dissipated. "Come forward that your family can be recognized."

"The Ojibwe are a family," the official said as Benjamin, his wife and children lined up, hands clasped, in front of their neighbors and friends. "Extending from the newest babe to the most worn elder. We live alongside one another in peace and togetherness, coming from all directions: north, south, east, and west. What happens to one of us happens to all of us."

The audience sat silently, listening to the honorable lessons of the spiritual elder. As Benjamin soaked up his words, he felt both joy and sadness. Joyful to welcome a new member to his family, but sad that it came at the death of Makwa's father, Charlotte's brother, and his friend, Giizhigoon.

"Now, as you build your family, the Ojibwe community, which is already so vast and so strong, becomes stronger. Like a school of fish, we swim together. Charlotte, Benjamin; we now recognize Makwa as a part of your family. Protect him and we will protect you. And when you cannot protect each other, your Ojibwe family here today and across the land will also be your protection."

The silence was filled with applause and shouts of celebration. As Benjamin turned to hug Makwa he noticed the hint of a smile, an expression from Makwa that Benjamin had not seen in a long time.

The celebration continued with singing, dancing, and a feast. It was a great and joyous occasion that extended well into the night. Everyone was happy, talkative, and enjoyed the celebration with little thought to the troubles that had so recently surrounded the La Pointe community. It was a memorable occasion, and a wonderful celebration.

———————

It was not until August 13, a full two months late, that Agent Watrous arrived at La Pointe. By that time the number of Ojibwe had grown to about 1,000. Many had come with their families—wives, children, and dogs—and were prepared for a long stay. They put up their wigwams of birch bark near the shore of the lake and wandered peacefully throughout the island. The visitors joined in all aspects of life at La Pointe. They hunted, fished, gathered, even made their own little gardens. In the evenings, they joined in the passing of the peace pipe and danced alongside the La Pointe Ojibwe during traditional ceremonies. Some even took work at the lumber mills.

When the agent finally arrived and was ready, council was called. The council took place in Austrian's store, Benjamin's place of employment. The store was long and spacious. Hundreds gathered inside while hundreds more gathered outside.

On the left side of the room the chiefs and elders of the La Pointe and other bands sat on the floor with their blankets wrapped around them. They were painted and dressed in full native attire, many of them with long-stemmed pipes extending from their mouths.

On the other side was Agent Watrous, his interpreter and Reverend Boutwell. These men were much disliked among the Ojibwe, but they were the ones in authority.

"I have called you here," Watrous said through the use of his interpreter, "to discuss the terms of your removal."

The agent paused to let his words take effect. Benjamin was angry that Watrous made no reference to the lateness of his arrival or to the deaths at Sandy Lake which he almost certainly caused. He just stood, brazenly, as if unaccountable to the world around him. Looking on, Benjamin gritted his teeth with contempt.

"I come as a representative of your Great Father," Watrous continued. "I desire to convey to you only that which your Great Father wishes you to know. Namely, that you remove yourselves from the ceded lands and resettle upon the interior."

There was a pause as the interpreter translated. This was followed by an audible grumble. *How could the removal orders continue?* Benjamin thought.

"I understand that you are upset, but this is for your own benefit as well as the benefit of your Great Father's white children. This land is no longer useful for you but is needed by your Great Father's white children that they may till the soil, harvest the timber, and mine the copper. These are all things for which you have no use. That is why your Great Father wishes you to move to the interior. There you will not be bothered by the white man's presence nor tempted by his fire-water. There the lakes abound in fish and rice and the forests teem with wildlife. There you will be safe and will not hunger, both now and for many years to come. This is what your Great Father wants for you."

There was a general silence as the elders conversed among each other. They took several minutes deciding what they wanted to say. The agent looked on impatiently.

"We will not go," Kechewaishke said speaking in his native Ojibwe. "We have been to Sandy Lake and we were welcomed with death and despair. We will not return to that place."

The agent responded immediately. "I understand your reticence. I was ill-informed and unprepared. Nor could I predict the flood that spoiled your food or know of the delay that prevented your payment. I have since been more diligent in order to assure your health and happiness. Furthermore, I shall leave you no choice. I have called upon a company of infantry of American soldiers to force your removal if you do not remove willingly."

"We do not fear violence," retorted the warrior Blackbird. "This would be a more honorable way to die than to be left in the cold and empty forest."

"If you and your families wish to receive your annuities," the agent said with a rather calm demeanor, "now or at any point in the future, then it must be done at Sandy Lake."

Tensions were growing in the crowded store as both parties seemed unwilling to negotiate. Benjamin seethed with contempt. How could this man be so brazen, so careless?

After a few moments Kechewaishke raised his arms and silenced the murmurs of anger and discontent.

"We do not wish to incite violence," the elder said, looking at the agent but speaking to all present. "We only desire that our wishes be heard. Go back to the Great Father and tell him to keep the money and his goods. We do not want them, but we wish to be left in peace. Tell him we will not move from the land that is our own, that we have always been peaceable and were always happy until the white man came among our people and sold bad medicine to us."

Kechewaishke was speaking of alcohol, which was often sold illegally to the native peoples.

"We know that you represent the Great Father," he continued, "and we act according to his authority."

"Then you will continue to suffer," Agent Watrous said. "Because the Great Father lives in Washington, a place far off where you cannot go. That is why he has placed me here. I understand and carry out the wishes of the president. My authority is given to me by him."

Why not travel to Washington? Benjamin thought. Yes, it was a great distance, but it had been done before. The removal order had originated there, and it was only there that the removal order could ultimately be put to rest.

"Let us send a delegation," Benjamin blurted.

The agent turned his head toward Benjamin, staring hard. "Excuse me?"

"Let us send a delegation of chiefs and elders to Washington to meet with the president. Let the Ojibwe express their grievances before the president that he might decide what is to be done."

"This is not so simple. The president is very busy and funds must be appropriated through Congress. The process would take too long, and you should already be removed by then."

"I agree with this request," Kechewaishke said. "Let us stand before the Great Father himself. Let us tell him of our needs and the needs of our wives and children. He should know of our poverty and suffering that he might end it. This is our request."

"I will take this into consideration," Watrous said, tightly folding his hands in front of him. "But this does not alter our arrangement. You are to remove to Sandy Lake along with your families. If you do not, payment will not be made, and infantry will be sent to force your removal."

Kechewaishke did not back down. "We have not agreed to such terms. Fond du Lac is as far as we shall go. We also desire a request be made that we should send a delegation to Washington to speak with the Great Father. These are our terms from which we shall not be shaken."

Those Ojibwe gathered showed support for Kechewaishke by banging their chests and slapping their thighs.

"We have counseled enough today," concluded the great elder, Kechewaishke. "When we meet again, you can tell us if you accept our terms."

Kechewaishke rose slowly, as did the other chiefs and elders. They departed the store to shouts of hope and confidence. Benjamin was impressed and encouraged by their defiant stand, but he was nervous, too. It was his request that they go to Washington, and it might ultimately be his responsibility.

The council, which ended abruptly, was resumed the next day and again the next day after that. For five straight days, the Ojibwe and the agent negotiated until it seemed no agreement could be met. At that point Watrous threatened to leave, having no agreement reached or recorded. This led to the sixth and final council. A compromise was reached, written down by the agent, and laid down before the assembly. Benjamin, glancing over Kechewaishke's shoulder, was able to read the agreement. It was an agreement of Mr. Watrous' intentions, not the Ojibwe.

1st—I agree on removing to Fond du Lac, to make your monied payment of 1850 and 51 at that place.

2nd—To provide you with twine, fish hooks, and nets, and feed you for one year from the time the removal commenced; to open farms and build houses as fast as the means placed at my disposal will allow.

3rd—To ask permission and to recommend that the chiefs be allowed the privilege to visit Washington in company with myself sometime during the winter.

Pleased with this compromise, Kechewaishke shook hands with the agent and bid him farewell. Watrous, and his small group of supporters, left quickly appearing much displeased.

"This is well for our people," Kechewaishke announced. "It is a good compromise, preventing us from going to Sandy Lake."

———

A few weeks passed and life at La Pointe was busy and unsettled. Some of the Ojibwe bands remained at La Pointe while others went home. Still others went west to Fond du Lac where they expected to receive payment from the agent. But all were unclear about where they would live and how they would prepare for winter. Although the agent had promised money and supplies that would last for up to one year, everyone knew that it was a great risk to take Agent Watrous at his word.

One day in September, while Benjamin was out collecting dried wood, he was approached by a young Ojibwe named Yellow Beaver. Benjamin was acquainted with Yellow Beaver though he did not know him well. He dressed in the manner of the whites and had taken up farming. Only recently had he made these changes, in hopes of appeasing the government so that they might not require the Ojibwe to move from their homes.

"Mr. Armstrong," he said cautiously while he moved through the trees nearby.

"Yellow Beaver!" Benjamin was taken by surprise.

Yellow Beaver raised his finger to his lips as he moved slowly toward Benjamin.

"What seems to be the matter?" Benjamin asked in a more hushed tone.

"The agent's assistant, Mr. Boutwell—he gave me a telegram," Yellow Beaver said speaking Ojibwe, his voice wavering. "I am acting as a messenger and I am to deliver it to Mr. Watrous at Sandy Lake."

"Why have you brought it to me? Is this why you are being so secretive? Is it because you have this official document?"

"Yes," answered Yellow Beaver as he looked around cautiously. "Mr. Boutwell told me to take it straight to Sandy Lake and to show no one. I do not know what it says, I cannot read. I want you to read it."

Benjamin was startled by the request, but curious. What could it possibly say and why was it meant only for the agent?

"You were right to come to me," Benjamin said with unexpected confidence.

"Kechewaishke trusts you, and therefore I trust you too."

Yellow Beaver handed Benjamin the telegram. It was in a small envelope with a wax stamped seal.

"Never mind the seal," Yellow Beaver said, sensing Benjamin's hesitation. "I will take care of that."

Slowly, Benjamin pulled the note from the sleeve and began reading the telegram. It was from the Commissioner of Indian Affairs, Luke Lea.

Suspend all actions regarding the Removal of the Lake Superior Bands of Ojibwe immediately. Such portions of those bands as may desire to remain for the present in the country they now occupy may do so. Any further actions will be determined by the president.

Benjamin's eyes became wide with shock, looking up from the telegram.

"What!? What does it say?" Yellow Beaver asked.

Benjamin looked at him excitedly. "The removal order has been suspended."

Yellow Beaver's face lit up with a smile. "That is great news!"

"It is, you're right, it is. We must tell the others."

"You can't!" commanded Yellow Beaver as he grabbed Benjamin by the arm. "No one can know that I have shown you this or I will be punished. I will lose my job, I will be denied my annuity. I can't afford that."

"But others must know. They must know of this victory. They must also know so that they can properly prepare for the winter."

"Just wait, please Mr. Armstrong." Yellow Beaver clung tightly to Benjamin's arm, his face now filled with desperation. "Wait until I return. Wait to see how the agent responds. Please, wait."

Benjamin was torn. He did not want Yellow Beaver to lose the trust of the agent or Mr. Boutwell, nor did Benjamin wish to jeopardize the young man's livelihood. But Benjamin wanted desperately to share the good news. It would give renewed hope to the community. But what if Yellow Beaver was right? What if the agent ignored the order? That hope would be futile.

"Go quickly," Benjamin said. "Tell me when you return."

Yellow Beaver nodded in agreement, put the telegram back in his breast pocket, and then turned and ran.

Looking around, Benjamin saw no witnesses. He took a deep breath realizing that for now he had to live with a secret.

CHAPTER 15

Alexander Ramsey walked into the Officer's Quarters at Fort Ripley and casually sat down. He was followed by the agent, John Watrous. The military garrison, which was located along the Mississippi a few miles south of the Crow Wing River, had been established just one year earlier to support settlement on the frontier and act as a buffer between the Ojibwe and Dakota peoples. It was a convenient meeting place for Ramsey and Watrous. Ramsey had just completed the Sioux treaties and was on his way north to negotiate the Pembina treaty. Watrous had a brief respite before heading to Fond du Lac to approve the delivery of provisions for the upcoming payment.

"The Ojibwe of La Pointe were exceedingly reluctant at our recent council," Watrous explained. "I refused them as long as I could, but to refuse them longer would have endangered the success of the removal."

"But they did agree to meet at Fond du Lac?" Ramsey asked.

Watrous removed his cap and wiped his forehead which had become sweaty from the late summer heat. "Yes, they did," he nodded. "But they were most adamant on one condition."

"Condition?"

"I had to pledge to ask permission and to recommend that the chiefs be allowed to visit Washington. They complain of many wrongs, and they are of the opinion that everything would be adjusted if they could visit their Great Father. I've determined that this request should be granted to safeguard the return of these people to their homes."

Ramsey took a deep breath. "That can be arranged, but I doubt if it will be granted."

"This has proven most difficult," Watrous said with a shake of his head.

"Whatever transpires," Ramsey said, "be of good cheer and try to conquer all obstacles in the way of removal."

CHAPTER 16

A few weeks passed, and Benjamin reluctantly held his tongue about the telegram with orders to terminate removal. He told no one; not Mr. Austrian, not Reverend Hall, not even Charlotte. Holding back such important information left him feeling guilty, but he also knew that it was information he was never intended to see. Yellow Beaver put his trust in Benjamin and that was something he did not wish to betray.

Meanwhile, life at La Pointe edged along slowly. People remained in a state of uncertainty. All of them wanted to remain on their homeland but were much in need of government annuities.

Benjamin spent his days running errands and fulfilling obligations for Austrian's store which remained a place of steady commerce. He also spent time at the Bad River Mission helping Reverend Wheeler with various tasks for a small salary. Charlotte stayed busy with the children, especially with Makwa who had taken ill. He had a high fever and was bedridden for some time. Charlotte worried much over his condition but could not determine what ailed him. Makwa remained silent the entire time.

"Did you hear the news?" reverend Wheeler asked as Benjamin helped him tend one of the large gardens at Bad River.

"News?" Benjamin tried to remain casual. Over the last few weeks he felt as if everyone knew he'd been hiding something.

"The Lake Superior Journal has reported that all actions regarding removal have been ordered stopped."

Benjamin froze in place, his back to the Reverend. He was relieved that his secret information had finally been let out. "That is great news!" he said, trying to sound surprised.

"Yes and no," Reverend Wheeler said. "I have very little confidence in the agent. Somehow, I doubt if he will abide by the order."

"The agent can't be trusted, that much we know."

"But the Ojibwe are pleased," Reverend Wheeler said as a few raindrops began to fall.

"What do you think will happen?" Benjamin asked, setting his garden tool aside and looking toward Reverend Wheeler.

"Well, the Ojibwe see it as a victory and are now headed to The Soo for a Grand Jubilee. They wish to celebrate, but I think it is too early for that." Reverend Wheeler paused as he struggled to uproot some weeds. "The elders have asked me to travel to Fond du Lac with them to attend the payment and advise them in their trying circumstances. How the Ojibwe are treated at the payment this year will be a good indicator of what the agent intends to do moving forward."

"It should not be left to him!" Benjamin said. "He has caused so much suffering already. I just wish this would all end."

"Of course," Reverend Wheeler agreed. "But it will not end easily. There just aren't enough good men."

Like a bell, the reverend's statement rang through Benjamin's mind. *There just aren't enough good men.*

———————

Having earned a certain amount of respect among the Ojibwe elders, Benjamin was invited to travel with the Ojibwe to Fond du Lac for the scheduled payment in early October 1851. However, Benjamin decided not to go at the request of his wife and his own better judgement.

"Better to forgo payment than to put your life at risk," Charlotte told him.

"I agree with you. For now, I think we should forgo our payment."

Following the good news that the removal order was to be stopped, the Ojibwe were in relatively high spirits. They were optimistic about receiving payment for 1850 and 1851. They also hoped, as everyone did, that by the same time next year the payment would be resumed at La Pointe as it had in years past. Benjamin could only wait and hope, in the meantime providing for and protecting his own family.

———————

Returning from Fond du Lac in late October, Reverend Wheeler looked tired and upset. "It was a complete disaster!" he said. "It was criminal."

"What happened?" Benjamin asked anxiously while feeling grateful he did not make the trip to Fond du Lac. "Do not tell me there was more death."

"No, thankfully. Death did not visit us this time, but only thanks to the foresight provided us by last year's experience."

"Then what was it? What happened?"

"The payment was not made!" Reverend Wheeler raised his voice in anger, something Benjamin had never heard him do before.

"Not made? How can that be? Under what pretense?"

The reverend's face turned red and he gritted his teeth. "Watrous had a variety of excuses," Reverend Wheeler said with tightened fists. "But I know his duplicitous reasoning."

"Do you think he intentionally delayed payment again?"

"Yes, I do. He wished, once again to delay payment so late in the season that the winter would set in and trap the Ojibwe in Minnesota."

"Again!" Benjamin said, horrified to think that the agent would apply the same plan that had recently caused so much death and suffering. "But how? How could he possibly think he could induce the Ojibwe to wait and risk the same outcome?"

"He planned two payments," Wheeler said, now with his hands on his hips and his shoulders drawn back. "He intended to make the 1850 payment early in October, then to go to Sandy Lake to pay the Pillager, Mississippi, and Mille Lacs bands. He said he would return to Fond du Lac to make the 1851 payment."

"So, he thought he could bait the Ojibwe to stay by making the first payment, but withholding the second," Benjamin said, trying to understand the agent's nefarious reasoning.

Reverend Wheeler was fuming. "Exactly! But we did not take the bait. Watrous refused to make the first payment and then left for Sandy Lake saying he would return. The Ojibwe became so upset and disillusioned with the agent that they returned to their homes before it was too late."

Benjamin pondered this for a moment, disgusted at this continued deceit and wrongdoing.

"I still don't understand," Benjamin said raising his hand to his forehead, staring at the pinewood floor. "If he wanted to persuade the Ojibwe to stay, why did he not make the first payment?"

"It is hard to determine because his reasoning is so . . . so wrong! But he said he would not make payment while alcohol was present. Whiskey dealers were everywhere at Fond du Lac. Also, the St. Croix bands led by William Warren had not yet arrived and he refused to pay anyone until all bands were present. Even then, he said that he required their families to be present, too."

"So, despite the death and suffering last fall," Benjamin said with the same unsettled anger as the reverend, "despite the order to cease removal, he continued to carry out all removal policies?"

"Yes," replied Reverend Wheeler in a tone of disbelief. "The agent has continued removal efforts just as we suspected he might."

Benjamin replied in a stern, determined tone. "This has to stop! It has to stop before we lose everything."

Reverend Wheeler paused and took a deep breath. "We are planning a council in two days' time," he said. "The La Pointe and L'Anse bands will meet to discuss and write down the objectionable behavior of Agent Watrous."

"Write down?" Benjamin asked, looking for clarification.

"A petition. A petition will be made regarding the conduct of the agent and the needs of the Ojibwe. You should attend this council. I am certain Kechewaishke wants you to be there. Your input will be useful."

"Yes," Benjamin answered. "I will be there."

It was a cold day in early November. A dusting of snow covered the ground and whirled through the air with each frozen breeze. Three dozen or so Ojibwe chiefs and elders gathered for the council, all covered in blankets and buffalo robes. They were joined by Reverend Wheeler, Reverend Hall, and Benjamin. Compared to others, this was a more intimate council held about a mile or so from the village. Along with the La Pointe Ojibwe there were also several members of the L'Anse band.

Once the peace pipe had been passed, Reverend Wheeler stepped forward to begin the council. "Gentlemen, chiefs, and elders, the time has come for action." The reverend gave his speech in the Ojibwe tongue, which he spoke well. Often, he held religious services in both the Ojibwe and English languages. "I do not call for actions of violence, but for a concerted effort to rescind the removal order and protect our rights. It is not enough to sit back and hope that all of this will go away."

The reverend's voice carried well through the thin, winter-like air, echoing off the trees in the backdrop.

"That is why we must consider every possible course of action. Your payment has not been made for this or the previous year. Your agent has ignored orders to cease removal. If you are to receive your payment and be left to remain in your homes, we must take action against the agent."

The Ojibwe chiefs and elders sat silently, showing neither dissent or agreement with the words of Reverend Wheeler. They were thoughtful and stoic as they often were.

"I have been called before you to write a petition on your behalf, and to draw up charges against the agent. It is with honor and duty that I have accepted this responsibility. Come forward now and express your grievances that they may be recorded."

The chiefs and elders were again silent. Reverend Wheeler took a seat at a table he had placed there previously for the purposes of writing. He was ready with his ledger and pen, his hands covered by thin gloves.

"I will tell you what to write," said one of the L'Anse elders while seated cross-legged, his chin held upright in a serious manner.

"I have heard there was a white chief from Washington. He came to visit our enemy, the Dakota. The white chief made a deal with the Dakota. He gave them much money and a place to live near their current homes. We want this white chief to visit the Ojibwe and to make a deal with the Ojibwe. That is all I have to say."

The L'Anse elder was speaking of Luke Lea, the Commissioner of Indian Affairs. Just a few months earlier Lea had negotiated a treaty with the Dakota of Minnesota in which the Dakota sold their land west of the Mississippi River in exchange for annual cash payments and a reservation along the Minnesota River.

"The petition will be addressed to the white chief you speak of," Reverend Wheeler said. "He will hear and understand your needs. If he is wise, he will come visit the Ojibwe."

There was a brief pause; then the La Pointe chief Oshoga rose to speak.

"Add this to the petition," Oshoga said as he pulled a long-stemmed pipe from his mouth. "We feel wronged and full of grief. The agent promises to give but then takes away. We traveled to Fond du Lac where the agent promised money and supplies to feed and clothe our families. We told our agent that we had come and now wanted our money. He asked us if we had all come and brought our things with us. We told him we had not brought our kettles and some of our friends we had left behind sick."

Oshoga moved his hands through the empty air, gesturing with nearly every word. He turned from side to side making eye contact with each participant, making sure his words were heard.

"The agent said he should only pay those that had come and had brought their things with them to stay. At the next council, we told him we wanted our last year's payment, that our children were cold and that we had no money to buy them clothing. He said he could not pay us until all the Ojibwe had arrived who were still behind. As I stand here today, the agent has not yet paid us our money."

Oshoga sat back down as the Ojibwe chiefs and elders chattered amongst each other in agreement.

"I will make this known," Reverend Wheeler said, never looking up from his ledger.

Then, Kechewaishke stepped forward. "I will now speak for the Ojibwe."

The chatter ceased as they all looked to the respected and revered chief and elder. He could barely be seen through his thick, ruffled hood, only his nose and mouth being visible.

"These are things that are true," Kechewaishke said, speaking his native Ojibwe. "But there are many more things that I want you to tell our Great Father. Remind the white chief in Washington City of the agreement we made some years ago when we sold what was on the land, but we did not agree to move from it. Remind him that we were told we could remain for fifty to one hundred years. Remind him that we have lived well and done all that has been asked of us. That we have committed no wrongs and continue to abide by the changes the white government wishes us to make."

Ho, ho called out the chiefs and elders.

"But mostly," he said with a pause, his head tilting toward the endless blue sky. "Tell the chiefs in Washington about the conduct of our agent."

Ho, ho again came the calls of the Ojibwe.

"We were deceived and wronged at Sandy Lake. We were fed flour that had been soaked in water which made us sick. We were made to throw away our canoes and walk through the bitter cold of winter. We were made to die because of the lies and deception of the agent."

All the chiefs and elders were clamoring now. As Benjamin witnessed their passion he, too, could feel emotion stirring inside in support of Kechewaishke and the Ojibwe leaders.

"We do not trust the agent. We think he goes against the wishes of the Great Father. We want to see with our own eyes the order telling us to remove with the Great Father's name affixed to it. Only then will we be satisfied with the intentions of the order. But now, we think it is only the agent and the traders."

Benjamin was startled, not because he did not believe it was true, but because he was associated with the traders. He felt guilty for that association. Unfortunately, there were many traders who took advantage of every circumstance they could with the Ojibwe.

"The agent, being a former trader, never did right by us. Now he acts on behalf of the traders, making the payment when and where they desire. When he withholds payment, the Ojibwe are forced to run up a greater debt with the traders. We also think goods and money have been deposited in the traders' stores instead of being given to us."

Kechewaishke paused, thinking upon his closing statement. Again, he looked toward the sky as if to admire it. A gust of wind blew a ribbon of snow over his head.

"Tell them that we will do what the Great Father desires, but we wish to see him ourselves. We wish to visit him at our own expense. Tell the representatives of our Great Father in St. Paul that we demand our promised annuities. We will come to Fond du Lac, but we demand our payment."

A resounding *ho, ho* rang out from all the chiefs and elders. Some began pounding the snow and frozen ground in support of Kechewaishke's demands. Pounding his own chest, Benjamin could feel a sense of community and comradery. If felt good to be a part of something.

"I have now heard your statements and made note of them," Reverend Wheeler said, frantically writing his final notes. "I will convey your wishes in a formal petition and then send it to the Commissioner of Indian Affairs in Washington. He's in close contact with your Great Father, and he has authority over the agent. Rest assured, your wishes will be heard, and your suffering will not be made to continue."

Reverend Wheeler maintained a strong and satisfied gaze at the elders in front of him. Then, the chiefs and elders began to applaud, recognizing the missionary for his contribution.

With that the meeting adjourned. But before departing, each man stepped forward to Reverend Wheeler's table and signed his name to the bottom of the prepared document.

As Benjamin turned to leave, feeling quite satisfied, he was approached by Kechewaishke.

"Mr. Armstrong my friend," the old man said in English while slowly walking toward Benjamin.

Benjamin stopped, and, realizing who it was, he quickly walked toward the great chief to spare him any further steps.

"Boozhoo," Benjamin said. *Hello.*

"Thank, thank," Kechewaishke replied, not fully grasping the manner in which the English words were used. "You are good to the Ojibwe," he said followed by a smile. "You have written our petition before. You have come to Sandy Lake and suffered with us. You hunt the moose and save us from starvation. You have adopted an Ojibwe boy. My eyes are old, but I see you are good."

Benjamin was filled with pride. There could be no higher praise than the support of Kechewaishke.

"This community took me in when I was sick, welcomed me even though I was an outsider and an orphan, provided for me all the things that I needed. It is the least I could do," Benjamin said with a true and honest sense of gratitude.

"Some things happen as they are meant to. You see, you know, we have been wronged and hurt. We still need help. You will help us?"

"Of course," Benjamin said without hesitation. "The Ojibwe are my family."

"Good, good." Kechewaishke smiled, making his deep wrinkles even deeper. "You spoke out to the agent. You said we ought to visit Washington."

"Yes," Benjamin nodded, straightening his shoulders in preparation of the elder's request.

"The time nears. Our condition gets worse. Our agent and traders take everything from us. We have no food to feed our children. I ask you who is smart. You are like the moose who is aware of all things. You know the way of the white government. I ask, organize and lead chiefs to Washington City. We cannot wait for permission."

Benjamin's eyes widened, and he could feel his heart pounding harder. *Could he really do this? Could he lead an expedition to Washington to meet the president?* Despite his doubts, how could he say no?

"I can," Benjamin said. "I would consider it an honor."

Kechewaishke smiled once again and looked deep into Benjamin's eyes.

"I have seen many suns rise and fall and I will not see many more. When I leave for Spirit World, I want that it happens here. I want that my children and grandchildren visit me here. Not just my home now, my home always. Home for all Ojibwe."

"I know," Benjamin replied softly. "I want the same."

———————

Shortly after the November council, charges were filed against the agent, just as Reverend Wheeler had suggested. They were made by the L'Anse Band of Ojibwe. Like the Ojibwe at La Pointe, the L'Anse were quite dissatisfied that the agent refused to make their payment unless they removed. The L'Anse band requested that Agent Watrous be terminated and they listed several charges against him. The charges included repeatedly breaking promises and daily deception; that he was guided by self-interest and followed the advice of the traders; that, prior to his appointment as agent, he was himself a petty trader; and finally, he was accused of attempted bribery and making chiefs of those who helped him in his measures.

The charges, which were very serious in nature, were forwarded to David Aitken, the Indian Agent at Sault Ste. Marie. The goal, as stated, was to have the agent removed and replaced. The L'Anse Band believed that only if Agent Watrous was removed from office would the Ojibwe receive their rightful payment and be allowed to stay upon their current lands.

As for Benjamin, he set to work right away organizing a delegation to Washington. He decided that before traveling to Washington, it would be wise to travel first to St. Paul and visit Minnesota Territorial Governor Alexander Ramsey. Not only was Ramsey the governor, but he was the Superintendent of Indian Affairs for the region and therefore the direct supervisor of Agent Watrous. Nothing happened regarding Indian Affairs in the region without first being ordered or sanctioned by Alexander Ramsey. Furthermore, Benjamin knew they might never be allowed to arrive in Washington without first gaining approval from the governor.

Benjamin and a small group of La Pointe chiefs traveled to St. Paul in December. Their mission was clear: to demand payment of the 1850 and 1851 annuities and to directly request that a delegation to Washington be approved. Kechewaishke was unable to travel because of the risks involved in traveling during winter. Since he could not travel, Benjamin requested that he write a letter directed toward Governor Ramsey, which he did. Arriving in St. Paul, Benjamin laid the letter on the governor's desk and made his request.

"I understand your grievances," Ramsey said, "and I have sent your request to Washington."

Ramsey looked every bit his role of a politician, seated as he was behind his heavy oak desk. He wore a heavy black frock coat, his face stern and determined, not yet wrinkled by time. His hair was brown with distinct looking mutton chops tracing the outline of his jaw.

"Then you understand that the agent has not made payment for two years."

"Yes," answered Governor Ramsey with a noticeable Eastern accent. "I have instructed the agent to make your payment as soon as possible. And he will, at Fond du Lac this January. But," he said with a finger raised, "your people must agree to remove first thing in the spring."

"That can only be determined by our chief, Kechewaishke," said Oshoga, who had traveled as a part of the delegation.

"I have much to do and haven't much time to discuss it," the governor said, barely acknowledging Oshoga. "I will read and respond to your chief's letter and I will send new instructions to your agent, Mr. Watrous. Understood?"

Benjamin nodded, somewhat satisfied but still very skeptical.

"Being that you have traveled so far, I will arrange a wagon for you filled with supplies." The governor got up from his desk to shake hands. "Pork, flour, sugar, tea, tobacco. The wagon will be filled with them."

The delegation seemed pleased, though Benjamin was worried. *Was he only putting on a show? Was this act of kindness genuine or just another political maneuver?*

Regardless, Benjamin and his delegation accepted Ramsey's offering and then departed St. Paul as quickly as they had arrived.

Returning home in late December, Benjamin was greeted by his wife.

"How was the journey and the meeting with the governor?" she asked.

Benjamin let out a hard sigh of relief to be home. "Travel was harsh," he said. Looking around the house he could see the children, Samuel and Marie, were fast asleep. Makwa, too.

"How has Makwa been? Has he shown any signs of improvement?"

"At times," Charlotte said as she poured Benjamin some hot tea. "He still has a nagging fever and he will not eat much."

"The poor boy. The stress of all this is too much."

"What of the meeting?" Charlotte asked as she handed Benjamin the tea and looked with curiosity into his eyes.

"It was favorable, I think. Ramsey said that he has requested permission for a delegation to visit Washington and he would instruct the agent to make payment as soon as possible."

"Do you think he was being honest?"

"He seemed a little too agreeable, as if he were avoiding something. I just don't trust him."

"I would not trust him either," Charlotte said. "And the removal?"

"It's hard to tell." Benjamin paused to blow the steam off his hot tea. "He wishes us to remove in the spring but seems less unyielding than the agent. He seems willing to agree to our requests and allow us payment, but still wishes to keep it at Fond du Lac, not at La Pointe."

"Then you will go to Fond du Lac?" Charlotte asked with a hint of sadness in her voice.

"Charlotte, you know that I must," Benjamin said, putting down his tea and pulling her close. "We need whatever we can get, especially now during winter. And I have confidence that the payment will be made this time."

Though Benjamin spoke with confidence, he had his doubts. He feared failure—for his family and for himself.

"I know you must," Charlotte said, her dark eyes gleaming in the candle light. "But what if something goes wrong? What about Washington? Will you have to travel to Washington? You have been absent more often than you have been present."

Benjamin wanted to assure Charlotte that everything would be okay, but he also wanted to be honest. Survival was precarious, and they truly had to fight to make it through, whether he ended up traveling to Washington or not.

"I'm sorry it has to be this way," Benjamin said with a sense of remorse, but also a sense of duty. "The request has been made several times and I don't know if it will be approved. First, we will go to Fond du Lac. If things go well and the government officials and agents recognize our right to remain at La Pointe, then we may never have to go to Washington. But if things do not go well..."

"Then you will go," Charlotte said as she wiped away a tear forming in the corner of her eye.

"Then we will have no choice. We will be forced to go to Washington."

Charlotte stared back at him.

"Listen," he said, wanting to break her somber stare, "everything will be okay."

Charlotte pushed herself away and turned her back. She looked toward the children who slept peacefully. "Don't forget your duty to this family. Don't forget to provide for them."

Benjamin reached for Charlotte reassuringly, but she pushed his arm away. He wanted so badly to provide for his family and protect the community. Standing there, he wondered how could he do both. How could he do right by his family and the Ojibwe? How?

CHAPTER 17

John Watrous paced apprehensively in front of Governor Ramsey. "This entire ordeal has been an unmitigated disaster. At best two hundred have been removed; the rest are determined to visit Washington, and now charges have been made against me."

Ramsey leaned back in his chair and stroked his long sideburns. "We have to make concessions, John. Without concessions matters will get considerably worse."

Watrous stopped and looked intently at Ramsey. "I was embarrassed and broken at La Pointe. It can't happen again."

Ramsey nodded as an expression of sympathy. "It is unlikely that they will see the president. I've written to Lea and convinced him that removal was a partial success. As for the charges, I am confident they will die in a long line of bureaucracy."

Watrous turned his head away and continued his anxious pacing.

"Listen," Ramsey said. "We may have to concede to some of their wishes, but payment will never again be made in the ceded territory. It will be made here in Minnesota where it will benefit Minnesotans and if they want it they have to come get it. Over time they will all be removed. Meanwhile, I will see that your reputation stays intact and you keep your position. Once the sub-agency at La Pointe is closed, you will become a full agent along with all its benefits."

Watrous paused and looked out the window at the streets of St. Paul. "I hope so, Alex. I hope so."

CHAPTER 18

Expecting to receive their annuity payment for the years 1850 and 1851, a large party left La Pointe bound for Fond du Lac in January, 1852. By this time the community at La Pointe was much in need of food and provisions and were wholly upset with the continual efforts of the Indian agent to force their removal from their homes.

Fond du Lac was an agency not much unlike that at La Pointe. It was located at the very tip of Lake Superior where it reached its farthest western point. It was the home of the Fond du Lac band of Ojibwe and was for centuries the access point for travelers and merchants seeking to enter the interior of the country. From La Pointe it was a few days' overland trip.

The assembly of La Pointe Ojibwe, along with Benjamin, arrived at an agency that, despite being the dead of winter, was filled with activity. Many Fond du Lac Ojibwe were present, rather than going on winter hunts, while other Lake Superior bands had gathered to receive payment. In addition, there were many traders and merchants who had come from all over the region in order to collect on their debts. Some of the more mischievous merchants brought with them alcohol while others were intent on inducing the Ojibwe to gamble away their payment.

After several days of waiting, the agent arrived. Immediately he was bombarded with Ojibwe demanding their payment.

"It is the dead of winter and we are cold and hungry," declared the Ojibwe men and women. "You owe us two years' money and we want it now."

Stepping out from his carriage, covered in a thick coat and heavy boots, the agent looked curiously over the landscape of traders, merchants, and native Ojibwe. "I have come to make your payment," he said while trying to create some room between himself and the indignant crowd.

"We need the payment now!" said half a dozen Ojibwe men followed up by various shouts from the crowd.

Agent Watrous lifted his hands above his head to quiet the gathering crowd. "Payment will be made in due time!" he shouted. "I am waiting upon specific instructions from Governor Ramsey. First, however, I need all those Ojibwe still residing upon the ceded territory to sign this document."

Watrous pulled out a paper from underneath his coat and handed it to his interpreter who then handed it to Reverend Wheeler who was standing nearby. There was silence while Reverend Wheeler reviewed the document.

Wide-eyed and open-mouthed, Reverend Wheeler looked up. "This is completely unjust and will not be signed!"

"What does it state?" Benjamin asked for the benefit of those gathered.

"It is an agreement that in return for payment, the Lake Superior Ojibwe agree to remove from the ceded territory in the spring without any further order."

The Ojibwe reacted with boisterous and powerful shouts, venting their anger toward Agent Watrous.

"This goes entirely against the promise of Governor Ramsey," Reverend Wheeler said as he held the document high in the air. "He told us not to sign any further documents and that we would only be required to remove at the request of the president."

Benjamin was surprised. This is not what he was told when he met with the governor. Yet, he did not doubt what Reverend Wheeler claimed. Politicians, it seemed, often talked out of both sides of their mouths.

"I have received no such instructions from the governor," Agent Watrous said with a cold stare. "Once the removal was put in action there was no halting it."

Reverend Wheeler stretched his arms out in frustration. "No such instructions! The telegram sent in September is no secret. It has been made public."

"I saw it with my own eyes," Benjamin said, finally admitting his secret.

Reverend Wheeler looked at Benjamin, but then continued his argument. "Under what authority do you have to ask the Ojibwe to remove after the order has been suspended by the Commissioner of Indian Affairs?"

Watrous casually shrugged his shoulders. "I have only been ordered to suspend active operations."

"Does this not appear like active operations?" Reverend Wheeler held the document in his hand high above his head for all to see. "You are asking the Ojibwe to leave La Pointe and Bad River in the spring and to start with their canoes, families, and all their effects for Fond du Lac. That seems to me the very definition of active operations."

"I cannot suspend what has already been put in motion," responded the agent. "The removal has been a success and needs only to be completed."

"A success!" Reverend Wheeler said in a tone of sarcasm. "At best only two hundred Lake Superior Ojibwe have been permanently removed. That is hardly a success, which is why operations should be suspended and reversed."

"There will be no reversal! I can assure you of that. The Lake Superior Ojibwe are living upon land which they ceded in 1842 and they agreed to remove at the pleasure of the president. The pleasure of the president is now."

The two men stood toe to toe, as if no one else was there, as if throngs of hopeful natives and eager traders were not standing by. All the crowd could do was watch.

"Even if the president wishes for removal to continue, are you prepared to sustain the Ojibwe during this time? Without aid from the government, there would be great difficulties for these people once they arrived at Fond du Lac. Do you remember your promises to feed them for a year and to have farms open and ready? Would these be prepared by spring? How much land have you cleared and planted?"

"I have done what is necessary," Agent Watrous said, evading the questions. "Had the Ojibwe followed orders they would find themselves well and provided for on the unceded lands."

"It was your ineptness that caused all this," Wheeler said without pause or hesitation. "It was your plans and the plans of the governor gone awry."

"A rather critical remark for a preacher," the agent said.

"It was not I who caused the death of four hundred," accused Reverend Wheeler.

There was a pause. The agent had no sly response in mind this time.

Benjamin was still and attentive as he watched Reverend Wheeler courageously take on the agent, neither backing down nor making concessions.

Watrous shrugged. "If you will not sign the document, then you must draw one up yourself. But it must include some agreement to heed instructions or I cannot hand out payment."

Wheeler looked around, caught off guard by the agent's concession. "Very well. I can tell you right now what it will say."

"And just what is that?"

"The Ojibwe will agree to move, but only upon the direct wishes of the president. Provided that and only that the government extend to them that aid which the health, comfort, and well-being of their families are required. This means farms, homes, and subsistence for one year."

"Have it written up and signed," the agent said as he turned away quickly, his face tightened with frustration. "Then we may proceed with this payment."

Silence permeated the grounds, only the hurried steps of the agent filling the air as he walked away. Reverend Wheeler just watched, until, moments later, an applause began. Cheers rose up for the reverend and finally, moving past his anger, he smiled.

———————

The long-awaited day of payment had finally arrived. It was a relatively warm day for January, but layers of snow and ice still covered the grounds giving the agency a somewhat barren look. The Ojibwe gathered outside the payhouse. They were anxious but organized, being familiar with the payment process. The payhouse was a small log cabin with two doors and one window, generally used for housing a stockpile of furs.

As Benjamin neared the payhouse to receive his family's payment, he could see that the Ojibwe entered through one door and exited through the other. As he observed and drew nearer and nearer the payhouse, he could see that upon exiting, most of the Ojibwe carried a much smaller payment than expected. Benjamin was concerned.

Finally, after hours of patient but distressful waiting, Benjamin was inside the payhouse. On one side, near the entrance, was a table at which were seated Agent John Watrous and John W. Bell, the enrolling agent at Fond du Lac. This is where each man's payment was determined and doled out. At the other end of the room, near the exit, was another table at which were seated Clement Beaulieu, a prominent trader, and his clerk. Benjamin did not know what their purpose was. Between the two tables were George Nettleton, another prominent trader, and Vincent Roy, Jr. Benjamin knew Mr. Roy well because he had previously worked alongside Vincent at Austrian's store. This was until 1848 when Vincent married and moved on to manage posts of his own at Fond du Lac and then Vermillion Lake. In addition to the two tables and Vincent Roy, there were various men of mixed, American, and European descent. All of them were traders or contractors of some sort.

Confused at first, it did not take long for Benjamin to determine why the payroom was filled with so many men with various purposes. As he observed what was happening, Benjamin was shocked. From what he could tell, the men received their payment from Agents Watrous and Bell in gold coin along with various goods such as blankets and tools. But, as they approached the exit, they were stopped by the trader Clement Beaulieu. There, an exchange was made. Listening closely Benjamin could hear Beaulieu repeat the words, "Now we are square; the account is settled." It became clear to Benjamin that as soon as the Ojibwe received their payment they were required to give it up! *How can this be?* Two years without payment only to have it taken away without ever leaving the payroom! Some Ojibwe became clever to this ruse and tried to exit out the same door they entered, but they were inevitably stopped and forced to approach Beaulieu's table. Then Benjamin witnessed Nettleton receive payment directly from Agent Watrous. When the enrolling agent called out the name of Michael Bazinet, Nettleton stepped to the pay table.

"Mr. Bazinet owes me sixty dollars," Benjamin heard him say. Then he presented the agent with a document which appeared to be a legal paper of some sort. The money was then handed to Nettleton without Bazinet ever having been present.

Power of Attorney! Benjamin concluded.

"Mr. Armstrong. Benjamin," the enrolling agent called out.

"What is going on here?" Benjamin asked as he stepped to the pay table. "The traders are being paid the greater portion of the money."

Agent Watrous did not answer. He didn't even look up. He kept his eyes fixed upon his ledger as he examined the rolls.

"Armstrong, Armstrong," he muttered as he looked down the list. "That's five heads at eight dollars per head. A total of forty dollars is owed you." He marked his ledger with several checks and then finally looked up.

"Eight dollars per head!" Benjamin exclaimed. "After two years' payment and we are only entitled to eight dollars per head. That is not enough to sustain us."

"It is not meant to sustain you," the agent said coolly. "You of all people, a non-native, should know that."

"Be that as it may, it is not right."

"I am not here to determine right and wrong. I am here to dole out the annuity payment as agreed upon in the 1842 treaty between the United States government and the Ojibwe bands."

Exasperated, Benjamin could see that arguing would accomplish nothing. He took his payment and moved away from the table.

Vincent Roy interceded his path. "Benjamin!"

"Hello, Vincent," Benjamin said, trying to be polite but fuming with anger. "It has been a while. I trust you are well."

"Quite," Vincent said followed by a smile revealing bright white teeth beneath his dark complexion.

"What can I help you with?" Even though Vincent was an old friend, Benjamin was not in the mood for small talk.

"I understand that you are still working for Austrian," he said as he revealed a document he held in his hand.

"Yes, that's right." Benjamin suspected something wasn't quite right.

"I am here collecting debts on behalf of Austrian, and his records indicate that you owe a sum of twenty dollars."

"I owe no such thing," Benjamin said in disbelief. "Surely Julius would have told me himself."

"Perhaps you should check with your family," Vincent said in a less friendly tone than before. "They incurred quite a debt while you were away. Food, blankets, even fishing supplies."

"If that is the case I will straighten the account myself."

Vincent brought his hand up. "Benjamin, I can't have you leave the payroom without settling your debts."

"This isn't right, Vincent. You're taking our money before we even have a chance to put it in our pockets. Are we not poor enough?"

Vincent tightened his lips but did not answer.

Resigned to the facts, Benjamin dropped twenty dollars' worth of coin into Vincent's outstretched hand, then quickly departed the payroom.

"We all have to make a living," Vincent called out as Benjamin was departing.

Now outside the payroom Benjamin leaned over his knees, beside himself with anger and frustration. The entire payment process was fraudulent, unregulated and unjust. Whatever debts the Ojibwe had were the result of poor treatment that forced the Ojibwe to borrow. The traders swarmed the payhouse and took the Ojibwe money at will, with no one to evaluate claims or verify documents. Not to mention the gamblers and whiskey sellers who sought and often succeeded in obtaining whatever money the Ojibwe had left. The Ojibwe, who were already poor, were left even poorer. Even those Benjamin considered friends exploited him and the community. Maybe he ought to give up fighting, Benjamin thought. The future was too bleak.

————

A few days later, Blackbird stood in front of several hundred of the Ojibwe gathered at Fond du Lac. "The payment has come and gone," he said. "Still we are very poor. Still we are very wretched. We haven't even enough to feed ourselves and cannot be expected to feed our families."

By now the traders and agents had left Fond du Lac. They made off quite well while the people who needed it were left with very little. The Ojibwe, like Benjamin, were disgusted and discouraged.

"I propose a ball game," Blackbird suggested. "Rather than have all of us leave here with very little, some should have enough to care for their families. We ought to place our goods and money in a pile. We should choose twenty of the best players from the Interior bands and twenty from the Lake Superior bands. They should compete here on the ice and the winner should take all."

There were no objections from anyone in the crowd. They were so distraught that they did not seem bothered by the wager.

"Then it has been determined. Our goods shall be placed together in a pile. The owner of the pile will be determined by the winner of a great game of stickball."

The crowd roared like a flame coming to life, accepting the stakes at hand. A game between the Interior bands and the Lake Superior bands. The winner would take all; the loser would get nothing.

Twenty men were chosen from each side. Most were young, athletic, and filled with competitive energy. Some were older, wiser, and confident in their abilities. The men took their places on the ice as they looked spitefully across the dividing line at their opponents. Each man held a stick in his hand of varying lengths, curled at the tip, with a web-like net attached to the end. A ball, which was made of deerskin filled with fur, was flung high in the air and the game began.

The men raced back and forth with remarkable balance and agility. The smooth, glassy ice caused them no difficulty whatsoever, each man cutting left and right as if he were on grass. The ball was thrown from the net of their sticks an incredible distance and with superb accuracy. If it was caught the player would meander through opponents toward the goal line while maneuvering his stick side to side to secure the ball. If the ball was dropped or missed its mark, a huge melee ensued as the players fought each other for possession of the small, round object.

And so, the game proceeded back and forth over a stretch of ice that must have been a mile long. A point was awarded any time a player crossed his opponents' goal line with possession of the ball, but this proved most difficult as the players vigorously defended their end.

The game continued, not just for a few hours, but for a few days! The players rarely took breaks, appearing inexhaustible. By the time they finished, the Interiors won and laid claim to the entirety of the annuities. In the meantime, while the game was being played, councils were being held almost continuously. There was much dissatisfaction over the payment.

"The agent is working on behalf of the traders," argued one of the Ojibwe men. "This has been made clear to us now."

"We tried to become allies with the white government," another argued, "but their chiefs treat us unfairly. They make promises that they cannot keep. They take without giving. They see us starving but do not share. They do not hear our wishes or petitions. There can be no alliance with the Americans. There never was. There can be no peace."

Benjamin could see that the Ojibwe were more agitated than ever before and more prone to retaliation. If something was not done soon, trouble of a serious nature would inevitably follow. Violence, maybe even war. Benjamin knew now, that whether approved or not, a trip to Washington was their only choice.

CHAPTER 19

Stillwater was quiet on a pleasant Sunday afternoon. The sun felt warm even though the temperature was still in the low 30s. People walked about in their church clothes, their heavy shoes clapping against the boardwalks while carriages moved slowly through the softening, muddy streets.

Reverend Boutwell, who had come to Minnesota along with his seminary colleague Sherman Hall in 1831, sat down to write his annual report to the ABCFM. He sat alone working diligently by the light of the afternoon sun. He was startled by a knock at the door. It was Agent John Watrous.

"Agent Watrous," Boutwell said with a look of surprise. "To what do I owe the pleasure?"

"I have need for your signature," Watrous said as he let himself into the room.

"Signature? Of course. For what purpose?"

Watrous, now inside the room, turned so the two men were facing each other. "No doubt you have heard of the charges against me. They are completely unfounded, and I am working to clear my name. I've taken the liberty to write a letter on my behalf and I only need your signature before sending it to the commissioner in Washington."

Watrous handed the letter to Boutwell who opened it slowly and began to read.

As a result of working with Agent John S. Watrous on the removal efforts, I am intimately acquainted with all his movements and saw nothing to convince me, but that he acted with fidelity as a public officer and I do not believe that the charges against him are founded in truth. I would remark, the removal itself was an unpopular measure with all the Whites and Mixed-bloods residing on the Lake from the fact that a great portion of the subsistence of the latter is obtained from the Indian annuities, the former furnishing them with large quantities of whiskey. Most of the Whites and a large majority of the Mixed-bloods are of a class that would originate and circulate any charges against a public officer however misfounded they might be in truth.

Boutwell lowered the letter and looked up at the agent, his face plain and without emotion. "You know that I cannot sign this."

"Why not?" Watrous asked, raising his voice.

Boutwell shook his head. "Governor Ramsey already asked me to write such a letter, but I declined him. I sympathize with you because I know you are only carrying out the orders of the government, and it is true that the removal is an unpopular measure, but I don't agree with this statement. The Ojibwe have suffered greatly under your care and because of that I cannot justify supporting your cause. I feel guilty enough already for the part I played in removal."

Watrous stared hard at Boutwell as he took a small step forward. "I will be exonerated whether you sign or not, William. I have already acquired two affidavits in my favor and I am certain the commissioner and governor will dismiss the charges. But still, I suggest you sign."

Boutwell paused as he looked down to avoid Watrous' stare.

"William," Watrous said as he lightened his tone. "We have worked closely together, and I consider you my friend."

Boutwell lifted his head, attentive to the agent's next words.

"It would be a shame if people found out that you were paid off to assent to the removal. But no one has to know. You just need to sign." Watrous took hold of the pen on the desk behind him and then held it out in front of the reverend.

Boutwell looked at the pen for a moment or two. Taking it, he moved to his desk and signed the letter then handed it to Agent Watrous.

"You've done the right thing, William," Watrous said as he tucked the letter inside his coat. "You've done the right thing."

CHAPTER 20

The winter of 1852 was filled with anxiety for the people at La Pointe, much like the previous years had been. The assembly returned from Fond du Lac with little money and no provisions. But, life continued as best it could. The men carried out their winter hunts. The women gathered firewood, repaired clothing and moccasins, wove fishnets, and prepared for spring. The children helped their parents and grandparents with cooking and making snowshoes, and when they were not helping their elders they could be seen playing, rolling down the snow-covered hills or having snowshoe races. If one had just arrived at La Pointe, one might think all was well.

Councils continued to be a daily occurrence as the chiefs and warriors argued over their next course of action. Some, such as Kechewaishke, favored diplomacy; others had decided that war was the only viable option remaining. Thankfully, no decision for the Ojibwe was made in haste or without the approval of all community members.

Before winter had passed, Kechewaishke again reached out to Territorial Governor Alexander Ramsey asking for his approval to visit Washington and see the president. But again the governor withheld his approval, telling Kechewaishke that he should not go and that if he did he would be turned away. For Benjamin, this made it clear that the time had come—the time that he follow through on his promise to guide an Ojibwe delegation to Washington, with or without government approval.

"If you are taking a delegation to Washington, then I want you to take Makwa with you," Charlotte urged Benjamin as she stood straight, hands on hips, her posture matching her tone of conviction.

Benjamin had become so caught up in his own activities he had forgotten about Charlotte's needs. He knew that she had grown tired of his coming and going. She had grown tired of uncertain circumstances and Benjamin's ambition to run to the aid of Kechewaishke rather than to the immediate needs of his own family. He could see it in her eyes, so caring yet determined. Benjamin felt indebted to Charlotte for the selfless manner in which she accepted and endured his persistent absence and withdrawn attentions.

"But he is still just a boy and he remains quite ill," Benjamin said, putting aside his sympathies. "How do you suppose he could endure such a long and painstaking journey?"

In addition to Benjamin's absence, Makwa had become a source of great stress for his family. Makwa had not yet spoken since his father's death and his health continued to decline.

"It is because he is ill that he should go." Charlotte stepped forward as she spoke. Her posture remained determined and her voice was clear and unbroken. "I have been here with him day after day. It does him no good to be trapped within this ... this ... this unmovable tepee. He needs fresh air. He needs a purpose. He needs to move on."

Benjamin thought upon those words. He owed Charlotte so much. He owed Giizhigoon even more. Yes, he had given Makwa a home and a family, but perhaps the turmoil was too much. Makwa was born into a world that was free and vast and filled with life. Now, all around him, all around La Pointe, was uncertainty and anger and loneliness. A world split in two between the needs and wants of one group of people versus the needs and wants of another. There was no easy fix, but Benjamin knew that he did not want for his children what had befallen him. A life of change, a life without family, a life uprooted. Benjamin had found his life at La Pointe and he wanted to keep it there. He wanted a future for his family free from uncertainty.

"I will take him with," Benjamin finally answered. "Maybe you are right. Maybe the fresh air will do him well. Maybe the comradery will help him open up."

———————

The day of departure finally arrived. The ice on the bay had withdrawn from the shores and now covered only the shallowest and most still of inlets. Snow covered the ground, but only in small piles where drifts had formed over the long winter months. In between the piles of snow, the earth was saturated and muddy. In the dryer spots, flowers had begun to bloom and rise slowly toward the glowing sun. It was a warm April morning which felt welcoming and pleasant.

A crowd gathered at Old La Pointe in the shadow of the Catholic church. Established by Father Claude Allouez in 1665, the old building stood tall and dark, looking like a relic of years gone by. In more recent times it was operated and cared for by Father Frederic Baraga. He resuscitated the mission some years ago after a long absence of Catholicism on the island. Now, it loomed over the old town as a reminder of the lasting presence of the white man throughout the region.

A crowd of witnesses gathered to wish good luck and good fortune upon the small delegation. The shore of the island was littered with folks of all kinds, young and old, Ojibwe and white. All were anxious and hopeful to put these hard times behind them.

"Don't accept no for an answer," Reverend Wheeler said with young Julia at his side, clutching his arm.

Benjamin felt a great deal of pressure. The future of the community seemed as if it rested entirely on his shoulders. If he should fail, they might permanently lose their homes. If he should succeed, his prolonged absence might cause him to lose his family. It made Benjamin sick to think about it. But he decided he had to go. There seemed to be no stopping the evil intentions of Ramsey, Watrous, and the long list of traders and businessmen who wanted their land and their homes for exploitation and who sought their annuities for the taking. Since there was no compromising with these men, since they completely disregarded the value of an Ojibwe life, and since the people at

La Pointe were left with no other option, Benjamin and a small contingent prepared to embark on an impossible journey. Impossible for its great distance, yes, but also for the lack of money and government support. They were not granted permission and it was possible they could be turned away at any or all points. Even if they made it as far as Washington, they might never be afforded the opportunity to meet the president or so much as lay their grievances on his desk. Benjamin could not bear to think they might fail, that they might return poorer and more distraught than ever before. He could not bear to tell this to his family or his community.

The delegation consisted of just seven men. There was Benjamin, the ninety-three-year-old Kechewaishke, Chief Oshoga, Blackbird, two warriors named Each Side of the Sky and Little Current, and Benjamin's adopted son Makwa. Makwa showed no resistance when asked to join the delegation, but no enthusiasm either. Benjamin could only hope the journey would do him well.

A great cheer was raised by the crowd as the delegation set off from shore. Benjamin waved to his wife and children feeling sad for leaving them, but resolute in saving his home and the home of the Ojibwe.

The vessel that carried the La Pointe delegation was a new birch bark canoe made specially for the occasion. It was called a four-fathom boat that was twenty-four feet long with six paddles. It was a proud, sturdy canoe with high tips at the stern and bow, and was low and wide in the middle with just enough room for its passengers and cargo. It was clean, with no scratches or scuffs and its color was a pure light brown which appeared almost amber. It was, at the outset, flawless.

The delegation carried a small amount of provisions—only crackers, sugar, and coffee. For the remainder of their needs they would depend on game and fish for meat. That and, of course, the generosity of those they would encounter. And though the men did not know who they might meet over the many days and many miles they knew the kindness and compassion of strangers would be paramount to the success of their journey.

Benjamin sat in the stern of the vessel and directed its course eastward along the coast of the great Gichigami. Makwa sat in the middle alongside Kechewaishke. Though he was still a young man, Makwa paddled as energetically and persistently as any of the men on the voyage. Lift, push, pull; lift, push, pull. The water sprayed against the sides of the long and heavy boat, but it did not deter the men who pulled it forward in an almost automatic fashion. Even Kechewaishke, the old elder, pulled his paddle in and out of the water as fast as the vibrant warrior Blackbird. Looking back at Kechewaishke, Benjamin could see the hint of a smile, probably recalling the days of his youth when the lake, the canoe, and the paddle were an everyday characteristic of his life, a life he sought to reclaim though he was in the twilight of his days.

"Steady ahead, the course is clear!" Benjamin shouted as the canoe cut through the wind and flitted across the water, his excitement brimming with the beginning of a once-in-a-lifetime adventure.

By the morning of the third day the small delegation reached Ontonagon, a settlement not much unlike the one at La Pointe. The region was home to the Ontonagon band of Ojibwe but had, many years since, been infringed upon by merchants, traders, and miners of all kinds. Like La Pointe, it was a vibrant community that clung to its traditional Ojibwe heritage while mixing with, and, at times, resisting European and American influences.

"We should portage a few miles ahead," Benjamin said. "We will save many miles by going across the Keweenaw Peninsula rather than around it."

The men agreed without hesitation.

Benjamin had brought along a petition he had written which urged people to support their bid to end all removal efforts and to reinstate payment at La Pointe. The petition was addressed to the president, Millard Fillmore. As they passed through the small but growing communities of Ontonagon, Houghton, Hancock, and Portage Lake, they could not find a single man or woman who refused to sign it. Even the men of the copper mines considered the Ojibwe of no detriment and agreed that they should be allowed to continue living within their own country.

Occasionally, Benjamin met men who claimed to be an acquaintance of the president.

"We practiced law together in Buffalo," one man said. Or, "I knew him as a young man when he worked on a farm in Upstate New York," another said. "Surely he will recognize my signature when he sees it."

The success of the petition filled Benjamin with confidence. The journey was off to an encouraging start having received much support and no setbacks. Also, Benjamin was happy to see that Makwa was fitting in and that his health was improving. Makwa's face was no longer sullen, and he moved with energy and purpose, something Benjamin had not seen since before the passing of Makwa's father.

Following the portage across the Keweenaw Peninsula, the delegation continued in their canoe for many miles along the rocky southern shore of Lake Superior. Other than to camp, they stopped only at Marquette to circulate their petition and gain more signatures. After several days, they arrived at Sault Ste. Marie, an ancient meeting place for the Ojibwe and the crossroads of the long fur trade route between Montreal and the northern regions of Minnesota Territory. While at "the Soo," the delegation once again circulated their petition. In doing so Benjamin met a man named Brown, editor of the newspaper at Sault Ste. Marie. He gave Benjamin several letters of introduction to helpful parties in New York. These, he assured Benjamin, would provide the delegation great assistance upon reaching the huge eastern city.

Before departing the Soo, Benjamin and his Ojibwe delegation had to pass by the American fort. Here they were met with their first obstacle.

"I cannot let you or your delegation pass," the commander said bluntly. "You must turn around and go back to your homes."

"You cannot turn us away," Benjamin argued. "Though we do not have the government's approval, we have received tremendous support from our countrymen. Here," Benjamin said, pulling the recently signed petition out from his breast pocket and showing the commander the long list of signatories.

The commander turned his head with a sigh and waved his hand to indicate that Benjamin should put the petition back in his pocket. "I do not wish to see your petition. As a matter-of-fact no delegation shall proceed to Washington without the government's permission.

Furthermore, we have received specific instructions to deny all Indian delegations from passage."

Benjamin was stunned by this new predicament. He expected obstacles, but not so soon and not so insurmountable. To give up this trip would be to abandon the last hope of keeping that turbulent spirit of the young warriors within bounds. Right now, they were still inclined toward peace and would stay that way until the delegation's mission should decide their course. As long as the delegation was on its way to Washington there was still hope that the wrongs done to the Ojibwe would be made right, but to return without anything accomplished and with the information that the Great Father's officers had turned back the delegation would be enough to rekindle the fire that was smoldering into an open revolt for revenge. Violence, Benjamin feared, would be the outcome.

Benjamin pleaded with the commander. "Sir, you must understand the situation in Ojibwe country."

Though openly desperate, Benjamin talked patiently and long with the commander, explaining the state of affairs. Knowing the commander may not care what happened to the Ojibwe, Benjamin explained that it was not a pleasant task for him to take the delegation to Washington. Without pay or hope of reward, he would never have attempted it if he had not considered it necessary to secure the safety of the white settlers in that country.

"I would never resist an American officer, nor disobey the orders of the government were it not absolutely necessary to spare lives," Benjamin said, being as dramatic as he could. "You must allow us to go as far as possible in order to protect the frontier settlements."

The commander was reluctant. He shook his head and muttered something under his breath. After much thought, he changed his mind.

"You may proceed," the commander finally said. "But you will certainly be stopped at some place, probably at Detroit. The Indian agent there and the marshal will definitely oppose your going further."

His warning did not matter because Benjamin now knew that this was just the first of many obstacles. From the start, Benjamin was not sure how they would reach Washington, and if they did, how they would arrange a meeting with the president. But Benjamin and his delegates were determined to try. Successfully overcoming this challenge was the first step.

The delegation proceeded by steamer to Detroit. The trip was quite pleasant for the men, this being the first steamer the Ojibwe had ever traveled upon. The boat fascinated the men who were struck by the huge vessel's ability to move effortlessly through the water. Benjamin simply tried to enjoy this moment of calm in an otherwise stressful and worrisome situation.

As Benjamin rested one day upon the deck of the boat, Kechewaishke came to his side. Kechewaishke appeared content wrapped in his buffalo robe and carrying his walking staff. His old, deeply wrinkled face carried an expression of satisfaction, perhaps in the way his eyes twinkled, or his cheeks reddened. As he came up beside Benjamin, he bent low, crossed his legs, and sat softly on the deck.

"I have survived many seasons," he said, speaking Ojibwe, his eyes looking straight ahead at the shoreline in the distance. "I have seen many changes and I have encountered many challenges. None perhaps more challenging than our current circumstance, than our past few years of uncertainty."

"Yes," Benjamin said, nodding in response, curious about what the elder had to say.

"I can see that you are worried, like a bear cub without his mother. I can see that throughout our uncertainty you have been lost."

Benjamin was struck by the elder's wisdom. *He is right,* Benjamin thought, but only looked at him silently.

Kechewaishke laughed, perhaps sensing Benjamin's thoughts.

"Do you know the wisdom of the Seven Grandfathers?" he asked.

"I have not heard of such things."

Kechewaishke continued to look out at the shore, watching the trees as they appeared to be moving past of their own volition. "Our existence is more important than the outcome. It is about how we live in unity and respect with the world around us."

"How so? How can we overlook the outcome?"

Kechewaishke took a deep breath and closed his eyes.

"The Seven Grandfathers are represented by the animals living among us with whom we share this existence. They teach us many things....

Humility—Humility is represented by the wolf who lives life for his pack. Humility is to know that you are a sacred part of creation.

Bravery—Bravery is represented by the bear because the mother bear faces her fears to protect her young. Bravery is to defend what you believe and what is right for your community.

Honesty—Honesty is represented by the raven who accepts himself and knows how to use his gifts. To be honest is to accept who you are.

Wisdom—Wisdom is represented by the beaver because he uses his natural gifts wisely for survival. To be wise is to use your inherent gifts and to live your life by them.

Truth—Truth is represented by the turtle who lives in a slow, meticulous manner because he understands the importance of both the journey and the destination. To be true is to show honor and sincerity in all that you say and do.

Respect—Respect is represented by the buffalo who gives every part of his being to sustain the human way of living. To be respectful is to not waste and to be mindful of the balance of all living things.

Love—Love is represented by the eagle who has the strength to carry all teachings. To know love is to view your inner self from the perspective of all teaching.

"This is the wisdom of the Seven Grandfathers."

Benjamin listened intently and thought deeply upon the words of Kechewaishke. But as he thought, he could not understand why the elder sought him out with this wisdom. Why in this moment of chaos and tragedy for his people? Why now when the future was so uncertain?

"You have shared great wisdom, but why now, why me?" Benjamin asked.

Kechewaishke paused, never taking his eyes off the distant shoreline. "You are young and you cannot see like I can see. You have been good to my people. You have been good to our land. You already embody the teachings of the Seven Grandfathers. You needn't worry about the outcome. You needn't worry so much. You have done well, and you need only continue to do well. The world will conspire in your favor. And," he added, "what you have done for young Makwa is invaluable. His health and his spirits are improving. Just give him time, he is still in mourning. You have shown great mercy to the boy and it has not gone unnoticed by him."

Benjamin felt a sudden alleviation, a loss of pent-up pressure. He was flattered by the leader's praise and heartened by his encouragement. Never before had someone recognized his inner conflict and so graciously provided the support that he needed. Not even his wife. In that moment Benjamin was rejuvenated and he was able to set aside his worry, knowing it was trivial. Kechewaishke, Benjamin realized, was becoming like a father to him.

———

When the delegation arrived at Detroit, which was a small but burgeoning city, they were met immediately by the Indian agent who commanded that they go no further. Though Benjamin and the delegation were prepared for such an outcome, it was discouraging to hear. As before, Benjamin pleaded with the agent to hear him out before concluding that they should not go further. The agent resisted but agreed to put them in a hotel for the night and to meet with Benjamin in his office later.

"I am afraid I cannot allow your delegation to proceed to Washington." The agent was seated behind his desk with the marshal standing alongside him. The two appeared staunch in their decision.

Trying to appear respectful and meek, Benjamin sat upright with his hat in his hands. "We have been told the same thing by our sub-agent at Sault Ste. Marie and we are aware of the unlikelihood of meeting the president. But I cannot stress with enough urgency the importance of our journey. Not only this, but I have a petition with thousands of signatures to support our cause."

The agent and marshal looked at each other as if having their own personal conversation in their minds.

"Please, if you'll allow me to explain our dire circumstances I think you will understand."

The agent hesitated but eventually agreed.

Benjamin gave in full detail the history of their circumstances and the reasons for which the delegation was traveling to Washington. He told the agent about the deaths at Sandy Lake. He told him about the annuity payments that had been withheld or stolen. He told him about the conduct of the agent, Mr. Watrous. Benjamin also explained that they had reached out several times to the governor for his support and approval to visit Washington. Finally, he explained that they had no choice but to make the trip and to make it now. And, like he had before with the agent at Sault Ste. Marie, Benjamin explained that if they were turned back he did not consider that a white man's life would long be safe in the Indian country under the present state of excitement.

The agent and marshal pondered Benjamin's statements, a look of concern on their faces. Then they turned to each other to discuss the matter. They spoke quickly but quietly, not allowing Benjamin to hear their discussion. They were nearly convinced, Benjamin suspected.

"Sirs," Benjamin said, "if we are made to return without seeing the president it will start a fire that will not easily be quenched. The result could mean war in the Indian country."

They looked at Benjamin, their eyes steady, their faces pensive.

"You have made a convincing argument," the agent finally said. "One that I cannot ignore. I have little choice but to allow you and your delegation to proceed."

"Oh, thank you!" Benjamin smiled and stood as he reached his hand forward to shake the agent's hand. "Thank you, sirs. You have made a wise choice."

The agent did not return Benjamin's smile nor his enthusiasm. "It may be the right decision," the agent said, "but I seriously doubt you will ever reach Washington with your delegation."

Benjamin only nodded, feeling undeterred, and left the room.

When he returned to his comrades with the good news, they all responded with joyful shouts, praising the Great Spirit for their good fortune. The next morning, they would depart on the next leg of their journey. The delegation was headed toward New York City.

CHAPTER 21

Alexander Ramsey sat alone in his office pouring over the details of the charges against Agent John Watrous. As the Superintendent of Indian Affairs, it was his job to investigate the charges and provide his opinion of the case to the Commissioner of Indian Affairs in Washington. On one side he had a stack of papers accusing Watrous of wrongdoing while on the other he had a stack of papers exonerating Watrous, stating that he had merely carried out his orders as a government official. Ramsey knew all along that he would write an opinion in favor of the agent and his conduct. He had to; it was politics. Any scandal involving Watrous would reflect poorly upon Ramsey. At the moment, the great Sioux Treaties of Traverse des Sioux and Mendota were being deliberated in Congress. Ramsey needed all the support he could get to ratify the treaties and so he desperately sought to avoid a scandal. Now, as he sat with his pen in hand, he thought carefully about how to word his opinion in a manner that exonerated Watrous but was exceptionally judicious.

By the light of a candle, Ramsey penned his remarks.

The efforts of Agent Watrous to affect the removal of the Ojibwes have elicited against him much opposition; and while these efforts have not been crowned with the full success which the Department or myself could desire, it is with bad grace that the very men who have raised every obstacle to the removal, should now attempt to use the opposition they have created, to the agent's prejudice.

Owing to these and other causes of like nature, during the past year Agent Watrous has been subjected to much censure from Indians and others. The rivalry and jealousy of opposition traders, which is ever prone to unjust favoritism, if not corruption, to an agent, does much to increase opposition to him.

Sandy Lake, the temporary seat of the Ojibwe Agency, is distant some three hundred miles from St. Paul. It is impossible, therefore, that I should know, other than in a general way what transpired in the extensive region in charge of Mr. Watrous. So far as my information does extend, I think he had acted faithfully to the Government and in kindness and honesty to the Indians.

In conclusion, I beg leave to report to the Department my belief that the charges of the L'Anse Ojibwe are unfounded in truth and in my opinion that so far as it has been in the power of Mr. Watrous, he has honestly endeavored to do his duty as Agent of the Ojibwe Indians, and deserves the commendation, rather than the censure of the Government.

CHAPTER 22

From Detroit the delegation traveled by sail across Lake Erie to the town of Buffalo. In Buffalo they boarded a train which took them to Albany. This was the first train any of them had ever seen, and they marveled at the huge machine's power, speed, and endurance.

"It is like a horse that never grows tired," said Each Side of the Sky watching the black puffs of smoke move across the sky while mesmerized by the massive, inexhaustible wheels. "It requires no wind to push it nor oxen to pull it," he observed.

It was a remarkable experience for each man.

After arriving in Albany, the delegation traveled by steamer to New York City. The men were growing tired, but no less determined to reach their destination. Unfortunately, by the time they arrived in New York they had just one ten-cent silver piece of money remaining. Benjamin, being in charge of the money and travel, became rather anxious not knowing how they might pay for travel or a place to stay. At the port, he handed the bus driver several Ojibwe trinkets and asked if he would haul them and their luggage to the American House Hotel across the street from the Barnum Theater. The driver, who looked curiously at the Ojibwe delegation, was eventually persuaded. Benjamin was relieved, but still faced the embarrassment of having no money upon arriving at the hotel.

"Oh, consider it no embarrassment!" the landlord said. "Perhaps some other means of payment can be devised."

Much to Benjamin's surprise, the landlord of the hotel put up no objections. Instead he smiled heartily as he looked over the Ojibwe delegation greeting them with a handshake and a nod.

"I have letters," Benjamin said. "The acquaintances in these letters should provide us with financial support to pay our bill. If not," Benjamin thought for a moment, "if not, the Ojibwe, dressed as they are in their native regalia, can put on an exhibition. This way we can raise the necessary funds to pay our bill and carry us to our destination."

"A capital idea!" agreed the landlord, again showing no objections. "And I believe you and I are just the ones to carry it out."

As the men settled into their room, Benjamin went out in search of the parties for whom he had received letters from Brown, the editor of the Sault Ste. Marie newspaper. New York, he marveled, was the largest city he had ever seen and on his own he might have become quite lost, but, he received some helpful directions from the landlord.

Arriving at the address noted on the letter Benjamin knocked firmly against the door, feeling nervous but undaunted. It was a three-story, brick row house and looked similar to all the other houses that lined the street.

After a few moments a gentleman of obvious stature answered the door. He was dressed in a finely tailored suit with bowtie and vest, his hair neatly combed and his mustache well-groomed.

"Evening," he said.

Skipping the usual formalities, Benjamin immediately explained the purpose of his visit.

"Good evening, sir. I represent a delegation of native Ojibwe men traveling to Washington to meet the president. We have traveled very far with very little money. Along the way we met an acquaintance of yours—Mr. Brown, editor of the paper at Sault Ste. Marie."

The man smiled. "Yes, I know Mr. Brown. A capital fellow."

"Well, he provided me your address and asked me to give you this letter." Benjamin removed the letter from his pocket and handed it to the man. Without hesitation, the man opened and read the letter. Benjamin waited patiently, gripping his hat tightly with nervous anxiety.

Benjamin's anxiety quickly melted as the man, a stockbroker by the name of Smith he said, smiled and invited Benjamin into his home. After allowing Benjamin to explain, in full detail, their desperate circumstances, Smith agreed to return with Benjamin to the hotel to meet the Ojibwe delegation. Without further arrangement, Benjamin and the stockbroker were on their way to the hotel.

"What a great pleasure!" Smith said upon meeting the delegation. "Never in my life have I seen such natives of the wilderness. You are all right," he said. "Stay where you are, and I will see that you have money to carry you through."

This was a great relief, but it came at a cost. Taking Benjamin aside, Smith discussed with him a plan in which he advised Benjamin to put "your Indians," as he called them, on display in the hotel lobby. He said that many people would come and pay to see the native peoples. He assured Benjamin of it.

Benjamin explained the idea to the delegation, but they were not pleased. "We will not be paraded around like zoo animals," Oshoga said.

"We don't have a choice," Benjamin said. "We are without money and if we wish to continue we need to obtain funds. Otherwise, we have journeyed all this way for nothing and we will return as failures."

Oshoga wasn't convinced. "There must be another way."

"There is no time!" Benjamin said, raising his voice with a sense of desperation. "And this *will* work."

Before Oshoga could respond, Kechewaishke stood to address the men. He looked out-of-place in a New York City hotel, wrapped in his buffalo robe. But that did not matter; when Kechewaishke spoke, people listened.

"Do you not see this forest of buildings that surrounds us? Before the white man, this was a land of trees and rivers, of prairies and lakes. That was not so long ago. But the reach of the white man is far, and his children are numerous. They spread like bees, pollinating every flower they find, spreading their influence across the land. We cannot stop their spread. We cannot stop them from pillaging our lakes of fish, from plundering our forests of trees, or from mining our rocky shores of copper. At one time, I thought we could. But now I see that all we can do is negotiate. Survive. The power, the vast and endless power, runs through the Great Father. Whatever we wish for ourselves and for our children we may only achieve before him. We must risk everything, at times even our pride, so that we may lay our wishes before the Great Father. That is all I have to say."

The men answered with silence and shame, looking at their feet like scolded children. As the men stood there, Makwa quietly sat down as a sign of concession. The rest of the men did the same.

———

The next evening the men dressed in their finest regalia including feathers, beads, sashes, and leggings, and they assembled in the hotel lobby. Benjamin dressed in a dark suit with a vest and tie and he combed his hair and beard neatly, looking the part of an Easterner. The men had only one drum and a few bells with which to make music.

As the delegation readied themselves Benjamin began to worry that no one would come to watch their dance. He watched as people throughout the luxurious hotel lobby engaged in conversation or passed by rapidly as if they had somewhere important to go. Looking outside the streets were a melee of noise and activity that never stopped. The streets and sidewalks were always flooded with people while horse drawn cars and buses went by with astonishing regularity. Benjamin feared the city and its bustling crowds were too busy to notice a few Ojibwe doing an old-fashioned native dance.

The drumbeat echoed through the lobby as the men began their dance. They moved about in a circular fashion hopping from one foot to the other while lifting their arms on one side and then the other, in unison with the beat. As they moved, their beads clattered and jingled. Then, adding to the drumbeats and bells, the men began a rhythmic wailing. It grew louder and louder and after a few minutes they sounded more like a symphony than just a few solitary voices. Around and around the men danced, together on every step, in unison on every hoot and wail. It was remarkable to witness, Benjamin thought, forgetting how important it was to draw a paying crowd.

A few people gathered at first, most of them guests at the hotel. But within minutes people poured in from the streets in an endless line until the lobby was completely full. All of them gazed upon the native dancers with curiosity and joy, pointing and smiling and speaking gleefully to their neighbors. They were, it appeared, amazed by the sights and sounds of the traditional Indian, something that had passed away from view in the eastern region of the country many years before. In their astonishment, most of them contributed freely to the fund that would provide for the rest of the delegation's journey. Benjamin's heart began to flutter. Despite his outward display of confidence and perseverance, this was the first time he actually believed they might reach Washington City.

The men continued dancing, without break, for what seemed like hours until the crowd eventually dispersed. Among those departing were the stockbroker and his wife.

"Wonderful show!" Smith exclaimed as he came to congratulate Benjamin. "What a magnificent crowd and a magnificent dance."

"I have never seen anything like it," his wife added.

Benjamin thanked Smith for his advice and support for putting on the show while Smith continued to express his gratitude for having seen it.

"My wife, Sarah, and I would like to invite you and your delegation to our house tomorrow afternoon. I have a number of friends and their acquaintances who would love to see your Indians without the embarrassment they would feel at the showroom."

Benjamin knew he could not decline. The invitation may have been patronizing, but after the genuine kindness shown by Smith and his wife, it would be too rude to say no.

"Of course," Benjamin said, masking his apprehension. "We would be delighted."

———

Rather than walk, Benjamin decided they should use a horse-drawn bus to carry them from the hotel to the stockbroker's house. But, immediately upon stepping outside the hotel in the bright afternoon sun, a large crowd gathered around them.

"Red Men!" Benjamin heard a small boy shout. "Real Red Men!"

The crowd grew and grew as the gawkers pointed gleefully at the native Ojibwe. To them, Benjamin supposed, these men were more of a relic, something they had only read about in storybooks. It soon became obvious that they could not push their way through the crowd and had to return to the safety of the hotel.

After some careful thought, the landlord devised a plan to take the delegation safely and obscurely to the stockbroker's home. First, he had a message sent to Smith requesting that the dinner be postponed until evening. Then he negotiated a bus to pick them up from the alley after dark where they would not be seen. Carried out this way, the plan sent the delegation whirling through the streets with shaded bus windows to the home of the broker, which they reached without any trouble.

The delegation was met at the door by a young lady of beauty and tact. She welcomed the men with a brimming smile and a certain ineffable style and grace. Within the home were thirty or forty young people, all ready and anxious to see the red men of the forest, as they called them, at a white man's table.

All were fashionably dressed. The women were quite elegant in their wide, domed skirts, their shiny pearls and brooches, their lace shawls, and their hair pulled tight in a bun or braid. Likewise, the men were stylish with their dark frock coats, their white turnover collars, and their top hats. The home was equally fashionable with its jewel encrusted candlesticks, elaborately designed furniture, and countless pieces of delicate artwork.

After some general introductions, everyone was seated at the numerous tables—one large and several smaller tables to accommodate all the guests. The Ojibwe men, not being accustomed to chairs or tables did not know quite how to sit, some sitting too close to the table, others too far. The New Yorkers giggled under their breath.

"I apologize for our lack of refinement," Benjamin said feeling embarrassed. He had never learned the etiquette of high society, nor had his Ojibwe delegation.

"Nonsense," Sarah said. "You're our celebrated guests, and we understand that life is very different where you are from."

Benjamin was uplifted by the graciousness of her response. Turning to the Ojibwe men, Benjamin translated the hostess' words. For the New Yorkers at the table, this brought sudden and great delight to hear a white man speak a native language.

"We want you to feel right at home," Sarah said in a dignified tone and manner. "In truth, your visit was contemplated for the purpose of seeing you as nearly in your native ways and customs as possible, and we take no offense at any breach of etiquette. On the contrary, we should be highly gratified if you should proceed in all things as is your habit in the wilderness."

Although it may have been demeaning, Benjamin understood that it was their polite duty to agree to the wishes of the hostess. Therefore, once dinner was brought out, Benjamin told the Ojibwe that they should rise up, push their chairs back, and seat themselves on the floor, taking with them only their plate of food and knife. They did this nicely and the meal was taken in true Indian style, much to the gratification of the guests. When the meal was completed each man placed his knife and plate back upon the table, and, moving back toward the walls of the room seated himself upon the floor with legs crossed.

"Oh, how delightful," the women said as they chatted over tea.

For some time, the Ojibwe kept to themselves, seated as they were against the wall. But after a while, the guests began asking questions of the men. "What do you eat? Where do you sleep? How do you survive in the wilderness?" Things of that nature. Eventually, Oshoga decided he ought to make a speech.

Getting up from the floor and pushing his long dark hair behind his shoulders, Oshoga began his speech. "Thank you for your kindness," he said in Ojibwe as Benjamin translated. "Though we are not of your clan you have welcomed us and made us to feel that your home is our home. You have made our bellies full with the spoils of your hunt and you have brought us under the roof of your wigwam where it remains warm and light all through the hours of darkness."

The guests were almost giddy, hearing the foreign words of a native while they tried, out of politeness, to withhold their chuckles and merriment.

"We are much impressed by the manner of the white people. Not only by their kind nature, but by their affluence of culture and riches. Never before have we seen a village with more people than can be counted and more buildings than trees in the forest. The vastness and power of the American city is beyond our own comprehension. Yet your kindness and gentleness of nature makes us feel as if we are among our own people and our own lodges."

Oshoga sat down while the guests replied with an uproarious applause. As the applause grew louder and more boisterous some of the Ojibwe were forced to cover their ears to shield themselves from the noise.

"Who is the young man?" one of the guests asked, pointing at Makwa.

"That is Makwa," Benjamin said. "He is my adopted son."

Makwa turned his head but gave no other reaction.

"Your son! How marvelous. Has he anything to say?"

Benjamin looked toward Makwa. He had not spoken in over two years.

Mawka kept his eyes to the floor.

"He prefers to keep silent," Benjamin said after a long pause.

"I would like to speak," Makwa said in a sudden, clear voice.

"Have you enjoyed your journey?" the guest asked, as if nothing unordinary had occurred. Meanwhile, Benjamin was stunned.

Makwa raised his head and looked across the group of dignified party-goers. His eyes moved cautiously as he examined each face, perhaps wondering how to express himself in front of such a strange and captivated audience. After a few silent moments he began to speak.

"The Ojibwe are a proud people, a strong people," he said as he picked himself up from off the floor. "Anishinaabe we are called. The First People. At one point in time everything that belongs to you had belonged to us. In turn, we belonged to it. From here to the Great Lakes and stretching north as far as a man can travel. But we migrated west over many centuries in search of food, in search of a home. We found that home around Gichigami, the greatest lake. We moved farther west still, conquering the Nadouessioux and forcing them south. Still we maintained our home, our culture, and our livelihood at Moningwunakauning, the place the French speakers call La Pointe."

The party-goers were silent, hanging on Makwa's every word.

Benjamin thought of interrupting the boy to stop him from offend-ing their hosts, but Kechewaishke held his hand out, signaling that he should not.

"But now our home is being taken from us and we have nowhere left to go. Where once there was an alliance between the Americans and ourselves now there is nothing. Your lies and the lies of your gov-ernment have left us hungry and sick and dying. Even now we are like little birds begging for a worm. No amount of kindness or gifts or generosity can make up for the loss my people experience."

Benjamin clenched his teeth, afraid their hosts would become deeply offended. But he also felt proud to hear Makwa speak out.

"What did you expect? A few coins and a bus ride? Some special attention? Do you think we can just forgive and forget? It is not that simple. It will never be that simple. Nothing you say or do can bring my father back to life. Our world has been changed forever and we cannot have it back."

Silence fell over the room. How could Benjamin explain the frank-ness of a boy who was suffering before a crowd of innocent spectators. He couldn't.

"Profound words for such a young man," Smith said, breaking the silence.

"Forgive the boy," Benjamin said cautiously. "He has been through a lot. We have all been through a lot."

"It's quite alright," Smith said with a look of compassion. "It is quite alright."

"An intelligent young man and quite eloquent," Sarah said.

After a few moments the smiles began to return to the faces of the men and women. Then, they approached Makwa and the other men, happy and joyous as if not in the least offended.

Mawka recoiled from the attention and kept his back turned to the numerous conversations around him. Benjamin sought to comfort his nephew, but Kechewaishke instructed him otherwise.

"Let him be," Kechewaishke said. "He must discover his own way."

Late in the night the men returned to the hotel after what was, for the most part, a splendid evening. At the first opportunity, Benjamin consoled Makwa, but the boy retreated into his private shell.

"Think of the stories you'll have to tell," Benjamin said.

"I am no longer a storyteller," Makwa said, still brooding from his speech. "All of our stories are gone now."

Saddened, Benjamin knew that he could never completely understand Makwa's suffering. He could only do his best to empathize. For who could possibly understand what it was like to have your world robbed without having a chance to fight back.

CHAPTER 23

John Watrous entered the office of the Commissioner of Indian Affairs, Luke Lea. He removed his hat and nodded respectfully. In his hand he held a tri-fold letter several pages thick.

Lea remained in his chair looking up at the agent and puffing on a cigar. As he exhaled a puff of smoke slipped out the window at the side of his office which overlooked the Potomac River.

"Is that your refutation to the charges?" Lea asked as his eyes widened looking at the letter in the agent's hand.

"It is," Watrous said, handing the letter to the commissioner. Without opening it, Lea placed it on his desk in front of him. "I have written a clear refutation to each charge and I think you'll agree that the charges against me are very highly colored and most of the charges entirely unfounded in truth," Watrous said, clutching his hat nervously.

"Why have you come all the way to Washington to deliver me a letter?" Lea asked, suspicious of Watrous' intentions.

Watrous looked down to the floor as if he were a child ashamed of something. "They have sent a delegation, sir. They are on their way and they wish to meet with the president."

Startled, Lea put his cigar down and leaned forward in his chair. "This has become quite a mess," Lea said as he shook his head. "Your annual reports have made the removal look like a success, but if the delegation reaches the president, Congress is sure to discover the charges against you and then examine the removal efforts. They will determine it has failed and at great expense. You must intercept the delegation."

Watrous nodded, "I agree."

"Keep this as quiet as possible," Lea continued. "I will write up my recommendations to Ramsey. Don't worry about the charges against you; just make sure you intercept the delegation and escort them back to La Pointe."

"Yes, sir," Watrous said. "I will, and I will continue with the removal. I am convinced that if the original order of the Department be strictly adhered to, of paying annuities only to those that reside and live in their own country proper, that two years will not elapse before all will remove of their own accord."

"Very well," Lea said as he picked his cigar back up and looked out the window at the slowly flowing, glassy waters of the Potomac.

CHAPTER 24

The Ojibwe delegation from La Pointe arrived in Washington City on June 22, 1852, more than two and one-half months after departing their island home. This in itself was an improbable accomplishment. Their next task and challenge was to arrange, by some means, a meeting with the President of the United States.

Arriving in town, Benjamin watched the Ojibwe delegation who were spellbound by the sights and sounds of the busy and bustling American capital. Everywhere there were neatly dressed Americans scurrying from one place to the next. Buildings and roads covered every inch of space with barely room for a spot of grass. All around bells rang, people shouted, carriages rambled, and construction— construction was endless. In the center, upon a hill, was a huge white building made of brilliant, glossy marble and marked by numerous Greek columns. Scaffolds lined its perimeter, as it, too, was under construction. Nevertheless, it was both beautiful and imposing, unlike anything any of them, including Benjamin, had ever seen.

But, as Benjamin insisted, there was no time to dally. They had an important mission with very little time and very little money to carry it out. So, rather than take in the sights and sounds, Benjamin led the delegation straight to the National Hotel. Upon their arrival the men requested a room on the first floor telling Benjamin that they did not like to get too high up in a white man's house. The landlord agreed to this request and, using the money they had earned in New York, they were soon provided lodging and made comfortable with just a few mattresses.

The morning following their arrival, Benjamin set out in search of the Interior Department of the government to find the Commissioner of Indian Affairs. Rather than go straight to the President's Executive

Mansion, Benjamin decided to request a meeting with the commissioner in order that he might impress upon him the urgency of their situation and in doing so obtain a meeting with the president.

After a short but relaxing walk among the broad, tree-lined streets of the city, Benjamin located the Interior Department building. It was a long, three-story wooden building with many windows and a huge double-door entrance. Entering the building, Benjamin was directed downstairs to find the Bureau of Indian Affairs.

"Pardon me," Benjamin said as he walked up to a woman with short brown hair and a collared dress who was seated at a desk near the entry.

"Yes," the woman said. "How can I assist you?"

"I'd like to request a meeting with the Commissioner of Indian Affairs."

"Of course," she said with a muted smile then reached for a pencil and paper. "What is the nature of your business?"

"I have traveled from Ojibwe country along with a delegation of chiefs that we might request an important and necessary meeting with the president."

A man walked hurriedly by but was slowed by the nature of Benjamin's explanation. Before rounding the desk, he stopped and asked, "Did you state that you have brought a delegation?"

Startled, Benjamin turned his head to answer. The man appeared middle-aged with graying hair and goatee. The buttons of his vest strained to withhold his expansive belly while his silk neck tie expressed a refinement of position.

"Are you the Commissioner of Indian Affairs?" Benjamin asked.

"I am," he said. "Commissioner Luke Lea. Who are you? What's your business here?"

The commissioner held tightly to a stack of papers, never lowering them to shake hands or exchange pleasantries.

"My name is a Benjamin Armstrong. I've come from La Pointe in Ojibwe country along with a delegation of chiefs led by Chief Buffalo. We have recently been ordered to remove..."

"I beg your pardon," the commissioner interrupted. "But have you received permission from your agent to come to Washington? Have you received permission from your superintendent?"

"Our situation is dire. The Ojibwe at La Pointe haven't received annuities for two years and if the situation becomes worse, I fear those less understanding will resort to violence."

"I have read the reports from Ojibwe country, and I know your circumstances. But had your superintendent deemed it necessary, he would have granted permission for your delegation to visit Washington."

A nervous anxiety began to fill Benjamin's mind and body. "What are you saying?"

"I'm saying that you should not have come here. You must have had a long and tedious journey, but you must understand how things are done. We are busy with other matters and cannot see your delegation until you've received permission through the proper channels. I'm sorry, but you should take your Indians and go home."

The commissioner turned and headed toward his office without waiting for a response.

Benjamin felt hot and uncomfortable as he watched the commissioner walk away. "But, sir," Benjamin said, calling loudly so he could be heard by the retreating commissioner. "We have traveled many miles at our own expense. If you'd only let me explain how important it is that we meet with the president, you would understand why we came without permission."

The commissioner paused, then turned his head quickly. "I have seven superintendencies to oversee. Among each there are half a dozen agencies and dozens of sub-agencies, each with its own unique characteristics. Each with its own set of circumstances. I have other matters to attend to right now, and I suspect the President of the United States does as well. Please, talk with your agent. Your agent will talk with your superintendent, and your superintendent will talk with Washington. Are we clear?"

The commissioner stared at Benjamin like a supervisor at his subordinate. Slowly, Benjamin nodded his head. Just as soon as he did, the commissioner continued into his office and closed the door behind him. Benjamin looked toward the secretary who merely raised her eyebrows and shrugged her shoulders apologetically.

Discouraged, Benjamin lowered his head in failure and exited the building. On the sidewalk, as city life continued all around him, he began pacing back and forth pondering his situation. Had they come all this way for nothing? Even if they chose to return home, they had no money to get there. What options did they have?

Resolute, Benjamin did not give up hope. For a while he wandered around the city and then walked to the Capitol thinking he might find someone he had seen before—thinking he might find someone that could help. But, finding no one, he decided to return to the hotel. Feeling defeated and utterly depressed, he wondered how he could confront the men with such despairing news? As he walked slowly back, reminiscing on the last few years of heartache and obstacles, he realized the narrative had to change. Or rather, he had to change the narrative.

When Benjamin arrived at the hotel, he found Kechewaishke surrounded by a crowd of people, all of whom were asking questions of the Ojibwe leader. Kechewaishke was hunched over with his arms in front of him, recoiling from all the attention. Overwhelmed, he directed their questions toward Benjamin.

"Who is this Indian?"

"Where have you come from?"

"Why are you here?"

Benjamin, being in such a foul mood, answered all their questions as directly and briefly as possible.

"He is the head chief of the Ojibwe of the Northwest," Benjamin said plainly.

"Why don't you take him into the dining room with you," suggested the hotel steward. "Certainly, such a distinguished man as he, the head of the Ojibwe people, should have at least that privilege."

Benjamin considered the suggestion and found it agreeable. And, he decided, it would be an appropriate setting to deliver the disheartening news to Kechewaishke.

A few hours later Benjamin invited Kechewaishke to the dining room. The old chief accepted and, as Benjamin and Kechewaishke entered the dining room, they were shown to a table in the corner. As they were seated, all the patrons turned and looked upon the native Indian as if they had never seen such a thing. Gasps and awe and chatter of all kinds could be heard throughout the restaurant.

Within minutes two distinguished looking gentlemen came from across the room and stood hopefully in front of Benjamin and Kechewaishke.

"If you have no objections, my colleague and I would like to speak with you."

Kechewaishke did not understand and looked toward Benjamin.

"We have no objections," Benjamin said.

Simultaneously, the middle-aged men pulled chairs up to the table and seated themselves. Without further introduction they began with the customary line of questioning. Having rehearsed his responses many times Benjamin answered quickly and with as little detail as was necessary. But the men were more inquisitive than usual. Benjamin thought they might be reporters.

"My name is Representative Briggs of New York, U.S. Congress. This," he said pointing to the man next to him, "is Secretary Stuart of the Interior Department. We are both Whigs and we work closely with President Fillmore."

Suddenly, Benjamin was pulled from his cynical stupor, feeling a great dash of hope upon learning the names and positions of these men. These were important politicians that might be able to help them. With a change of attitude, Benjamin proceeded to explain their situation in great detail trying to persuade them of the urgency of the matter, making sure to emphasize the necessity of meeting with the president.

"That is completely unjust," Representative Briggs said after hearing Benjamin's explanation. "You and your delegation and the entire Ojibwe community deserve justice. Such wrongs cannot be allowed to continue. Such wrongs must be made right."

"You have my condolences," Secretary Stuart said, nodding toward Kechewaishke who gave no response.

Then, Briggs leaned over and began to speak privately with Secretary Stuart. As Benjamin watched and waited he felt an intense excitement he could barely withhold. This, he knew, could be their pathway to the president. Benjamin observed Kechewaishke who appeared unmoved and emotionless, as if he had expected such an outcome.

The men completed their private discussion and shifted their attention back toward Benjamin and Kechewaishke.

"We will undertake to get you and your delegation an interview with the president," the representative from New York said. "We will notify you here, at the hotel, when a meeting can be arranged."

"Thank you!" Benjamin said as he stood up to shake hands with his new political advocates, unable to suppress the smile from his face.

Getting up from their seats, the men bid farewell to Kechewaishke and departed, their conversation already changed to another matter of business. Turning toward Kechewaishke, Benjamin's smile grew larger and larger. "I think our fortunes have changed!"

The elder replied confidently, "The Great Spirit is with us."

It did not take long before Benjamin heard back from the two politicians.

"We have arranged your meeting," Representative Briggs said in a telegram. "Arrive at the Executive Mansion at 3 p.m. tomorrow afternoon."

Immediately, Benjamin told the men who were overwhelmed by the good news. They were excited and anxious for the hard-earned and long-awaited encounter with the Great Father.

When the delegation arrived at the Executive Mansion they were greeted by Representative Briggs and ushered into a large study characterized by several elegant lounge chairs and numerous bookshelves. After a short time, all assembled, with the exception of the president. This included Benjamin, the five Ojibwe delegates, Makwa, Representative Briggs, Secretary Stuart, Commissioner Lea, and several other staff and aides.

Before the meeting could begin, Kechewaishke insisted that the peace pipe be passed. It was an Ojibwe tradition, he explained, as a sign of peace and respect that should not be overlooked on such an important occasion.

The pipe, which was brought for just that purpose, was filled and lighted by Kechewaishke and passed to Representative Briggs. He took two or three puffs and politely asked, "Who is next?" The pipe was passed until all had a puff. Rather than hand the pipe back to Kechewaishke, it was taken by the stem and handed to Benjamin for safe keeping, only to be used for special occasions.

The pipe having been passed, the old leader rose from his seat. Following his example everyone else stood and marched single file to the office of the president.

The president, who was there waiting, stood and greeted the men happily. General hand-shaking followed until everyone had been seated.

As Benjamin shook hands and observed the polite formalities his heart was racing with excitement. Having grown up a poor boy in Alabama and an orphan after that, he had never expected to be in the office of the President of the United States of America. Yet, there he was.

"I understand you gentlemen have traveled a great distance to see me," President Fillmore said as he leaned forward and looked attentively toward the Ojibwe delegation.

The president was a large man with a round face and narrow eyes. His hair was full on his head, but stark white, except in places around the ears and neck where it remained gray. He dressed stylishly, not ornamented like a king, but in a nicely fitting dark suit, neck tie, and silver chained watch. He looked every bit the part of a Great Father.

"Thank you, Great Grandfather," Kechewaishke said in a slow, deliberate manner trying hard to enunciate the English words. "We travel many day, many night. We know your power reaches all the way from there to here. But your power is lost on the way and your agents forget what you say. Now we see you so we can hear your words ourselves."

Kechewaishke turned, looking at Oshoga who was seated at the side of the room. Kechewaishke nodded subtly and Oshoga nodded back.

"Great Father," Oshoga said as he stood to address the president, speaking in his native Ojibwe. "We have come many lengths, covering the span of two whole moons, giving up our time of hunting and gathering foods, with the hope that you would right the wrongs done to our people, that you would quiet the excitement in our country."

All attention was turned toward Oshoga as he continued speaking for nearly an hour describing all the painful misdeeds done to the Ojibwe. He began with the treaty of 1837 and showed plainly what he understood the treaty to be. He next took up the treaty of 1842 and said he did not understand that in either treaty they had ceded away the land. In both cases, as he understood it, the Ojibwe were never to be asked to remove from the lands, provided they were peaceable and obeyed the laws of the land and this they had done. Why now, asked Oshoga, had the Great Father become displeased with the Ojibwe and though they had been peaceable, why had he asked them to remove?

When Oshoga had finally finished his speech, the president sat quietly as he thought on what to say.

"I understand you have a petition for me," he said looking up toward Benjamin.

"I do," Benjamin said quickly and then he laid the paper down on the table in front of President Fillmore.

"Yes, yes," he nodded as he examined the petition and pointed to various signatures. "I know this man."

After completing his examination, he placed the petition in his breast pocket, looked up, clasped his hands together, and inhaled deeply.

"Being the head of a great and powerful nation has opened my eyes to the needs of a great many people." The president looked poignantly upon the Ojibwe men and he appeared to be speaking from the heart. "Some needs, because of my position, I can satisfy. Others, I can only sigh in sadness, making my heart weary and keeping me up at night. It is obvious that your people have endured great wrongs and enormous suffering. What disheartens me nearly as much as your suffering, is that it has come at the hands of the government, the very government I am entrusted to represent. For this I apologize. But also, because of this, I believe I can help you."

"First things first," the president said, now looking toward Commissioner Lea who had nearly hidden himself in the back of the room. "Say to the landlord of the hotel that their bills will be paid for by the government. Second, ensure that this delegation has the freedom of the city for a week."

Commissioner Lea nodded obediently. "Yes, sir."

"Now, as to the more important matter. I will countermand the removal order and I will instruct the agent that the annuity payment shall hereafter be made at La Pointe. I know this does not reverse your suffering, but it should at the very least eliminate any further cause for complaint. Hopefully, your community may move forward in peace and relative comfort."

While translating the president's words Benjamin could hardly contain himself. A great load was lifted from his shoulders. Finally, he thought, this marked the end of the long and tedious struggle that he had made on behalf of the Ojibwe and his family. And though it could not bring back his dearest and truest friend, Giizhigoon, it meant that he had not died in vain.

"Thank you, thank you," the Ojibwe men repeated as they began to comprehend the good news.

"We know you are good," Kechewaishke said to the president as both men stood to shake hands. "You will keep your promise."

The men stood and then one by one reached toward the president to thank him. As Benjamin looked to Makwa, he was shaking hands with the president and he was smiling. He looked happy. The entire delegation gleamed with a positive radiance that Benjamin hadn't seen in many years. It was a great and satisfying moment.

———

Over the next few days the delegation was able to enjoy the grandeur and beauty of the capital city. They were, for the first time in many years, free and light-hearted, confident that the future was brighter than the past. It was an extraordinary feeling, an incredible relief.

But, much to Benjamin's dismay, he encountered the agent, John

Watrous. Benjamin was alone at the time, walking down the city's main thoroughfare, Pennsylvania Avenue.

"Do you know what today is?" the agent asked, without saying hello as if their meeting had been predetermined.

"I beg your pardon?" Benjamin had no idea why the agent asked him such an abrupt and ambiguous question.

"Today is the day the Dakota treaties have been ratified."

Benjamin looked at the agent curiously.

"The treaties of Traverse des Sioux and Mendota. Thirty million acres of rich and abundant land has exchanged hands from the Dakota Indians to the United States government. It is something the men in the Indian Bureau have worked very hard for over many years."

"I hardly see your point, Mr. Watrous. What has this got to do with me?"

"This has everything to do with you and your delegation," Agent Watrous said, his voice hardening.

"Aren't you under investigation, Mr. Watrous?" Benjamin asked. "Charges of a serious nature were brought against you for your misdealings during the entire Ojibwe removal effort."

"I *was* under investigation. Those charges went straight to Governor Ramsey who saw to it that the charges were dismissed. And besides, I was merely doing my job. I am moving this country forward."

Benjamin was shocked. "What! After all that's happened, the charges have been dismissed? Your exploitation of the Ojibwe caused the deaths of hundreds in our community. You caused the death of my brother-in-law. How could there be no consequences?"

"Mr. Armstrong, the natives of this land will be wiped away sooner or later. With the Dakota lands acquired it is only a matter of time before the northern portion is ceded and Minnesota becomes a state. There is no room for your Indians. You must recognize the inevitability of it all."

"If there is one thing I've learned about the native peoples, it's their ability to endure," Benjamin said, incensed by the agent's insensitivity. "There is no inevitability that they cannot endure and overcome."

"I would beg to differ, Mr. Armstrong. Like the seeds of a dandelion your native people will weaken and wither until they are blown away. They are a relic of the past. Even you must recognize that. Even you may come to exploit them."

"That's absurd."

"Is it? I have used them to advance my financial and political standing. You, to gain prestige among their community. It is only a matter of perspective."

Benjamin was frustrated by the agent's accusation. He paused trying to think of a way to change the subject. "You must know why we are here," Benjamin said. "You must know why we came all this way. We met with the president and we had a tremendous victory. The president himself assured us that we would not be removed from La Pointe. He told us that our annuity payment would hereafter be made at our PERMANENT island home!" Benjamin leaned forward as a gesture of confidence to match his confident tone.

Watrous was unmoved. He shook his head and stood his ground.

"I'm not sure there was a meeting," he said, questioning the truth of Benjamin's statement. "But it would not matter anyway."

"It wouldn't matter? We have the assurance of the president."

Again, Watrous held firm, doubtless in his convictions. "The president may say what he wishes, but the removal effort is not as you believe. It is not a decision for the president to make. It is done at the discretion of the governor."

"Excuse me? Discretion of the governor?"

"If you did in fact meet with the president, and if he did give you such promises, those promises will go no further than the Commissioner of Indian Affairs. And even if they get passed along, they will go to the Superintendent of Indian Affairs, who just so happens to be Governor Ramsey."

"But we have his promise," Benjamin said, clinging to hope. "And if you refuse to instate his policy you will be dismissed from your position and high standing, as you ought to be."

"Not quite, Mr. Armstrong. Promises do not equal policy change. And your country—Ojibwe country—receives very little attention in

Washington. There are much larger issues at stake such as building and maintaining the Union. The words of the president will dwindle and die in the bureaucratic system and there will be no one to ensure that such meaningless policy is enforced. My job, I assure you, is safe and the removal effort will continue. The removal effort will be completed."

Benjamin crumbled inside. He felt defeated, broken, undone. What could he say? His efforts, like so many before, meant nothing.

"If you'll excuse me," Watrous said. "I have business to attend to."

As the agent walked away, Benjamin asked one more desperate question. "Have you no heart, sir?"

Watrous turned, looked up plainly, and said, "If the Ojibwe were cold and asked for my shirt, I would not even give them that."

CHAPTER 25

"Congratulations," Agent Watrous said as he entered Ramsey's St. Paul office on a warm summer afternoon. "Although the Pembina treaty was not ratified, you must be very pleased over the Sioux treaties. The new land will bring a large amount of money into the territory and will certainly boost your political standing."

Ramsey sat back in his chair, pleased with the accomplishment but still unsatisfied with current political matters. "Yes," Ramsey finally said, "it is a shame to lose the Pembina treaty and I remain concerned with matters of the Ojibwe removal." Ramsey paused and stroked his chin and seemed to look off into the distance, pensively.

"Give it time," Watrous said. "The removal will be completed."

"Yes, but if the public learns of our failure to this point, I will face censure for expending so much public money for no purpose. My accomplishments will be for naught."

"You have built this territory. Just look out your window at the rapid growth of this city. Soon it will be a great northern state—because of you and the work you have done bringing business, commerce, and settlement to a once lonely and backward frontier."

"Hmm," Ramsey nodded, still deep in thought. "That may be."

"How shall we proceed?"

"Proceed?"

"With the Ojibwe? Do you agree with my recommendations? They have made their trip to Washington and now await your orders."

"Yes," Ramsey said breaking out of thought. "Lea had no objections and neither do I. Move the agency to Crow Wing. Tell the Ojibwe—insist that it has become Indian law—that they have to remove from ceded lands if they wish to receive their payment."

"Good," Watrous said. "This may be a success yet.

166

CHAPTER 26

The delegation returned to La Pointe by the same route they used to travel to Washington. It was uneventful. And though he hated to do it, Benjamin had to tell the men what happened—he had to tell them that the decision to remove or remain was not in the hands of the president, but was instead, as Agent Watrous openly declared, in the hands of Governor Alexander Ramsey.

"Then we must make our plea before the father of Minnesota Territory," Kechewaishke said after hearing the bad news.

"You are not upset?" Benjamin asked. "We traveled so far and accomplished so little."

Kechewaishke remained calm and thoughtful. "An eagle cannot fly backwards," he said plainly. "Our direction is forward and will always remain forward. We cannot see the path behind us and we will not know the benefit of our burdens until we reach our destination."

Despite Kechawaishke's wise words, Benjamin remained discouraged. "But Governor Ramsey has shown indifference for our situation. He will not hear us. He will not change his mind."

"Do you see the wrinkles on my face?" Kechewaishke said. "I have seen many days. Some were filled with sun; others were marked with clouds, sickness, and famine. But I have survived; my wrinkles give you the proof. I am not discouraged by failure. I am not defeated by suffering. I am only discouraged when I do not try. I am only defeated once I give up."

The men of the delegation praised Kechewaishke with subtle nods and soft tones of agreement and thanks. Benjamin was enlightened by the elder's words and grateful for their effect on him. He could almost feel his pessimism being lifted.

"I will write a letter to the father of Minnesota Territory," Keche-waishke said. "Oshoga will help me. Benjamin, you will send it."

"Do you know enough English?" Benjamin asked. "Shall I revise the letter before I send it?"

Kechewaishke shook his head. "Send it as I give it to you. Ramsey will understand my words."

As the summer moved along there was a certain uncomfortable silence that loomed over the island. No more councils were being held to discuss a course of action. No more chiefs and headmen could be seen collaborating or inciting action or influence. Instead there was a quiet reticence, a bitter acceptance. There seemed to be no changing the future, no delaying the inevitable march of progress. Still, moving their homes from the island was out of the question. Rather, people began hunting and trapping more, trying to obtain much-needed sustenance and income. Unfortunately, much of the hunting grounds had been depleted or the habitats destroyed by lumbering and mining. Men returned with little game and what furs they had, had lesser and lesser value. The island was becoming poor and destitute. Benjamin feared things would only get worse.

"Have you heard the news?" Benjamin's employer, Austrian, asked one day in his thick German accent.

"News? I'm afraid I haven't." Benjamin, who was translating documents, stopped to listen.

Austrian did not immediately respond, and Benjamin could tell something was wrong. Being accustomed to bad news, Benjamin braced himself.

"The agency is moving," he finally blurted.

"Moving? That's impossible," Benjamin said. "There are still hundreds of Ojibwe living here."

"That may be, but the government has made it clear that they don't want them here. It seems they have every intention to continue endorsing the effort to remove all Ojibwe from the Lake Superior region. The St. Paul *Minnesotian* has even reported it."

"Where will the agency be moved—do you know? Fond du Lac? Sandy Lake?"

Austrian shook his head and pursed his lips with a look of regret.

"Farther? Beyond the Mississippi?"

"Crow Wing," he said with reluctance. "Beyond the Mississippi."

Benjamin dropped his shoulders and almost fell to his knees, shocked and dismayed at the news. Apparently, the governor had shown no compassion, not even compromising by putting the agency and all its necessary services at Fond du Lac. Crow Wing was more than twice the distance from La Pointe, making it nearly impossible to travel there and travel back with annuity payments and goods.

"I'm afraid that's not all."

That's not all. That's not all. Benjamin's mind raced. *What else could possibly go wrong? How much worse could my situation become?* Benjamin could not bear another failure, another setback. He had done all he could these past few years and nothing came out right. Raising his head, Benjamin prepared for what he was about to hear.

"I'm so sorry, but I have to terminate your employment."

It hit him like a frozen winter breeze, penetrating his entire body. Without a job, he, too, would become poor and destitute. He, too, would suffer and so would his family. Benjamin would be at the mercy of the government annuities.

"The trade has dwindled and with the removal of the agency it will become next to nothing. I no longer have a need for a clerk, and I must look ahead. The times are changing, and I must change with them. The future is in land speculation and mining, not the fur trade."

Benjamin wasn't listening. He had known this time was coming; still he was not prepared for it.

"I understand, Julius."

Feeling numb Benjamin set down his pencil and closed his ledger, then looked at Austrian for some form of reassurance. Austrian merely looked back at him apologetically.

"I'm sorry, Benjamin. You have been a dedicated, hard-working employee. I know you will find a way to care for yourself and your family."

For many years Benjamin had depended on his job and depended on the fur trade. He had supplemented his income with hunting and fishing and a small garden, but alone that was not enough. Surely, he could not depend on the annuities; no one at La Pointe could. Benjamin lowered his head and walked slowly out of the store, worn down by his misfortunes, frightened by his new and harsh reality.

Returning home, things suddenly became much worse. Benjamin discovered Charlotte packing a wagon with supplies. Anxiously he asked, "What are you doing? Where are you going?"

"I am leaving."

Dumbstruck, Benjamin stopped in his tracks. "Why?"

"Mr. Austrian told me he could not continue your employment. He told me that you were going to be terminated." Charlotte moved hurriedly between the door of the cabin and the back of the wagon, loading supplies in haste. Marie and Samuel sat on the bench of the wagon with looks of apprehension on their faces. Makwa stood silently by the doorway. "You have been absent more often than you have been here. Now, without your job, you can no longer provide for us," Charlotte explained.

Alarmed, Benjamin ran quickly to his children as if they were something he could slip into his pocket and prevent from leaving. "Please, wait a day or two so we can talk and decide what to do." Benjamin was so nervous, so scared; he began to sweat.

Charlotte stopped loading the wagon and looked straight into Benjamin's eyes. "I am tired of waiting. You have become so headstrong about rescuing this community that you ignored your own family. I can no longer risk the livelihood of my children over the injustice that you strive to fix."

"But you know … you know my heart." Benjamin was desperately reaching for anything he could. "You know I would do anything for this community."

"Your duty is to your family."

Grabbing his children by the hands, Benjamin fixed his eyes on Charlotte's. "Have I done anything wrong? I have worked hard for this family and for this community. I have sacrificed everything and asked for nothing in return. You can't leave me. Not now. Not while things are so bleak."

"Gaawiin!" Charlotte exclaimed with her hands on her hips and her head held forward. *No!* "You do not know what it is like without you here, not knowing if or when you'll return. I cannot live with such uncertainty. I cannot raise my children without a father as a constant presence. Whether the government removes us from this island or not, I have to protect my children."

"But, please," Benjamin said as Charlotte began loading the last of her supplies in the wagon. "Please don't leave. Things will change soon. I will be here for you and the children. I will."

"I'd like to believe you, but I can't take that chance."

Charlotte hoisted herself atop the bench of the wagon and grabbed the reins. "We are leaving now, Benjamin," she said as she forced his hands from the children who whimpered and cried.

"Charlotte," he said as a desperate plea. "Daga." *Please.*

With the reins in her hands Charlotte turned and looked back toward Benjamin. "I know your heart, Benjamin. You care a lot about this community and its people, but something has changed about you. It has—" she paused to collect herself. "It has become more about you than about the island. It is more about you than the people. It has become your story when it should be theirs."

Charlotte cracked the reins and the wagon started slowly down the trail. All Benjamin could do was watch, his heart breaking. Benjamin waved cheerlessly to his daughter Marie who looked back until the dust had covered her sightline. Turning, Benjamin found Makwa who had sidled up beside him. Seeing Benjamin's suffering, Makwa put his arm over Benjamin's shoulders. Now, they had both lost those they loved.

———

Benjamin was depressed and heartbroken. For days, he never even left the house. At night he could not sleep as he meditated on Charlotte's words—*It has become your story when it should be theirs.* What did it mean? Was she right? The only thing that kept Benjamin going was his responsibility toward Makwa and his well-being. For that Benjamin was grateful, but he was not sure how much longer he could continue. He felt as if he had nothing left to live for. He needed something good to happen. He needed a purpose.

One afternoon, Benjamin was visited by Michel Cadotte, a well-known and respected trader in the region. Cadotte and his family had been at La Pointe for many years. It was his grandmother Madeline from which the island took its namesake.

Michel did not stay long. He merely informed Benjamin that Kechewaishke had requested Benjamin's presence at what he called "an important council." Benjamin did not feel inclined to attend, depressed as he was, but he was not one to deny the chief elder's request. Reluctantly, Benjamin decided he would attend.

It was a small gathering, almost private. It included Benjamin, Reverend Wheeler, Reverend Hall, Michel Cadotte, Kechewaishke, Oshoga, and Mary Warren. Benjamin was surprised to see Mary. She was the sister of the mixed-race agent, interpreter, historian, and politician William Warren. Sadly, William had passed away from tuberculosis earlier in the year. His sister Mary lived at Bad River and was adopted into the Wheeler family. She was a woman of just eighteen at the time. Benjamin could not imagine what her presence might indicate.

"We were saddened by the news that the agency is to be moved," Kechewaishke said, speaking directly to Benjamin rather than addressing the group. It was as if those present knew something that Benjamin did not. "This appears to end all hope of keeping our ancient home here at Moningwunakauning, the place given to us by the Great Spirit, the place where food grows upon the water."

Kechewaishke paused and handed Benjamin a document. "Read," he said.

August 10, 1852

Oshoga and Buffalo,
You learned in your late visit to Washington, that it is still the

wish and purpose of your "Great Father" that you should remove from the lands you sold him in the treaties of 1837 and 1842.

But I hereby promise you, and you may show this promise to your agent, that if it is, as you have indicated in your letter, your desire not to remove further than Fond du Lac, you shall be permitted to remain at that place.

It will be better for you to remove there quietly and contentedly and receive regularly your future annuities.

Respectfully Yours,
Alexander Ramsey

"This is the response to your letter by Governor Ramsey," Benjamin said with a sense of grief in his voice. "But it is NOT the Great Father's wish! What good is this man's promise!"

"We know, we know," Reverend Wheeler said trying to calm Benjamin. "All of us here have accepted our defeat at the hands of Watrous and Ramsey. We think you should, too."

"That's why you called me here! Acceptance? Quiet acceptance of evil and wrongdoing. Acceptance of the loss of an entire people and their ancestral homeland. My home."

Distraught and outraged, Benjamin could not be so easily persuaded. Fuming from within, Benjamin felt more determined than ever before.

"No!" interrupted Kechewaishke. "You are overzealous. You have forgotten the wisdom of the turtle who buries her eggs in the sand, so they cannot be discovered, or the patience of the moose who can stand still all day to outlast her pursuer. Not all wars are won with death and mayhem, with strength against strength. Some require wisdom and cunning."

The surge of energy that had moments ago filled Benjamin's body, now emptied like an open wound. The great elder was not ready to give up, and Benjamin should never have assumed he might. Ashamed, Benjamin shrunk down, both in posture and in spirit.

"It's okay," Reverend Hall said, recognizing Benjamin's shame. "We understand why you are upset. We know you have great perseverance. We have a plan," Reverend Wheeler said.

As if on cue, all eyes turned toward Michel Cadotte. The aged trader and mixed-race Ojibwe stood, ready to present what was apparently his plan.

"Aware that you and the La Pointe Ojibwe have done all you could to reverse the removal order and to obtain your promised annuities, it has become clear that you cannot circumvent the plans of Alexander Ramsey and John Watrous."

Cadotte stood tall and though he had lived his life in the wilderness among travelers and natives, he was educated and well-spoken. He was fluent in many languages and was well-connected throughout the region. He was a man to be admired.

"Thanks to the American form of governmental democracy, we don't have to defeat their plans. This fall there will be a presidential election. As you know, Ramsey and Watrous are Whigs and both hold appointed positions. Therefore, if the Democrat, Mr. Franklin Pierce, wins the election as he is expected to do, new agents will be appointed and so too will the territorial governor. We believe that if they are replaced by new officials, these new men will recognize the terrible wrongs done upon the Lake Superior Ojibwe and will grant your request to remain at La Pointe and receive there your annuity payments."

Benjamin furrowed his brow. He was skeptical. "We cannot just hope this will happen. There must be something more we can do, something to ensure this outcome. Otherwise, we are just sitting on our hands."

"There is," Cadotte replied. "I have learned that my nephew, William, before he passed had a great disagreement with Mr. Watrous."

There was a pause as Cadotte gathered his thoughts.

"A few years ago, William was in favor of the removal efforts because of the economic benefit it would provide his home of Benton County, Minnesota. As a matter of fact, he was hired by Agent Watrous to facilitate the removal efforts. But, after working with the agent, William discovered his treachery. In an open and public letter, William accused Agent Watrous of arranging the annuity payment so that it would only benefit fur traders who were friends of his. He further accused him of deception and false charges. That's when William gave up his position as a removal agent and was voted into the Minnesota Territorial Legislature. He despised Watrous and wanted to put an end to his treachery and exploitation of the Ojibwe."

This all sounded very complicated to Benjamin, but somehow unsurprising. The more Benjamin had become involved in the politics of the Ojibwe country, the more jaded he had become to their nefarious and convoluted possibilities. Benjamin had never met Mr. Warren, but he had seen him at La Pointe and Fond du Lac before. He appeared to be a poised and intelligent young man. He often sat with a pencil and paper, interviewing the elders and recording their oral histories. He intended to write a complete history of the Ojibwe people but died before it could be published.

"Now," Cadotte said after a brief pause, "we are aware that Mr. Watrous is sly and cunning. If the Democrat, Mr. Pierce, wins the election, Mr. Watrous will try his best to keep his position. He may try to make it appear as if he were a Democrat all along."

"Also," Sherman Hall added, "I have become aware that his political friends would have him retain his job even in a new administration."

"That is where Mary and I come in," Cadotte explained. "As close personal relatives to William Warren, we will continue his legacy by lobbying his supporters in the Legislature to remove their favor and protection from John Watrous. With my personal connections in the region and William's political clout, we believe we can have John Watrous removed as agent to the Lake Superior Ojibwe. With a new governor and a new agent, there will be a new future for the people of La Pointe."

Benjamin swallowed hard. He was glad to know that there may be a way out, a way to make the future better than the past, but he had grown cynical. *Could this really work?* After so much that had gone wrong, after believing so many times that things would get turned around, was this opportunity any better than those before? *No*, Benjamin told himself. After all the petitions, after all the letters, after all the meetings, travel, loss and grief. *No. No. No.*

"Do you remember when you came to us?" Kechewaishke asked, sensing Benjamin's doubt.

Benjamin looked at him. He was an old man but had such a wise and vibrant spirit.

"You were near death. You were sick and starving and lost, without family, without a tepee or lodge, without a clan to provide for you. But the Ojibwe rescued you, gave you a tepee to cover your head and deer meat to fill your belly. Soon you thrived like a beaver atop his own dam. You are white, and we have cared for you. You are from another clan, the clan that strips our land of timber, that corrupts our men with poisoned water, that plants a stake at the graves of our fathers and calls it their home. Yet we welcomed you. Yet we trusted you. How much more would we care for our very own: for our own children, for our own mothers and daughters, fathers and brothers? You have lived through three years of heartache and deceit and now you begin to doubt! We have lived through a century of deceit and dishonor, but we do not choose to turn our backs and run. So now, even in this time of great despair you must trust us. You must trust the Ojibwe. You must follow us all the way to the end no matter the outcome. You must trust your brothers, your sisters, your family. If you belong with us, this is the only way it can be. If you belong with us."

Did he belong with the Ojibwe? Benjamin wondered. For the first time since arriving at La Pointe he wasn't sure. Nevertheless, he nodded in reverence and respect for the elder and his words. He would go along with their plan and he would give them his trust, but he was no longer sure why. He was no longer sure of who he was or what he sought to accomplish. Truly, Benjamin began to doubt his role.

CHAPTER 27

Nestled nicely along the river among a handful of wood-frame cab-
ins, Henry Sibley's Mendota home and trading post stood out like a
frontier palace. His deep beige, two-story stone house had stood as
the center of the fur trade in Minnesota since his arrival in 1834. On
a cold, February night he welcomed his friend and political cohort,
Alexander Ramsey.

"It is wonderful to be back in this lovely home of yours," Ramsey
said as he sat down across from Sibley in the parlor, a steaming cup
of tea at his side. "I wish I could visit more often, but the hazards of
governing a territory are exceedingly onerous."

"Progress is not without hardship," Sibley said in his formal,
business-like manner.

"Indeed. Before long I think you will know all too well what I
mean. Only you will be governing a state, rather than a territory."

Sibley grinned just slightly. "One can only imagine."

Pausing the conversation, Ramsey took a sip of his tea. "I have
come in need of a favor."

"I thought you might've," Sibley nodded. "If it is within my power,
I would grant any favor you ask."

"With the Democrat Pierce soon to take office, I fear that he will
replace Agent John Watrous of Crow Wing, a Whig. I've promised
John my support and, in turn, he has been loyal to me and the needs
of Minnesota. I don't wish to see him replaced."

Sibley nodded.

"The strategy is to make it appear that John has been a Democrat
all along. Already a petition has been signed and sent by the Democratic members of the Wisconsin Senate stating that John is a true and

unyielding Democrat. Since you have such great political influence in this region, I was hoping you could do the same."

"Of course," Sibley said without hesitation. "To whom should it be addressed? What exactly should I write?"

"The new Secretary of the Interior is Robert McClelland; address it to him. State that Watrous is a sound and consistent Democrat and would doubtless have been removed by the late Whig administration but for the fact that his activity and efficiency were so great, as to render it difficult for the Department to find a substitute in whom, as Indian agent, the same reliance could be placed."

"I will have it written by tomorrow evening, Alex."

Ramsey smiled before taking another sip of tea and looking wistfully out the window. "This truly is a lovely place to live."

CHAPTER 28

Winter came on quickly and conditions at La Pointe remained poor. Many families struggled to collect enough food to last the long and cold winter and those who depended on the fur trade could not find a way to transition into something more profitable. For many families at La Pointe, debts continued to rise, and the annual payment could not be depended upon and was almost impossible to obtain. Once again, for the third year in a row, the agent scheduled the Ojibwe payment in Minnesota. The previous fall, after much discussion, it was decided that only fourteen men would make the long journey to Crow Wing along the Mississippi where the payment was expected to take place. The rest decided to wait until spring in order to collect their money and supplies at that time.

Benjamin, who still aspired to have his own trading post and store, was lucky enough to obtain work through the kindness of Michel Cadotte. Since Michel would be occupied lobbying against Watrous, and because he knew of Benjamin's situation, he hired Benjamin temporarily to audit his books. The Cadotte family was quite large at La Pointe and they owned several businesses. Thankfully for Benjamin, this would keep him occupied for the time being, something he needed because he missed his family desperately.

Benjamin didn't have any knowledge of where Charlotte and the children had gone, and it seemed futile to go out in search of them. He had asked Kechewaishke, but the wise elder had told him to have patience. Benjamin knew in his heart that Charlotte still loved him and the best thing he could do was to try to create better circumstances if they should someday return. Still, he could not imagine his life without her, without them. Benjamin thought of his family continuously and was not sure how long he could go without them.

The days rolled on and Benjamin merely sought to keep himself busy. He needed anything to keep his mind off the absence of his family and the continuous removal troubles. One afternoon, Reverend Hall entered the store where Benjamin was working. The reverend glided across the floorboards like he hadn't a care in the world.

"Will you attend the celebration?" Reverend Hall asked.

"Celebration? What are you talking about?"

"You haven't heard the news? It is all over the paper." Reverend Hall began digging through his ledger, apparently searching for a copy of the newspaper. "Where did I place that?" he asked himself. "Oh, I can't find it. The election! The election results are in!"

"The Democrat, Mr. Pierce, won?"

Reverend Hall's face lit up with a brimming smile emphasizing all of the creases in his face. "Yes!" he said. "It was a landslide. Pierce with 254 electoral votes and Scott with 42."

"That is great news! But, perhaps it is a little early to celebrate?"

"Nonsense," Reverend Hall said, maintaining his vibrant grin. "We have to celebrate every victory we can get. Right now, I think that is the only thing keeping us going."

"I—I suppose ..." Benjamin stuttered and then trailed off.

"Of course!" the reverend shot back. "Put your worries aside for one evening and enjoy our victory. If for no other reason than to enjoy the island and this community while it is still here, before they take it away from us for good."

Benjamin sighed, reflecting on the reverend's unbridled enthusiasm. He made a good point, Benjamin realized. "I will be there reverend, you can count on it."

———

The joy and celebration over the election results were short-lived. Not long after the people at La Pointe had enjoyed the high spirits brought on by the Democratic victory they were reminded that things had not yet changed—that circumstances were still becoming more dire for the Lake Superior Ojibwe. The fourteen men who had gone on to

Crow Wing for payment had returned. They returned much later than expected and with devastating news.

Blackbird, who was one of the fourteen, explained. "We waited many weeks upon the agent. Without food to eat we relied on the credit of the traders and we became much in debt. When the agent finally arrived, we pleaded with him to pay our debts saying it was his fault we had to rely on the traders. But he refused saying he had no authority to do so. We asked him then to pay the traders out of our annuities which he did, but we think he paid them too much."

"It is the same story," Benjamin said with chagrin. "He forces us to travel many miles at our own expense, then keeps us there beyond what we are prepared to do and then he allows the traders to get rich off of our suffering. It is sheer fraud."

"What of the remaining annuities?" Kechewaishke asked. "What of those goods and monies owed the rest of us?"

"They are placed securely in the agency storehouse at Crow Wing," Blackbird said. "But I do not know how long they should stay. The agent is in the pockets of the traders and I think he gives out our payments and supplies to anyone he chooses."

The small but growing crowd grumbled with anger.

"The agent is a thief!" one man shouted.

"We must retaliate!" shouted another.

Benjamin, filled with anger, looked over to see that Kechewaishke ignored the shouts and grumbling. He sat silently, deep in thought. Perhaps he felt old and tired and finally ready to accept defeat for his people. Or, perhaps he persisted, knowing that although his time was close to an end, the lives of his children and his children's children would go on. For them and for their future, for the future of all Ojibwe, perhaps he would fight to his last breath.

Breaking his silence, Kechewaishke instructed his comrades. "We must form an expedition and go to Crow Wing as soon as possible. We must gather our annuities from the storehouse. We must bring them here before they are all used up."

Kechewaishke scanned the crowd as if he were looking for volunteers. As he looked the crowd became quiet. The cold winter air whipped off the nearby snowbanks creating a tornado of icy flakes.

"I will go," Benjamin said, raising his hand. "I have nothing to lose."

"I will go, too," Oshoga said.

"I will go," followed another and another and another.

Before long there were dozens who had volunteered to make the long winter trek. A small but determined group, they took a few days getting outfitted but wasted as little time as possible. Soon they were on their way once again to right a wrong, to overcome injustice, to gather their promised payment, and to protect their lives.

———

As Benjamin and the newest group of resisters headed west, they were joined by Reverend Wheeler who, throughout this difficult and sorrowful time, was an ever-present ally for the La Pointe Ojibwe. Makwa, who was quickly coming of age, also joined. Benjamin did not ask him to come, but he was glad that he did. Makwa was establishing his independence, though he still refused to speak.

Travel was slow and difficult. The perils of winter forced the group to travel overland by foot rather than the much fleeter method by canoe over waterways. It was about one-hundred fifty miles to Sandy Lake and another sixty to Crow Wing. But the group was steady and determined, headstrong on collecting their portion of the 1852 annuity payment. As they traveled they were assisted along the way by those at Fond du Lac and Sandy Lake who had received their portion at the December meeting. The Fond du Lac and Sandy Lake bands expressed their unhappiness with the annuity payment telling Benjamin and the La Pointe group that most of it had gone to the traders. They had only received five dollars a head which was hardly enough subsistence for one year. That knowledge only increased the La Pointe group's determination to reach Crow Wing and collect what belonged to them.

By the time they had arrived at Crow Wing they were tired and hungry and much in need from their difficult overland travel. The agency storehouse was locked and virtually impenetrable. Benjamin, having predicted this, sent a messenger to St. Paul to inform the agent

that the La Pointe Ojibwe were ready and eager to collect their portion of the 1852 payment. While they waited, they set up camp nearby
the agency storehouse.

The first night, as everyone slept, Benjamin was awoken by shouts
of ishkode! *Fire!*

Benjamin scrambled from his tent, Makwa beside him, to see a
heavy orange glow in the distance. *The storehouse, please not the storehouse!* "Stay here!" Benjamin commanded Makwa; then he ran in the
direction of the glow alongside many others who sought to discover
what had caught on fire. As Benjamin and the other men ran, the collective sound of feet cutting through the snow was soon matched by the
constant roar of the thick flames. The closer Benjamin got the louder
the roar became and the hotter and brighter the air grew. Trees which
were covered in darkness as he approached, appeared as if lit by the
noon day sun as he passed them by. The building was fully engulfed.

The men who had arrived before Benjamin stood and watched
both in terror and awe at the destructive power of the flame. Though
unrecognizable from its previous form, it was the storehouse and all
its contents that fed the fire. Men fell to their knees and cried as they
watched the flames dance high into the dark and endless night sky.
The glowing embers, like fireflies, drifted effortlessly toward the re-
lentless night sky, disappearing into nothingness like a cruel metaphor
of what had been lost. Benjamin merely stood in disbelief that everything that could go wrong, had gone wrong.

Looking to his side, Benjamin noticed Reverend Wheeler who was
in prayer huddled next to those now grieving. Whatever God or Great
Spirit there was, Benjamin thought, he had forgotten the Ojibwe. The
suffering was real, and it seemed endless.

As Benjamin fell to his knees in the wet, melting snow, Makwa
appeared at his side. Turning toward him, Benjamin was filled with resentment. He had sacrificed so much—lost everything—and the boy
never even thanked him.

"Have you nothing to say, boy!"

Makwa snapped his head, turning away from the fire and toward
Benjamin. His eyes narrowed in confusion and surprise.

"How long will you remain silent! What does it solve, what could it possibly solve! Can't you see! Your father is gone! He is not coming back!" Benjamin's heart beat heavy and hard like the quick patter of raindrops.

Makwa only stared back at him, silent and with a look of uncertainty.

Looking at Makwa, waiting for his reply, Benjamin knew he had made a terrible mistake. He knew that he had let his emotion take over.

Finally, after what seemed like an eternity, Makwa turned away from Benjamin and ran. He ran past the crowd of silent observers, past the remnants of the charred storehouse, and deep into the woods.

Benjamin's heart sank, farther and heavier than ever before. Ashamed, Benjamin did not chase after Makwa.

As Benjamin was kneeling there, beside the rising flames, Reverend Wheeler calmly stood at Benjamin's back and placed his hand on his shoulder.

"Nothing can be done tonight," he said. "Tomorrow, once the ash has cooled, we will search for anything that can be salvaged."

Benjamin nodded, though never lifting his eyes from the crystal-clear melting water flowing past his knees.

"Where there is love, there is forgiveness," the reverend said.

Benjamin dropped his hands in the water and cried.

———————

The following day, when the sun had risen over the trees and the air was clear and rigid, the men gathered around the ashes of the former storehouse. Makwa was nowhere to be found. At first glance, all that remained of the storehouse was a charred and disjointed frame above a heap of soot and ash. Among its backdrop of clear blue winter sky and pure white January snow, the black hole that once enclosed precious belongings looked uncomfortably beautiful, like a shipwreck upon a mountain top. The men slowly made their way within the ruins hoping to find silver coins that remained intact despite the furious fire. With sticks in hand they forced aside piles of ash and former implements of utility, now just whispers of their former shape. Every corner was searched, every crevice was revealed, but they scraped and scratched in vain. All that was found in that ruin in the shape of metal were two fifty-cent silver pieces.

"Our payment was never delivered here," one man, covered head to toe in soot, declared in frustration. "We would have found it among the ashes. Coins do not melt in fire."

By this time a great crowd had gathered. It was not only those who had come to collect their goods, but also those Mississippi Ojibwe from Crow Wing. Even those settlers living nearby came to witness the commotion created by the destructive flames.

"This fire was set deliberately," one man said as the Ojibwe grew more and more despondent, beside themselves with grief and anger.

As the clamoring and commotion grew, attentions were turned by the sound of a carriage. The carriage stopped abruptly and was accompanied by a dozen soldiers. The Ojibwe men quieted as they looked with curiosity at the carriage.

Then, the door pushed open and out stepped Agent Watrous. Quickly the soldiers dismounted and surrounded the agent, giving him only enough room to leave his view unobstructed. Agent Watrous looked at the men as he straightened his hat and then began walking toward the remains of the storehouse. The soldiers followed.

The agent strolled casually toward the ashes, calm and collected from within his brigade of well-trained, disciplined soldiers. As he examined the former structure men continued to shout insults, but the agent ignored them.

Finally, Watrous turned toward the crowd and raised his glove-covered hand and calmly waited for the commotion to settle.

"Unfortunate," he said. "This is indeed unfortunate. I vow to set in motion a full and complete investigation." His tone was steady and plain.

"It was the adaawewininiwag!" one man shouted. *It was the traders!* Then another man shouted. Then another, until the shouts were so numerous that they could no longer be distinguished from each other.

Watrous raised his hand once more. "I cannot understand your native tongue. Nor would I enter into a shouting match with one hundred angry men." The agent then turned his eyes toward Benjamin, knowing he was experienced as an interpreter. Apparently, thought Benjamin, their previous disagreements mattered little to the agent.

Putting aside his own mistrust and anger toward the agent, Benjamin sought for something constructive to come from this meeting. "Agent Watrous, I will speak for the group," Benjamin said.

"Very well." Agent Watrous shuffled forward, out from the shadow of the bayonets that had guarded him. "I see no reason for the disgruntled nature of these men. It is unfortunate that the storehouse burned down, but I will immediately begin an investigation and I will have all goods replaced in due time."

The agent's casual indifference angered Benjamin, but he tried to remain calm. "The men have accused you, Agent Watrous. You are culpable for this fire."

"Me!" he said, taken aback. "Under what motive?"

Benjamin was astounded. *How could the agent possibly be so imprudent, so unaware of his own role in this drama?* "Over the years, you have made your favor toward the traders obvious. You have in every instance set the time and place of the payment for the advantage of the traders. You starve the Ojibwe and force them to rely on credit. Then, when the time for payment comes, you give the greater portion to the traders for debts you created through your own manipulation. Even the goods and implements are given away and then resold to the Ojibwe to whom they rightfully belonged. We are not so blind to your ways. That is why we came here today, in the dead of winter. We did not want to lose our goods to the traders. We did not want to see you give our goods away. But now it seems you have burned the storehouse with the goods inside to benefit your friends and business partners. The goods will be replaced by them, won't they? And they will profit while we continue to go hungry."

Silence filled the cold winter air as the men gathered waited for the agent's response. For a few brief moments time stood still, and the entire scene remained portrait-like, steady and unmoving.

The agent stepped forward, out from the shadow of his guard. "You may be right about a few things, Mr. Armstrong. But I feel bad for you. I really do." The agent paused and took a few more steps forward so that the two men were now face to face. "I know of your attempts to prevent my return, your efforts to convince legislators to remove their favor from me. But it matters not what you accomplish. In the end, there is only one outcome for the native, whether you accept that or not. I will be followed by others like me, and they will be followed by others like them all marching toward progress in the name of profit under the flag of the United States. It is inevitable. It is the destiny of this great nation."

Despite his anger, Benjamin remained calm. "You are wrong," he said. "No inevitability will ever be met with silent acceptance. No injustice will go unpunished. Someday, the world will know what happened here."

"And then what?" Watrous said coolly. "Do you expect progress to stop? Do you expect their land to be given back or their traditions to be restored?" Watrous paused, staring at Benjamin through hard, determined eyes that suddenly began to soften. "I was once naive, too," he said. "I lost my wife to that Indian disease. I lost my reputation to the Indian trade. I decided that was enough. I was going to join the winning side. I was going to become a part of the future, rather than dwell in the past. So, don't think you are the only one who has suffered. It just happens that I was smart enough to learn from it."

Watrous turned and retreated slowly within his armed guard. Looking at him, Benjamin didn't know what to say.

"Go ahead and tell your story, Mr. Armstrong," Watrous said as he began his exit. "By the time it means anything, it will be too late."

"No," Benjamin said, desperately. "If I have learned anything from my time with the Ojibwe, I've learned that they persevere. They will outlast you, Mr. Watrous. They will outlast this tragedy."

As the agent continued his exit, men began to shout, some launching snow and ice toward the wall of soldiers. Then, Agent Watrous paused, turned toward Benjamin, and took one last look at the people he had forsaken. His eyes finding Benjamin's, he tipped his cap, and then he continued on like it was just an ordinary day.

———

The next morning, as the La Pointe group prepared for the journey home, Reverend Wheeler stood facing Benjamin. He was bundled tight, only his mouth, nose and eyes peeking through the hood of his robe. "The sun is up, the men have eaten, and we are all prepared and ready for the trek home."

"I just can't. I can't go with you. Makwa is out there somewhere, and it is all my fault. I can't leave without him."

"Don't be discouraged." Reverend Wheeler turned as he heard the last of the packs being picked up off the ground. "You have done the best you could for the boy," he said, turning back toward Benjamin. "Even the most courageous of us loses strength now and again."

Benjamin shook his head, still in shame over his words and actions toward Makwa.

"I will see you back at La Pointe," Reverend Wheeler said, placing his hand reassuringly on Benjamin's shoulder.

"Travel safely," Benjamin replied.

With a nod and turn, the reverend joined the rest of the men who waved and then headed down the path. Benjamin watched as they marched slowly into the blustery winter distance. As they disappeared behind a fog of white snow, Benjamin's thoughts changed back to Makwa. *Where could he be? Was he safe? Was he alive?*

Benjamin began by searching the trails which were numerous since he was so near the Crow Wing Agency. But, having gone north, south, east, and west, he did not find Makwa or any sign of him along the trails. As Benjamin wandered down and alongside the river his worry began to fester. Filled with guilt he thought over and over about what he had said to the boy. Then, Benjamin remembered his dearest friend's dying wish, Giizhigoon who only asked that Benjamin care for his son. He had failed. He had failed at the one thing that mattered. Looking back deeper, Benjamin remembered his own father and how his anger and neglect drew him away from home. Benjamin had grown up without a father, and now, he feared, he had placed Makwa in the same position. How could he have been so selfish, so heartless and wrong?

The river showed no signs of a human presence. No fires had recently been made, no shelters to hide from the biting wind. But suddenly it occurred to Benjamin to return to the agency, to return to the spot of the fire, the spot of his iniquity.

As Benjamin approached the agency, he could see through the trees a shadowy figure seated in front of the ruins of the storehouse. The small, crouched figure was covered by a buffalo skin robe with snowflakes building up on his head and shoulders. Benjamin approached slowly with both fear and hope.

"Makwa?"

The figure turned and looked as the previously undisturbed snow slid down his back. *It was Makwa!* His face was red, and his eyes looked cold and lost. Benjamin ran quickly toward him and stretched out his arms, embracing Makwa across both shoulders.

"I'm sorry," Benjamin said with desperation in his voice. "I am so, so sorry. I should have never said those things to you. I didn't mean it. I didn't mean it."

Both of them were panting now, breathing heavily at the relief of being reunited.

"You did nothing wrong..."

"No!" Makwa said, interrupting Benjamin. "No, it was my fault. You were right."

Benjamin released his embrace, kept his hands on Makwa's shoulders and held him at arm's length, amazed that he finally spoke. Benjamin looked into Makwa's clear, brown eyes ready to listen to his words, the words he had held inside for so long.

"You have been a wonderful uncle," he said. "I was scared, I was hurt. I didn't think anyone but my father appreciated me. I didn't think anyone but my father could appreciate me. I had no place in the world. I lived in resentment."

Tears were streaming down Makwa's face. He tried to look away, but Benjamin held Makwa's head steady.

"You have been through so much heartache and change. But you have endured. Your father would be proud of you, so proud of the man you are becoming, the Ojibwe man you are becoming. I am proud, too. I am so proud."

Makwa stared back at Benjamin, wiping tears off of his cheeks. "I'm sorry," he said, softly.

"It's okay, it's okay." Benjamin embraced Makwa tightly. Together they sat in the cold, unblemished snow, before the dark, tarnished ash of the storehouse. Together they reconciled their past and agreed to go blamelessly into the future.

CHAPTER 29

New Minnesota Territorial Governor Willis Gorman struggled to comprehend the state of Indian affairs left in the wake of Alexander Ramsey. In an attempt to sort out exactly what went wrong and exactly where, Gorman, a lawyer by trade, called upon several witnesses. One such witness was William Johnston, a low-level trader and interpreter in the Ojibwe country.

"What can you tell me about the state of affairs in Ojibwe country?" Gorman asked, his words smooth and deep, elongated by his Southern accent.

Johnston sat upright, eager to reply and excited to be seated before the governor. "Since the Indian annuities have begun, the present Indian traders are not human."

"Not human?"

"They grasp and cheat him of his all and mock at his degradation and silent despair."

Discouraged, Gorman let out a sigh from below his large, brown mustache. "Go on."

"The claims of Borup, Oakes, Beaulieu, and Nettleton are so large that there was no money for a small trader like me and I was forced to quit the trade. The agent made money, too. I know because he deposited $20,000 with Borup and Oakes and when they refused to pay it back, the agent was afraid to take legal measures because he might be exposed."

Gorman did not know how to reply. He was so discouraged he just sat there shaking his head.

"Do you know anything about the fire at Crow Wing?" Gorman asked.

Johnston paused and looked at Gorman sympathetically. "The burning of the agency at Crow Wing was done intentionally to bring an imaginary loss on the U.S. and upon the Indians. My information has come from trustworthy people."

"I believe you," Gorman said. "Thank you. With this information I will consider how I can clean up the Indian policy in Minnesota."

CHAPTER 30

On May 13, 1853, a new territorial governor arrived in St. Paul, replacing the previous governor, Alexander Ramsey. The new governor, Willis Gorman, gave a new hope to the Ojibwe at La Pointe. Though Gorman governed Minnesota, and La Pointe was in Wisconsin, Gorman was the Superintendent of Indian Affairs for the Mississippi and Lake Superior Ojibwe. Gorman was well-known for dealing fairly and justly with native populations. With Ramsey out and Gorman in, there was renewed hope that circumstances would finally change.

In the meantime, life remained difficult at La Pointe. Without their annuities for three consecutive years the Ojibwe were forced to rely even more heavily on their traditional economy of hunting, fishing, collecting maple sap, harvesting rice, trapping, and trading. But that was more difficult with each passing year. Land was being bought up by speculators, hunting grounds were depleted, and lumber companies were removing trees everywhere they could. At La Pointe, the American Fur Company completely removed itself making the fur trade almost obsolete. Julius Austrian, Benjamin's former employer, bought out the holdings of the American Fur Company making himself perhaps the wealthiest landholder in the region. All the while the Ojibwe scraped and scratched to get by and were still left with uncertainty about the future. By the summer there still had been no word on the policy of the new administration toward the Lake Superior Ojibwe.

———

"Right here," Mrs. Wheeler instructed Benjamin as she pointed to the stem of a turnip. "Dig out along the stems so that when the water flows it flows toward the root."

Benjamin smiled in agreement. It was summer, and Harriet and Benjamin were working in one of Odanah's numerous gardens.

"You have to be careful not to disturb the stem or it may not continue to grow. It is very delicate at this point."

Harriet moved back and forth through the rows of squash, corn, and tomatoes, ensuring the health and quality of all her plants.

"You are diligent in this," Benjamin said. "It is a marvel to watch an expert like you at work."

"Don't be so obliging," she said while leaning forward to tighten the strings that held her tomato plants. "Besides, one has to be diligent in these trying times."

"Indeed," Benjamin nodded.

A few minutes passed while Harriet and Benjamin worked quietly and contentedly among the dirt and plants of the garden.

"Can I be candid?" Harriet asked.

Benjamin was struck by the unexpected break of solitude. "Of course."

Looking up, Benjamin noticed the age in Harriet's face. She appeared older than he had remembered. Her hair had become distinctly gray along and behind the ears while her face had begun to sag almost forming the jowls of an elderly woman.

"I admire what you've done for this community," she said, turning her face away from the sun, hiding the age Benjamin had just observed. "I admire your persistence and dedication." Harriet lowered her head. "I am ashamed to admit this, but even though I know you and Leonard," she said referring to her husband Reverend Wheeler, "are often away doing such good things, it makes life so difficult at home. The last winter was one of the most dreary, lonely and trying ones we have ever spent in this country. The confused state of Indian affairs has thrown a gloom over the future. I have to admit, often I had to flee into my bedroom to hide the tears I could not control. And poor Leonard..." She paused in thought, or perhaps pity. "Poor Leonard has great burdens pressed upon him."

Benjamin nodded politely, just listening, though Harriet still had her eyes turned to the ground, now welling with tears that she held back.

"He is obliged to attend to all the secular affairs of our station and has charge of the property of the mission board here. Plus, he must monitor the Indian farming by giving out their seed and plowing the ground, and he is doctor for both places, Odanah and La Pointe, chairman of the board of county commissioners, besides numberless other things too small to mention."

Harriet raised her hand to her cheek, while she continued to try and hold back her tears.

"I'm sorry," she panted. "I'm sorry. You of all people know how difficult these times have been. You have sacrificed as much as anyone."

"It's quite alright," Benjamin said softly as he rose from the dirt.

"I sometimes look anxiously forward to the future when all of this is behind us."

Benjamin sympathized with Harriet. She, too, had made many sacrifices. Away from home, away from her parents and siblings, and often away from her husband, she was left to raise her family and to do what she considered her Christian duty, alone.

As Benjamin stood, thinking of what he ought to say, Julia, Harriet's daughter, came running up from behind the garden. "Mother! Mother!" she exclaimed with carefree joy.

Harriet wiped her tears and tried to collect herself. As she took Julia's hand and said, "What is it, darling?" she looked over at Benjamin with a thoughtful expression. Benjamin tipped his hat and lowered himself back to the soft, cool dirt. It was a subtle acknowledgment for both of them that life would go on.

In his dream Benjamin was racing through the snow. He was frantically trying to escape something, but from what he could not see. Behind him there was only darkness, ahead of him only a muddled, gray fog. He ran and ran, breathlessly and without fatigue, motivated not by fear but by necessity. Along the dark and empty path, he passed people he knew and loved. Charlotte, his children, Makwa, Kechewaishke... but they could not see him. They appeared lost and desperate, sad and alone. Their clothes were no more than tattered rags, their faces gaunt and lifeless, their bodies slumped and haggard. *Look out!* they cried, as if sensing a hidden danger at Benjamin's back. There was something behind him. Something pushing him forward, but he could not see it. He did not know whether to fear or embrace the presence that he felt gaining on him. Suddenly, it appeared. Sleek and graceful, robust and powerful, cutting through the snow like a fin through water. As it reached his side Benjamin could see its imposing fangs, its bulging shoulders, its glistening fur. It was a wolf. But this wolf, as it growled and snorted and heaved itself forward, did not attack him. Did not pounce on him. It did not strike fear in his heart. Rather, it led him. It guided him forward, past the tragic and woeful conditions of his friends and family. It led him beyond the darkness and toward the fog, the fog that grew brighter with each step. The wolf continued, never looking back but somehow urging him forward, pacing Benjamin stronger and faster. As Benjamin and the wolf grew closer and closer, the thick fog could no longer contain the brilliant source of light that sprayed forward like a thousand stars at once. Closer and closer. Closer and closer. The wolf leaped into the light. Benjamin did not stop. He did not slow down. He leaped, too.

"Wake up, Benjamin! Wake up!" Reverend Wheeler sat on Benjamin's bed, shaking him by the shoulder. The reverend had an insuppressible smile on his face and a boisterous enthusiasm in his voice.

"What? What is it?"

"A special agent has arrived."

"Watrous? Agent Watrous is here?"

"No," Reverend Wheeler said. "A SPECIAL agent. His name is Henry Gilbert, and he is here to deliver the annuity payment."

"You're kidding!" Benjamin quickly got out of bed and rubbed the sleepiness from his eyes. "Here? At La Pointe? And so early in the season? It is still just the second week of October."

"Yes, yes, yes!" Reverend Wheeler said, still grinning from ear to ear. "Come quickly. The whole village has gathered."

Benjamin left as quickly as he could, in disbelief that after three hard years the payment had come back to La Pointe. For many months, no one had heard a single word on the 1853 payment—when, where, or if it would take place or who would administer it. Alone and isolated, the La Pointe community was unaware if the change in administration would have a positive effect. Men went without work, families were starving, supplies were scarce. As another hard winter approached people began to lose hope; they began to realize that the coming winter might be a deadly one.

But, as Benjamin approached the town center, it looked as if all that were changing, as if hope and happiness had been restored. Hundreds had gathered, all of them singing and dancing, laughing and smiling. They appeared to be carefree and filled with unbridled joy.

"What is it?" Makwa asked as he followed closely behind. "What is happening?"

"I think the payment has finally returned to La Pointe."

Benjamin arrived to find the community beside themselves with joy and utter disbelief. Some were dancing, some were beating drums, some were kneeling, faces to the ground, shedding tears of great relief.

"Debwewin?" Makwa asked. *Is it true?* "Can we trust this agent? Does he seek our goodwill or only his own profit?"

"You are right to be skeptical," Benjamin said to him. "I truly don't know."

Benjamin wanted to be sure. He wanted to trust that this was real. After so much heartache and so much false hope he could not believe it. In any case, the excitement, the jubilation, the satisfaction of the moment was real. What Benjamin and others like him had fought for, what they had longed for, what they had died for, had finally come true. It had finally come true.

As Benjamin looked around he could see that the special agent was occupied, taking roll and accounting for every family that was to receive payment. Behind him were several wagons filled to the brim with goods. Barrel upon barrel of flour. Blankets, kettles, guns, and ammunition, farming implements of all kinds, quite literally overflowing from the back of the wagons. It appeared to be more than the La Pointe Ojibwe had ever been accustomed to. It appeared to be enough to truly sustain their community.

"It is magnificent, isn't it," Reverend Wheeler said as he walked up beside Benjamin.

"Most certainly! But how is this possible?"

"Ramsey and Watrous are out. The new governor, Gorman, recognized the wrong and suffering brought upon us and that is why he has sent Agent Gilbert. He has sent him to change all that. To right the wrongs of the past."

"Remarkable," Benjamin said, still in awe of the joy and celebration that surrounded him.

"The agent has called a council tonight. He will distribute goods tomorrow."

"Tonight," Benjamin repeated. "I should be very glad to meet Agent Gilbert. I would like to know what the future has in store."

"Of course," Reverend Wheeler said with an arm around Benjamin's shoulders. "And I think he would quite like to meet you."

The entire La Pointe band had gathered for the Grand Council with the new special agent. Men, women, warriors, chiefs, children and the elderly. All had come to celebrate a new hope and a new peace, maybe even a new life. Makeshift lodges were everywhere. People gathered around fires singing and telling stories, and in every Ojibwe the most perfect satisfaction was apparent.

Amidst the celebration, a circle of chiefs and elders gathered around the special agent. Benjamin was elected interpreter.

"I am pleased to see your people so happy," the special agent said as he passed the peace pipe.

"We are equally pleased," Oshoga said.

The special agent was a young man, not more than thirty. He carried himself with politeness and dignity. He dressed formally, sat upright, and was slow and calculated with his speech.

"My name is Henry Gilbert and I am the new Indian Agent for the Michigan Superintendency." Agent Gilbert paused, allowing Benjamin to translate. "Governor Gorman of Minnesota, recognizing your poor condition, has asked me to handle your affairs for the time being. That is why I am here."

The chiefs and elders were wary because of how they had previously been treated. They looked hesitantly upon the agent.

"Our agent before you lied, cheated, and stole our money," Oshoga said while looking intensely at the agent. "He led us to faraway places and promised food and shelter and then gave us nothing—left us to die like wounded rabbits in the snow."

"You are right," acknowledged the young agent. "The new governor understands your situation. He has recognized that more fraud and cheating has gone on within your country than he has seen or known anywhere else on this earth. He also knows of the promises made to you by the Great Father, the promises you traveled many miles at great sacrifice to obtain. He is greatly saddened by these things. That is why he has appointed me to set things straight."

"You speak like the others," Blackbird said. "How do we know you do not speak from both sides of your mouth?"

The agent paused, leaned forward and looked carefully at Blackbird. "Arriving here I was shocked and hurt by your condition. Your people, once flourishing, have been reduced to the very extreme of want and poverty." The agent spoke in a somber, conciliatory tone. "My heart is not without compassion nor my eyes blind to injustice. Surely, you can already see your improvements. I have arrived at an early date, I have not asked you to travel, and I have brought an abundance of gifts."

Blackbird's expression lightened as his skepticism was visibly withdrawn.

"And the removal?" Oshoga asked. "Has the removal order finally been revoked?"

"There is nothing official, but I wholeheartedly believe that the policy of removal ought to and will be abandoned."

"Official?"

"By official I mean that it should be communicated in writing. This would leave no doubt over the future of your homes and the location of the payment."

There was a stirring among the Ojibwe elders and chiefs. All seemed pleased by the agent's response. After the commotion had settled, Kechewaishke brought forth his concerns.

"We have signed many documents before," the elder chief said. "We have listened many times to the promises of the Great Father and the promises of the Great Father's children. But the documents we have signed have little meaning and his promises mean even less. We have learned to protect ourselves—to be wiser before shaking hands with the Americans like yourself."

"I understand," Gilbert said, undaunted by the elder's grievances. "Men have conspired to do wrong by you and your people. That I cannot deny. They have watched your families die and felt no remorse and faced no consequences. I wish to right those wrongs. I wish to correct those mistakes and erase those lies. When I give my report to the governor, when I visit the president in Washington, I will ask for a new treaty. I will seek a treaty that will do right by you and your people and your ancient and sacred homes."

All of the Ojibwe looked toward Kechewaishke, expectant for his response.

"You speak wisely," Kechewaishke said. "I think we shall be glad to call you our agent. We desire this new treaty, this new alliance. One that will assure the prosperity of my people now and for many generations to come. We seek a treaty that will not leave us cold and naked, one that will not give our homes away to those who seek to profit from it. This is what we desire."

Ho! Ho! the men and women shouted in agreement.

The agent stood, stepped forward and prepared to take Kechewaishke's hand. "Your fortunes have changed." The agent smiled and held out his hand.

There was a pause followed by an unmistakable hush. Using his staff as a crutch, Kechewaishke slowly rose to his feet. From within his robe he extended his arm and the two men shook hands and smiled.

The hush turned to joyous hysteria. It was a new day in the history of La Pointe.

———

As the night continued, no one slept. There was so much joy and excitement that no one wanted it to end. At some point late into the night, Benjamin observed a large crowd that had gathered around Kechewaishke. As Benjamin drew near he could hear the old chief was regaling the crowd with the story of their trip to Washington. He spoke of the petition passed around at Sault Ste. Marie, of the officers who stopped them at Detroit, of the train that took them across New York, and of the grand dinner party at the banker's house. Everyone leaned in and listened with great attention and pleasure. They laughed at Kechewaishke's description of the New York crowd's reaction to the native presence. They were in awe of his description of the endless jungle of buildings in the city, and they applauded the delegation's ability to earn enough money to finally arrive at the capital. They hung on Kechewaishke's every word. As the venerable chief continued, he bragged about his meeting with the Great Father, explaining how the pipe of peace had been smoked in the Great Father's wigwam.

"Now I wish to bring out the pipe of peace again," he announced to his audience. From under his robe he uncovered a long, fanciful and ornate pipe that glimmered in the light of the fire. The crowd let out a unified awe.

"In the name of our ancient and traditional ritual, I pass this pipe, not to be smoked, but to be admired." He paused, then looked toward Benjamin who was startled by the sudden attention.

"Benjamin Green Armstrong." Kechewaishke called out Benjamin's full name loud and clear. "Daga, indaashaan." *Please, come here.*

Benjamin could actually hear the crowd shift as all of the attention turned toward him. He felt embarrassed but did as the elder had asked, weaving his way slowly through scores of people.

"Mr. Armstrong came to us alone," Kechewaishke said though Benjamin did not know his purpose. "At a young age he left his home, his parents, became an orphan in the world. He wandered many years before he was led here, to us, to the Ojibwe. We welcomed Benjamin and he welcomed us. Since that time, he has become our ally and friend."

Benjamin blushed, but Kechewaishke continued in his grandfatherly manner and tone.

"He has respected our traditional life and culture—learned our language, protected our children, married into our family."

Benjamin felt a deep and sudden heartache as he was reminded of his beloved wife and children.

"He has sacrificed and fought for our benefit. He suffered with us at Sandy Lake, he confronted our enemy Agent Watrous, and he brought us across land and water, across mountain and valley, through city and forest, to the home of the Great Father, that we might plead to save our homes. That is why today, I announce to all gathered, that I am adopting Benjamin as my son."

A collective gasp rose out of the crowd followed by boisterous cheers and applause. It struck Benjamin like an ocean wave. He was stunned by the unexpected display of love and gratitude.

As the cheers grew louder Benjamin could feel his heart flutter in joy and surprise. This remarkable and surprising expression vindicated his suffering. Vindicated his sacrifice. It gave him true and permanent belonging to the place he loved and the people he respected.

Kechewaishke raised his hands to silence the crowd. "Come, kneel before me."

Benjamin walked slowly toward Kechewaishke feeling light and exuberant. As he got down on his knees, Kechewaishke placed his hands on Benjamin's head and began to pray.

"I'iw nma'ewinan, maaba asemaa, miinwaa n'ode'winaanin gda-bagidinimaagon..."

As he prayed, Benjamin remembered all of the strife he had encountered throughout his life. He remembered that day when Mr. Thompson arrived at his father's farm. He remembered choosing to walk away from his father and his childhood of neglect. He remembered the illness that prevented him from riding horses for show. He remembered saying goodbye to his brother and leaving for places unknown. He remembered Charlotte and that enchanting smile and innocent look. And he remembered Giizhigoon while suddenly realizing it was Giizhigoon he saw in his dreams. It was Giizhigoon who came up beside him and led him toward the light.

Kechewaishke lifted his hands from Benjamin's head. As he looked up, everyone and everything was silent except the crackling of the midnight fire.

"From now on you will be called Shaw-Bwaw-Skung which, in your language, means *The Man Who Goes Through*. Your name, like your spirit, shall signify persistence and thoroughness. This is what you have shown yourself to be, never giving up and never backing down. The Loon Clan welcomes you."

From out of the stillness came a huge cheer and an extended applause, this time louder than ever before. Benjamin rose to his feet and shook Kechewaishke's hand. An irrepressible smile came across Benjamin's face and tears rolled down his cheeks. Standing there, he felt like life had begun anew. The narrative had changed, and it fit him just fine.

"Though we celebrate tonight we are not finished here," Kechewaishke announced as the men and women seated themselves. "There is yet one more treaty to be made with the Great Father. I hope that in making it we shall be more careful and wise than we have been in the past." Kechewaishke spoke in a different tone than before. Now he spoke as he might in council, stoic and direct. "It is important that we protect our homes and reserve a part of our land for ourselves and our children. But I am an old man and I must leave this world soon. I cannot be with you forever."

The crowd of Ojibwe groaned in dismay though Kechewaishke's statement was true.

"I must pass along my wisdom so that others might lead you once I have joined our ancestors along the Great Spirit's starry path. And so, I ask Shaw-Bwaw-Skung to advise us in the next treaty, to speak for us, as he has in the past, to ensure that we do not sell ourselves out and be left without a home. I hope that when the treaty is brought forward to sign that you will listen to him and follow his advice, because in doing so I assure you that you will not again be deceived."

The crowd was silent, and Benjamin was once again surprised—surprised by Kechewaishke's incredible show of confidence in him that seemed to constantly be growing. And though Benjamin felt great pressure in representing the La Pointe Ojibwe, it was an immense honor and he trusted the elder's decision.

"Son, before me and this entire community do you accept this new and significant responsibility?"

Benjamin paused, not to think, but to revel in that beautiful moment. To be present in it. He closed his eyes and took a deep breath as the world around him melted away. Past, future, even present. It all just faded away in a moment of pure clarity.

"Yes," Benjamin answered. "I will be your advocate in the new treaty. I will be your advocate for years to come."

CHAPTER 31

Agent Henry Gilbert waited patiently in the governor's office in order to give his report of the recent payment at La Pointe. As he waited he admired the territorial seal which stood out prominently on the front of the governor's desk. A huge, bronze disc, the seal depicted a farmer with a plough in tow as an Indian sat atop a horse while galloping toward the setting sun. The farmer and the Indian were looking at each other as if in a gesture of apologetic acceptance. It was fitting, Gilbert thought, for the time and place he found himself.

Gorman burst through the door, disturbing Gilbert from his momentary meditation. "My apologies," Gorman said as he reached out his strong right hand to greet the agent. "A governor's work is never done."

"It's no trouble." Gilbert smiled, and the two men sat down across from one another.

"I'm anxious to hear your report of the payment," Gorman said as he leaned back and crossed his right leg over his left knee. "What can you tell me?"

Gilbert shook his head remorsefully. "I can tell you that it came at an opportune time. Many Ojibwe were reduced to the very extreme of want and poverty and without the aid furnished them many must have perished during the coming winter from cold and hunger."

"That is what I feared. What did the chiefs and elders tell you about the removal?"

"That it was a source of great distress and suffering. I hazard nothing in saying that they will sooner submit to extermination than comply with it."

Gorman's eyes widened.

"The missionaries told me that when the removal order arrived, the Ojibwe were in a more prosperous condition than they had ever been. Its effect has been to scatter them and render them distrustful of the whites and the government."

Gorman nodded. "Yes, the same is true of the Ojibwe at St. Croix. I went there myself to deliver blankets, leggings, strouds, and shirts. Without them, they would freeze over the coming winter."

"As an Indian agent, I never expected to see anything like this," Gilbert said regrettably.

"Neither did I," Gorman agreed. "I think there has been more fraud and cheating in the Indian trade in this territory than it has been my lot to see or know of anywhere else on this earth."

CHAPTER 32

In the far northern region, winter was the great equalizer. The 1853 annuity payment that was marked by great joy and fervent hope, was followed by a harsh, barren, inhospitable winter. Many long, dark days passed in which it was so cold that it was almost impossible to be comfortable. But what was worse—much worse—was an epidemic of smallpox that struck the region.

"I have come with bad news," Reverend Wheeler said as he stood in the doorway of Benjamin's home. He was covered head to toe in fur clothing which was coated with snow and ice. Outside the cold wind howled creating near whiteout conditions.

"Please, come in," Benjamin said, "it is dangerous to be traveling in this weather."

Makwa, who stood near the burning fireplace, nodded in acknowledgment as the reverend walked in.

"Forgive me for coming, but I thought you should know," Reverend Wheeler said as he lowered his hood and removed his gloves.

"Know what?"

"It's Oshoga," Wheeler said bluntly. "He has perished from the smallpox epidemic."

Benjamin dropped his head in anguish. "This cruel disease is not judicious. It will take anyone."

"I was told he became frantic in his final days. He threw off all his clothes and went alone into the woods where he froze. The disease took away his rational thinking."

"It is so sad," Benjamin said. "It tears families apart and now it has taken away one of our great leaders."

The fire crackled loudly filling the silence that followed Benjamin's lament.

"You'll have to remain isolated for the time being," Wheeler said. "It is the best way to avoid contracting the disease. But a vaccine is on the way, and it should arrive soon."

"A vaccine from who?" Benjamin asked.

"The governor of Minnesota Territory. He learned of the epidemic at St. Croix and he does not want to see it spread."

"Good. Good," Benjamin said. "He is more compassionate than the previous governor."

"He is," Wheeler agreed, then, looking about the room, he put his hood back up and his gloves back on. "I must be going."

"Thank you, reverend," Benjamin said. "Be safe."

"You, too. I suspect we will not see each other again until spring."

As winter melted into spring, and spring became summer, there was much talk of the coming treaty. Benjamin knew that the treaty deal was of utmost importance and was to be a grand occasion, especially for those Ojibwe who had been asked to remove in the previous years. Years of suffering had led up to this moment and the entire future of the Ojibwe, both near and far, hung in the balance of the new deal. Every day passed with anticipation. As the summer waned, various bands from the surrounding regions began arriving at La Pointe. These included the L'Anse, La Vieux Désert, Lac du Flambeau, Lac Court Oreilles, Fond du Lac, Grand Portage, and Ontonagon bands. Councils continued as the arriving bands made their desires known. Fulfilling the role laid upon him by Kechewaishke, Benjamin counselled the Ojibwe, trying to put matters in the appropriate light. As far as Benjamin understood, they were ready and anxious to make a deal, but they most ardently sought reservations that would suit their needs and that would afterwards be considered their bona fide homes.

"You have both an honorable and significant role before you," Reverend Wheeler said to Benjamin one afternoon. "The future of this entire region will be influenced by your decisions."

"I know. I fear I will mishandle things."

"Yes, but you are in this position for a reason," the reverend assured him. "You have done much to earn their trust and you know what is right. Do not doubt yourself."

By mid-September 1854, the U.S. commissioners arrived. This included the Commissioner of Indian Affairs George Manypenny, the Special Agent Henry Gilbert, Indian Agent for the Mississippi Ojibwe David Herriman, their secretary and clerk Richard Smith and several government interpreters.

Manypenny was dignified in his appearance. A former journalist, he wore a tailored suit with his hair slicked back and his beard combed. His posture and physique were impeccable. He looked like a proper man with whom to do business.

"Welcome to Moningwunakauning, our ancient and sacred home," Kechewaishke said in an official welcoming ceremony. "We are pleased that you have come to treat with us. Our peoples wish to secure a place for our children where they will remain for many years, where they can visit the graves of their fathers, where they can hunt, fish, and gather, in the land of their ancestors."

"Thank you," Commissioner Manypenny said. "We are indeed pleased to visit your beautiful and abundant homeland. We have heard and understand your grievances over years past and we wish to rectify those wrongs."

"We are all ready and prepared to negotiate at your convenience," Kechewaishke said.

"Negotiations will begin shortly, but I do not want to make a deal without the presence of the Mississippi Ojibwe. We shall begin once they arrive."

"We understand your desire to include the Mississippi Ojibwe but is it necessary to include those living far to the west whose lands are not under consideration here?" Kechewaishke asked, making no attempt to sound controversial.

"I've invited only the principal men of the Mississippi bands. I do not wish to make a treaty without representation from each of the Ojibwe bands."

Kechewaishke hesitated as he searched the eyes of the newest government official with whom he was to negotiate. "It is tradition to include all Ojibwe when making important decisions," he said. "We only fear it may cause a disturbance because their interests are so different from our own. You do not ask the eagle to share the sky with the fish, nor the fish to share the water with the eagle."

"I understand," Commissioner Manypenny said through the help of his interpreter. "But on this I cannot be moved. There will be no treaty without the presence of the Mississippi Ojibwe."

"Very well," Kechewaishke said with dignity. "We will be ready when they arrive."

———

After a few days waiting, the Mississippi chiefs and headmen arrived. Along with them came the traders of the American Fur Company and many of their employees. Before negotiations with the American commissioners could begin, a general council was called which included the Mississippi Ojibwe and the American Fur Company traders. It did not take long after they arrived for Kechewaishke's prediction to prove accurate.

As the Lake Superior Ojibwe laid out their intentions for the treaty, the Mississippi Ojibwe and the traders frequently objected.

"All of the debts should be paid at one time," the traders argued. "The annuities should be paid at Leech Lake," the Mississippi Ojibwe urged.

After several days, the Lake Superior Ojibwe found it impossible to get the Mississippi Ojibwe to agree to any of their plans or to come to any terms. Finally, having lost patience, Kechewaishke had a proposition.

"Being that we cannot agree, a division should be drawn between the Mississippi and Lake Superior Ojibwe separating each other altogether, and each should make their own treaty."

The proposition was not immediately agreed upon but took several more days of council. This was due almost entirely to the opposition of the American Fur Company traders who were adamantly opposed to having such a division made. They yielded, however, once they recognized that further opposition would do no good. The proposition was then accepted, and it was agreed that the Lake Superior Ojibwe would make their treaty for the lands south of and surrounding the great lake and the Mississippi Ojibwe would make a separate treaty for the lands west of the Mississippi at a later date.

What happened next came as a surprise to Benjamin. Kechewaishke, in the presence of all Ojibwe gathered, introduced a new proposition.

"Chiefs and elders of all Ojibwe bands," Kechewaishke said. "I wish to recognize the services of my adopted son, Mr. Benjamin Armstrong, known to us as Shaw-Bwaw-Skung. He has rendered services in the past that should be rewarded by something more substantial than our thanks and good wishes."

Benjamin was flattered by the attention and recognition. Already some chiefs of the nearby bands had offered him money from their annuities, but he had declined to accept it because of their poor and needy condition. He did not wish to exploit their situation like many others had sought successfully to do.

"Now that we are gathered here, now that we can negotiate with the representatives of the Great Father, now that we have hope for our future generations, we owe much to Armstrong, we owe much to Shaw-Bwaw-Skung, The Man Who Goes Through."

Benjamin felt humbled as some of those gathered began to cheer in agreement with Kechewaishke. But, feeling embarrassed, he wanted to slink away and hide from the attention.

"And now, I submit to you my proposition. As he has provided us and our children with homes by getting these negotiations set for us, and as we are about to part with much of the lands we possess, I have it in my power, with your consent, to provide him with a future home by giving him a piece of ground which we are about to part with. When we offered him money he did not accept because he did not want to take anything from us. But, this takes nothing from us and makes no difference with the Great Father whether we reserve a small tract of our territory or not."

The crowd started to get louder in support of Kechewaishke's proposal. They cheered and clapped and called out *Ho! Ho!* in agreement.

"And if you agree," Kechewaishke said trying to speak over the noise of the crowd, "I will proceed with him to the head of the lake and there select the piece of ground I desire him to have, that it may appear on paper when the treaty has been completed."

The cheering continued and grew louder as Kechewaishke completed his proposal. They showed overwhelming support, and, in that moment, Benjamin was filled with joy. For all he had done they were grateful. And though he had done it willingly, not seeking a reward, they sought to provide him one.

Finally, once the cheers died down, the chiefs began to vote. Eya! they shouted one by one. Eya. Eya. *Yes. Yes.*

"We, the chiefs and headmen of the Ojibwe are unanimous in our decision. Please, Kechewaishke, select a large piece of land that he might also have a home in the future as has been provided for us."

The proposal was accepted. The council adjourned. Benjamin was overwhelmed by their gratitude and respect—by their generosity and graciousness.

At daybreak the very next morning, Kechewaishke and Benjamin, along with four young Ojibwe men, set off in a canoe heading westward. Stopping only once for a short break, they traveled for several hours until reaching the head of St. Louis Bay where the St. Louis River emptied into Lake Superior. They rested and had their lunch before the old chief and Benjamin waded ashore and ascended a small plateau.

The air was cool, but brisk and comforting. The sun had risen to the center of a cloudless sky which created a serene and quiet setting.

Kechewaishke, his staff in hand, his mouth breathing heavy from the climb, turned to Benjamin and said, "Are you satisfied with this location? I want to reserve the shore of this bay from the mouth of the St. Louis River. How far that way do you want it to go?" Kechewaishke pointed southeast along the shore of the lake.

Amazed, Benjamin looked out over the huge, endless expanse of water, at the sloping, rounded shores, and across the pristine, tree-filled horizon. He wondered how all this could be possible. All this beautiful land, this boundless lake, offered to him as a gift. He felt like a king.

"You are too generous," Benjamin said with humility. "I should think it wise not to try and make my piece of land too large."

"You have earned it, son."

Once again, Benjamin was flattered, but being somewhat aware of the political process of treaty making, he knew it was a risk to include this parcel of land for himself.

"If the land is too large, the Great Father's officers at Washington might throw it out of the treaty," he explained. "I will be satisfied with one-mile square."

"Wise and humble," Kechewaishke said.

Benjamin could only smile in return, feeling the warmth of the late summer sun on his face.

As the two of them continued to look out across the land, they discussed the exact parameters of the square mile that would be provided for Benjamin. They determined the landmarks that would set it apart and proceeded to spend the next hour in relaxation upon the plateau and among their beautiful surroundings.

As Benjamin lay there warm, comfortable, and happy, amazed by the turn of events over the last year, he noticed a canoe entering the bay from the direction of the river. At first, he thought very little of this canoe, but as it grew closer he could see that the travelers within were a woman and two young children. Benjamin found this odd and it made him think of Charlotte, Samuel, and Marie. *Where could they be? Would they be gone forever?*

The canoe came very near the lake, close enough to shout and be heard. *Charlotte?* he thought. *This can't be!* Benjamin got up from his resting position and looked closely.

"If you are going to have all this land, you'll need a family to take care of," Kechewaishke said, a touch of grandeur in his voice.

"Charlotte!" he yelled.

Benjamin was filled with nervous excitement. He began running toward the shore of the bay. The woman and children in the canoe jumped out into the water and ran onto the shore. "Charlotte!" he yelled again. "Benjamin!" she returned. It was her, it was Charlotte and his two children.

As they came closer Benjamin never slowed down. They crashed together in a helpless embrace, both of them crying, both sobbing with joy.

"Charlotte, I love you so much. I'm sorry, I'm sorry..."

"Papa! Papa!" his children cried out.

"I'm sorry. I'm so sorry," Charlotte said, sobbing. Benjamin could feel Charlotte's sorrow as she held him tight. "We should not have left you."

"No, no, I understand," Benjamin said through his own frantic sobbing. "It's okay. But, how did you find me? How do you know I would be here today?"

Releasing his grasp, Benjamin bent down to hug Marie and Samuel. "They are so much bigger now."

Charlotte pointed toward the plateau. "Kechewaishke," she said. "Somehow he knew where to find us. He sent a messenger. He told us of all the good news. I'm so sorry for leaving. I'm so sorry for doubting you."

Benjamin breathed a sigh of relief, a release of his long-endured pain. He admitted to himself that he was hurt. That the prolonged absence of his family was insufferable, despite his attempts to ignore it. But he could not admit this to Charlotte. Not now, not ever. Benjamin did not want her to feel guilty for the choice she made. Whether he was deserving of such things or not, he only knew that it was over.

"I am just so glad you are back. I am so glad my family is together."

They embraced once more in a moment of complete forgiveness. As they separated, Kechewaishke came slowly to their side.

"We must care always for each other," he said. "Now our work is not done. Our Ojibwe family needs us. Let us return to La Pointe and do more good things."

"Together," Benjamin said. "Let us go together."

And so, they traveled east along the shore of the great lake to their island home, all day and into the night.

––––––––––

At 10 a.m. the following day all was ready for the negotiations between the Lake Superior Ojibwe and the United States government.
At old La Pointe, in the backdrop of the old Catholic church, gathered
the chiefs and elders of the Ojibwe bands near and far. Some put on
paint and feathers in their traditional style, while others appeared in
farmers' clothes with pants and calico shirts. The U.S. commissioners dressed in their formal attire and sat along a table underneath a
large tent. Around the table and mixed throughout the crowd were
various traders, interpreters, missionaries, La Pointe residents, men
and women of all kinds; even dogs roamed here and there. It was a
remarkably diverse crowd gathered and ready for a historic occasion.

When the time was right, Agent Gilbert stood and beat his gavel
against the table to indicate to all those present that it was time to
begin.

"Ladies and Gentlemen," he said through the help of an interpreter. "The United States has determined that it is right and necessary to negotiate a treaty with the Ojibwe of this region. First, to right
the wrongs of the previous administration, and second for the mutual
benefit of our two nations."

Before Agent Gilbert could continue, Kechewaishke, who sat no
more than fifteen feet away, raised his arm to interrupt.

"I am sorry," Kechewaishke said plainly in English. "We not want
anything said to us from the English language by anyone but my adopted son." Kechewaishke pointed at Benjamin. "There have always
been things told to Ojibwe in past that proved afterwards to be un-
true. Whether the interpreter was wrong or not I do not know. As we
now feel that my adopted son interprets to us just what you say, we
wish to hear your words repeated by him and when we talk to you our
words can be said by your own interpreter."

Agent Gilbert listened carefully appearing neither annoyed by or
in favor of the request. He simply listened.

"This way one interpreter can watch the other and correct each
other should there be mistakes. We do not want to be deceived anymore as we have in the past."

Agent Gilbert did not answer, looking instead toward Commissioner Manypenny for his response.

"What you have said mirrors my own views exactly, and I will now appoint your adopted son as your interpreter while we shall retain our own." Commissioner Manypenny then turned to the other U.S. officials. "How does that suit you, gentlemen?"

At once they gave their consent and the council proceeded.

Agent Gilbert cleared his throat, looked toward Benjamin, his new interpreter, and then continued his speech.

Agent Gilbert gave a dignified and respectful speech. He welcomed the opportunity to meet with and make a new treaty with the Ojibwe people. It was both eloquent and appropriate.

Blackbird spoke on behalf of the Ojibwe, echoing many of the sentiments of kindness and hospitality that had been set forth by Agent Gilbert. He then went on to catalogue the grievances of the Ojibwe going all the way back to the treaties of 1837 and 1842 in which the Ojibwe ceded their Wisconsin lands but did not give up the right to live upon and use that land. Blackbird then outlined the requests of the Ojibwe.

"We have several requests before agreeing to a new treaty," he announced while standing tall and firm before the U.S. officials. "We wish for payments to our mixed-race kin and land, so they may farm. We have agreed to sell our lands along the north shore for which we desire an annual payment. We have agreed and hope that you will recognize a split between those Ojibwe living near the great lake and those Ojibwe living west of the Mississippi River. From this day forward, we wish our annuity payment to be made here, at La Pointe, and several other locations as directed by our separate bands. Most importantly, we request a permanent home for all of our bands. A home set aside for each of us and our future generations. A home that we may select that may never be taken from us."

Blackbird went on to describe the lands that had been selected. To Benjamin's surprise, the La Pointe band had not selected land on the island, but rather they selected two spots just off the island. One at Bad River, south of the bay where Reverend Wheeler's mission was located; the other, at Red Cliff, west of the bay along its western shore. Additionally, Blackbird requested a reserve tract of land encompassing about one hundred acres lying across and along the eastern side of Madeline Island so that they would not be cut off from the fishing privilege.

For several hours, the terms were negotiated back-and-forth, but no real agreement could be met. Then, an argument erupted.

"The traders of the American Fur Company request a payment of debts be made directly out of the annuity funds," stated the secretary, Mr. Smith, as he brought up the issue of traders' claims.

"How much do they claim?" asked Loon's Foot, second chief of the Fond du Lac band.

"They request payment of claims amounting to $250,000."

Astonished, the crowd let out a unified gasp.

"Gaawesaa!" shrieked Loon's Foot. *Impossible!* "That is two to three times higher than what we owe."

"I beg to differ!" shouted the trader John Lynde. As Lynde stepped forward he slowly pushed aside the bottom of his open jacket revealing a pistol at his hip. He was followed by several other traders who did the same. "Your tribe owes at least that much, and we will settle for no less. Already you have split the tribe in two, minimizing what claims we may recover. We will not let you pay less than what you owe."

"Gentlemen, please!" Commissioner Manypenny shouted as he stood and raised his hands. "There will be no violence today, nor any day for that matter."

"We should be allowed to review the claims," Loon's Foot said. "We wish to pay only what we owe."

"Now I think would be a good time to adjourn," Agent Gilbert said seeking to relieve the tension. "We have talked a great deal. You have told us what you want, and now we want time to consider your requests, while you need time consider these claims. So, we will adjourn until tomorrow and we, the commissioners, will carefully examine and consider your propositions. When we meet tomorrow we will be prepared to answer you with an approval or rejection of those requests."

Agent Gilbert then directed his voice toward the traders who were still filled with anger. "As for you, I suggest you put away your weapons or you will get nothing. We will examine your claims and decide justly what is owed and what is not."

Though unhappy, the traders relented. Everyone else agreed happily to the adjournment, and they departed quickly to their separate camps. For the time being, negotiations were put on hold.

———————

That evening, a surprise visitor arrived at Benjamin's store. It was Commissioner of Indian Affairs George Manypenny. He came alone.

"Commissioner, to what do I owe this surprise visit?"

"You have a fine little shop here," he said as he walked forward and shook Benjamin's hand.

"Thank you, commissioner. I've recently opened my own trading post through the goodwill of Mr. Cadotte."

"I see. Call me George."

"George. May I offer you some tea?"

"Thanks, but that's not necessary." It was obvious by the commissioner's upright stature and firm tone that he came for matters of business.

"How then might I help you?"

The commissioner paused, breaking eye contact while considering just what to say. "The incident—earlier today—it nearly became ugly."

"Far too many traders have been allowed to exploit the Ojibwe in recent years. We are determined not to let it happen again." Benjamin was straightforward and confident. He had suffered through too much to behave otherwise.

"I know." The commissioner nodded, then shook his head. "That is why I have come to you. I am impressed with the manner in which you have conducted business for the Ojibwe. I see that they have confidence in you."

"It seems they do," Benjamin said.

"I believe the demands of the Ojibwe are reasonable and just. Meanwhile, the traders have filed claims that are far greater than what the Ojibwe contend they owe. This has been and will continue to be a major point of contention before a deal can be made."

"Certainly," Benjamin said, "but I assure you those claims are unfounded."

"Right," the commissioner said quietly to himself while thinking of a solution. "Do you keep a set of books?" he asked.

"Of course. I maintain a day book showing the amount each man owes me."

"Would you mind…"

"You'd like to look at it?"

"Well yes—I mean, if you don't mind."

"By all means." Benjamin proceeded to get his day book which was underneath the counter a few steps to his right. "Within this book is every claim, both paid and unpaid, I have accepted since opening my store in the spring of this year."

The commissioner paged through it quickly.

"You may take it with you. You or your interpreter may question any man whose name appears therein. I would accept whatever they say they owe whether it be one dollar or ten cents."

"Whatever they say they owe?" The commissioner was confused.

"George," Benjamin explained, "I have lived among the Ojibwe now many years. I have seen their condition continually worsen because of inflated claims and other conditions such as the illegal sale of spirituous liquors and the negligence of the government agents. I do not wish for that to continue. I will accept what they are willing and able to pay. I suggest you and the treaty commissioners should do the same."

The commissioner nodded to show that he understood and moved the book from the counter to the crux of his arm. "I am certain that some of the traders are making claims for far more than is due them. But for now, I will take the matter under further investigation."

As they shook hands the commissioner thanked Benjamin for his help and departed. Benjamin was pleased with the commissioner's visit and knew he and the treaty commissioners still had much work ahead of them.

———————

The next day everyone gathered once more, this time in preparation to review the treaty. The traders came with anxious looks but without their weapons. Everyone dressed neatly for the occasion, expecting that it might be the day the treaty would be signed. Revered Wheeler dressed in his slickest suit and stood alongside Harriet and his entire family. The chiefs dressed in their finest regalia with buffalo robes, ornate head dresses and colorful moccasins. Even Makwa, who rarely put on traditional garb, wore an elaborate sash and colorful beads. It was a pleasant scene, Benjamin thought, perhaps the most formal he had ever witnessed at La Pointe.

"I am pleased to see us all gathered and ready," Agent Gilbert said. "My fellow commissioners and I have listened to your requests and now put them down on paper in the form of a treaty. We expect that you will find it to your liking that it may be signed. As it gets later in the season we are anxious and hopeful to return to our homes, near and far, so we may prepare for the long winter. Before the treaty is presented, have you, the Ojibwe, got anything more to say?"

Kechewaishke rose slowly from his central position among the chiefs and elders. As Benjamin looked on from his spot at the interpreter's table, he admired the unique view he had—the old chief in front of him while in the backdrop were hundreds of onlookers of all backgrounds and ages. Seated at each side of Kechewaishke were the chiefs and elders, their necks turned, their chins upward, in reverence and respect of the greatest, wisest Ojibwe elder. It was a view, a moment, Benjamin would not soon forget.

"We are happy to gather here today," Kechewaishke said, this time speaking his native tongue. "And we too are anxious to make this deal. But I have already talked too much. I have asked Chief Nagonab to speak on our behalf. Let him tell you how we feel."

There was a rustling among the crowd as Kechewaishke sat and Nagonab stood, though it was nothing that would cause a disturbance.

Chief Nagonab came from Fond du Lac. He was neither old nor young, but well past the age of a warrior. He had a rounded face and somewhat curly, unbraided hair which he kept long like many of his Ojibwe kin.

"My friends," he said in a clear, strong tone. "Our wishes are now on paper before you. Before, this was not so. We have been many times deceived. We had no one to look out for us. The Great Father's officers made marks on paper with black ink and quill. The Ojibwe cannot do this. We depend on our memory."

Nagonab turned from the crowd and toward the commissioners.

"We often talk together and keep your words clear in our minds. When you talk we all listen, then we talk it over many times. This is the way we must keep our record. In 1837, we were asked to sell our timber. In 1842, we were asked to sell our minerals. Our white brothers told us the Great Father did not want the land, that we might remain to fish and hunt."

Nagonab became more adamant with each sentence. He wanted to make sure the Ojibwe were not deceived again.

"But by and by we were told to go away. We were told to leave our friends and the graves of our fathers. What does this mean, we asked? Did the Great Father speak untruth? But you could not tell us from memory. You go back to your black marks and say this is what those men put down when they made the treaty. We asked to speak to those men, but you do not know where they are. You say they are dead and gone. Now we know better. We know that only the black marks matter, not the words you speak or the promises you make."

Nagonab paused to catch his breath and then pointed toward Benjamin as he translated. "Now we have a friend who can make black marks on paper. When the council is over he will tell us what is written down. Now we know what we are doing. If we get what we ask, the chiefs will touch the pen to paper, but if not, we will not touch it. We will not touch the pen unless our friend says the paper is alright."

A series of *ho-ho's* followed Nagonab's speech as the Ojibwe men and women showed their support and acquiescence. Benjamin, too, supported Nagonab's statement, but felt a huge amount of pressure, having the weight of the entire treaty placed upon his shoulders.

"We know your history and we understand your concerns," Agent Gilbert said. "We think perhaps your friend the interpreter will need some time to evaluate our terms and conditions to ensure that they are to your liking. Therefore, your Father, Commissioner Manypenny, has ordered some beef cattle killed and a supply of provisions will be handed out to you right away. You can now get a good dinner and talk matters over among yourselves the remainder of the day and I hope you will come back tomorrow feeling good natured and happy. For now, we place the treaty in the hands of your friend, that he might be able to read and explain it to you."

The agent's statement was met by cheers and applause, everyone being very happy to accept the beef and provisions. Benjamin, however, felt more and more tense, realizing just how important his role had become. As he sat there, in a bit of a daze, Kechewaishke approached him with the treaty in his hands. Along with him were several other Ojibwe elders.

"My son," he said, "the chiefs of all the country have placed this matter entirely within your hands. Go and examine the paper and if it suits you it will suit us." Then, turning to the chiefs he asked, "What do you all say to that?" *Ho-ho* was their response. Turning back to Benjamin he said, "Go then and examine the paper."

CHAPTER 33

The commissioner, George Manypenny, and the agent, Henry Gilbert, sat quietly near their campfire while they enjoyed beef steak and corn for supper. The September air was brisk, and both men huddled under woolen blankets that covered their backs while they listened to the steady crackle of the fire. In the distance were softened sounds of native dancing and song.

"Where did you go tonight?" Gilbert asked, breaking the silence between them.

"The interpreter," replied Manypenny, his mouth full of steak. "He gave me a copy of his ledgers. Our clerk is evaluating them now."

"Good," Gilbert said setting his plate down and staring into the fire. There was a long pause. "I'm curious about your policy, commissioner. It is so business-like—each treaty you negotiate is just a copy of the one before it."

"You're right," Manypenny said without hesitation. "I am a businessman and my goal is to get things done."

"Get things done?"

"Indian policy in this nation has failed and I aim to change that. There is a lot to do."

"How?" Gilbert asked, looking over flames at the commissioner.

"It is quite simple, really." Manypenny paused to put down his empty plate and swatted the mosquitoes away. "Assimilation. I believe the Indians are fully capable of learning and can be prepared rather quickly for life in civilized society. To accomplish this, it is necessary first to protect them by concentrating them on reservations and then by teaching them English, mathematics, domestic skills, modern agriculture and husbandry, the value of toil, thrift, private property and the Christian faith—preferable of a Protestant denomination."

Gilbert swallowed hard, as an abolitionist he wasn't sure it was right to take away the Ojibwe way of life. "Learning, of course," he said, "but complete assimilation? Is there no place for them in this vast land?"

Manypenny smiled and glanced up at the moon. "One tribe after another, it is the only way to save them. If they hope to survive they will assimilate."

CHAPTER 34

Silence. Benjamin had never experienced silence like he had in that moment. While the rest of the island gathered to sing, to dance, to feast, to socialize, Benjamin sat alone in a small one-room office, closed off from the world. With a draft of the treaty before him, seclusion was necessary, but it was also intimidating. He had known all along that the Ojibwe would rely on him, their advisor and friend, to determine the correctness of the treaty, but it wasn't until he was struck by this deep, cavernous silence that the reality of it set in. Thousands upon thousands of Ojibwe men, women, and children now depended on his intelligence and decision-making—on his ability to see through the coercive tactics of the traders and politicians, to perceive both present and future effects, and to determine for everyone what was best. As Benjamin sat there, this incomprehensible task before him, he felt small. Insufficient. He groaned in dismay as he laid his head against the table.

You are to separate your paths. You must go a different way.

Benjamin heard a voice. His head shot up as he looked anxiously around the room. "Hello? Who's there?" No answer. The room was empty.

Each of you will be feared, respected and misunderstood by the people who will later join you on this earth.

He heard the voice again. This time louder, more distinct. "Who's there!" Benjamin thought it was his imagination, but then he heard the voice again.

Protect us.

Benjamin didn't know if he was truly in his friend's presence or if the words resonated in his memory, but they were the words of Giizhigoon as he lay sick and dying, that Benjamin heard. It was

Giizhigoon's story of the brother wolf and the future of the Ojibwe people. It was his final wish, his final command before Giizhigoon left the world of the living.

Still, as Benjamin eyed the words of the treaty, he felt uncertain. He had worked so hard and he believed he had done it for the right reasons. He had done it for his brother-in-law, for his nephew, for his wife and children, and for the community. But something was missing; something wasn't right. Was it enough, he wondered, to tell his story— to make his mark on history?

———————

"The treaty is all right," Benjamin said to Commissioner Manypenny as he returned from his temporary isolation, "but there are a few important changes that must be made before it can be signed."

"What did you have in mind?" the commissioner asked.

Benjamin laid the treaty document on the commissioner's desk and prepared himself for a potential argument.

"First, there is no provision for previous payments due. We demand that unpaid sums from previous treaties be paid in full."

To Benjamin's astonishment, the commissioner showed no objection. Benjamin paused and waited, but the commissioner merely lifted his eyebrows as if expecting Benjamin to proceed.

"Very good," Benjamin hesitated, but there was no response. "The treaty provides eighty acres of land for each of our mixed-race kin heads of family, but it should also provide for those who are single and over the age of twenty-one."

The commissioner nodded, again showing no objection. "Anything else?" he asked.

"Yes," Benjamin said, "and this is the most important stipulation. The treaty provides for future annuity payments to be made at L'Anse, La Pointe, Grand Portage, and on the St. Louis River, but it does not specify that they should not be asked to remove. It MUST specify that the Ojibwe shall not be required to remove from their homes hereby set apart for them."

As Benjamin finished speaking he laid his finger down against the desk as if to make a point.

"Very well," the commissioner responded calmly. "I will forward these requests to our clerk, Mr. Smith, and I will see that you are allowed to review the treaty once more with all adjustments included."

Finally letting go of his skepticism, Benjamin smiled. "Thank you, Commissioner Manypenny. Thank you."

"Thank you, Mr. Armstrong. You are invaluable to this treaty process, and you are indeed invaluable to these people. Believe it or not, I do not stand in the way of this treaty deal. I want the Ojibwe to be comfortable and happy with their circumstances. This is the only way they will be allowed to change and become a part of white, American culture."

Benjamin knew this was wrong. He knew the assimilation policy expressed by the commissioner would have effects no less detrimental than the removal policies they had just overcome. But, he decided, it was not the time and place to argue. They had regained their homeland—permanently. Instead of arguing, he shook the commissioner's hand, happy for the treaty outcome.

But maybe, he thought—maybe it was an inevitability. Maybe Watrous was right. The notion sank deep into Benjamin's subconscious.

————

The next day, Benjamin put the stress of the treaty negotiations aside and he enjoyed some time with his family. Charlotte, Marie, Samuel, Makwa and Benjamin went exploring about the island, enjoying its pebbled shores, its abundant, secluded forests, and its winding and numerous trails. For Benjamin, it was invigorating to forget his cares for a while and to be together, happy and healthy.

That evening Benjamin and his family joined the Wheeler family for dinner by campfire. Around them were dozens of other families camped out under the stars engaged joyfully in talking and eating while they all awaited the signing of the treaty. It was as serene and comfortable as any of them had been for many years.

"Forgive me for asking," Reverend Wheeler said as they sat together, watching their families interact, "but how is the treaty? Is it all right?"

Benjamin chuckled, seeing how anxious the reverend was. "Yes," Benjamin said, patting the reverend on the knee. "I requested that a few additions be made, but the commissioner seemed willing. The rest is just as we desire."

"Good. Good. That is good."

"Yes, it is."

"And not a moment too soon," the reverend said, his tone changing from nervousness to eagerness. "The treaty is not only necessary to right the wrongs of the past, but to prepare for the future."

"Change is upon us."

"Great change," the reverend said quickly. "Have you heard of the new town site, Ashland?"

Benjamin hadn't. "No, I have been far too occupied in the affairs of the island."

"Two men from Ohio. Whittlesay and Kilborn, I believe. They have platted a site at the head of the bay a few miles east of my mission. Just the other day they completed their first permanent structure."

"Really?"

"Yes, they've already invited me to hold services there."

"Are they expecting rapid growth?"

"Of course. Stories are spreading about this region. About its beauty. About its abundance. About the rich silver, copper, and iron mines along the southern shore of the lake. Already a steamer has landed at Ashland. Growth has been gradual until now, but that is about to change. In the next few years I think the population in this region will burst upward."

"Then the timing for the treaty is perfect. We need to secure reservations before all the land is claimed."

"Yes," Reverend Wheeler agreed. "La Pointe is no longer a faraway trading post. Soon this entire region will be a commercial center."

Benjamin shuddered at the thought, knowing it was true. The treaty was definitely a victory, but settlement and industry were coming. Though they had fought and suffered and won, never again would their community be the same.

_____

After several days passed, the commissioner finally came to Benjamin with the revised treaty. The requests he had made were added, but they were attached as separate documents.

"These requests are important," Benjamin told the commissioner. "The entire treaty must be rewritten as one single document."

The commissioner agreed and returned the treaty to his clerk for rewriting. A few hours later Benjamin was shown the completed and final draft.

"Yes," Benjamin said with confidence and gratitude, thinking of Giizhigoon and how he had led Benjamin all along. "This is right. The treaty is ready."

Benjamin proceeded to find Kechewaishke and the other chiefs and headmen. "All is ready," he told them. They nodded and prepared themselves to meet with the treaty commissioners.

_____

Once again, the stage was set as a crowd gathered just outside the shadow of the old church. The commissioners sat at their table and under the tent, somewhat shielded from the breezes that constantly swept in from the lake. In front of them were dozens of neatly dressed Ojibwe chiefs and headmen all ready to make a deal, all ready to put their trust in Benjamin.

Meanwhile, the peace pipe was passed, and the final historic council was ready to begin.

"There has been much talk and negotiation," Agent Gilbert said, projecting his voice so that all could hear. "But now, on this the thirtieth day of September, 1854, the Treaty of La Pointe, which shall be forever binding between the United States of America and the Lake Superior Ojibwe, is ready for your signature. Who shall be the first to sign?"

The agent held out a quill pen. In front of him was the treaty, and beside him was an interpreter prepared to help the Ojibwe make their mark.

Kechewaishke stood, being the most revered of the elders, he would be the first to sign.

"Today we begin a new alliance," he said, "one that shall not be broken."

As he took the pen and made his mark the crowd erupted with cheers and applause. The joyous noise filled the air. Like a warm blanket, Benjamin could feel the pride and excitement. He could see it in the faces of young and old, Ojibwe and white. Their long suffering, their hard work and determination had paid off. It had made all the difference.

The rest of the Ojibwe chiefs went forward to make their marks. One after another they continued in a near endless line to the table, eighty-five in total. There were many smiles and much hand-shaking. After everything was done, the commissioners gathered their things and boarded the steamer North Star and headed for home. As Benjamin hugged his wife and watched the crowds depart for their camps and homelands, he was visited by Kechewaishke.

"Mino," he said. *Good.* "Well done my son."

"All the credit is yours."

"You see now what this life requires. Patience and courage. Trust in your brothers. That will lead to a long and prosperous life."

"You have seen this outcome all along, haven't you?"

"I see many things and I am not fooled easily. As happy as we are today, I want you to know that this is not the end of the injustices for our people."

Benjamin lowered his head with the sad realization of that fact.

"I have fulfilled my role over many years and several generations. I have seen time pass and I know the changes will continue. But do not ever be defeated. Be strong and remember your Ojibwe brothers and sisters who have gone before you but concentrate on your Ojibwe brothers and sisters who will come after."

With a gleam in his eye, Kechewaishke, the oldest and wisest of the Ojibwe chiefs, turned and walked slowly toward the shore of the lake.

As Benjamin watched Kechewaishke's hunched, almost decrepit and shadowy figure, he admired his gracious spirit and he reflected on Kechewaishke's words. Silently, Benjamin captured the moment in his heart.

CHAPTER 35

Benjamin Armstrong paced slowly back and forth. At seventy-one years of age he had a limp in his step and a long, stiff gray and white beard. Seated at a desk beside him was his biographer Thomas P. Wentworth, a much younger man touted for his journalistic abilities. On the desk in front of Wentworth was a huge stack of papers that had been marked and remarked, crossed out and rewritten, read and reread.

"The preface is absolutely the most important part," Armstrong said as he stared hard at the floor. "Read it back to me, again."

Wentworth cleared his throat and held a paper lined with text in front of him.

> *This undertaking I begin, not without misgivings as to my ability to finish a well-connected history of my recollections. I kept no dates at any time and must rely wholly upon my memory at seventy-one years of age.*
>
> *Those of my white associates in the early days, who are still living, are not within reach to assist me by rehearsals of former times.*
>
> *Those of the older Indians who could assist me, could I converse with them, have passed beyond the Great River, and the younger ones, of whom there are many not far distant, could not assist me in the most essential portions of the work.*
>
> *Therefore, without assistance and assuring the reader that dates will be essentially correct, and that a strict adherence to facts will be followed, and with the hope that a generous public will make due allowance for the lapse of years, I am, Your obedient servant, Benjamin G. Armstrong.*

Wentworth laid the paper against the desk and looked up at Armstrong who was still staring hard at the floor with his hand to his beard.

"What do you think?" Armstrong asked.

"We've discussed this already. It denies culpability for any error in memory and establishes trust with your reader. I think it is a perfect way to start out."

Armstrong stood still, silent in thought.

"What is left to think about?" Wentworth asked.

Armstrong finally lifted his head and turned to his biographer. "It's just something someone said to me once. I can't stop thinking about it."

CHAPTER 36

When the time came, Makwa did not travel with Benjamin, Charlotte, and the children to their new home on Oak Island.

"Are you certain you don't wish to come with us?" Benjamin asked him before departing La Pointe.

"I am certain," Makwa said. "I will go with my great uncle, Ke-chewaishke, to our new and permanent home at Red Cliff. It is time for me to take care of myself."

Shortly after the 1854 treaty, most of the Ojibwe left the island and settled on their new reservations at Red Cliff and Bad River. Although the treaty was celebrated as a victory for the Ojibwe, it didn't elimi-nate many of the challenges they had been facing all along. The gov-ernment changed its policy from removal to assimilation while many traders continued to exploit the annuity system. Also, white settlement increased as nearby cities grew and industry expanded. Then, by the summer of 1855, less than a year after the celebrated treaty, the Ojibwe faced a new obstacle: tourism.

Returning to the island for the 1855 annuity payment in August, Makwa barely recognized his island home. Thousands upon thousands gathered at La Pointe. Many of them were the Lake Superior Ojibwe, but just as many were whites, dressed in their finest clothes. Men walked around in top hats and vests while women were adorned with colorful green, blue, and pink dresses. They looked, Makwa thought, just like the men and women he had seen in New York City.

"Look at that Indian young man!" a tourist exclaimed pointing at Makwa as he made his way to Austrian's store and the location of the annuity payment.

Makwa paused and looked at the man curiously. "What happened? Where did you come from?"

Lacking no enthusiasm, the man answered. "Don't you know?"

Makwa shook his head.

"They have completed the canal at Sault Ste. Marie. Lake Superior is now accessible to major luxury liners. I read about it in the paper and booked my ticket right away. Isn't it amazing! Fresh air, refreshing climate, enchanting scenery, and real Indians!"

Makwa was saddened by those words. As he looked around at the wealthy, content and carefree men and women, now invading his sacred Ojibwe homeland, his heart ached. The treaty to secure a permanent home, he realized, was made just in time to save his people from losing their land forever.

Arriving at Austrian's store, Makwa found hundreds gathered. There were men and women of all kinds, Ojibwe and white, traders and warriors, tourists and elders. At the front was George Manypenny, the commissioner who had come just a year earlier to negotiate the treaty. Near him were several interpreters and Ojibwe leaders such as Blackbird and Nagonab, but Kechewaishke was not among them. The atmosphere was contentious. Men, Ojibwe and white, were shouting toward the commissioner who shouted back.

Makwa could hear the cries of the Ojibwe. "That money belongs to the Ojibwe! It was promised to us!"

"Why are they arguing?" Makwa asked as he stood near an Ojibwe man dressed in trousers, calico shirt, and farmer's hat. He was a Bad River Ojibwe.

"They want to make the payment to the traders," he said in English. "Ninety thousand dollars they say."

"I thought they made a treaty for our benefit? Why do they give the money to the traders?"

"The traders want all the money for the things they gave us. The elders say we don't owe them so much."

The commotion began to die down and Makwa turned to see the commissioner standing atop a chair with his hands held high.

"I insist upon keeping order," Commissioner Manypenny said. "Let everyone of all nationalities and interests be seated on the ground and we will have a pleasant exchange."

The crowd, who was anxious to come to an agreement, wasted no time in finding a spot to sit. Once everyone was settled and quiet, the only two left standing were Manypenny and Blackbird. The commissioner looked at Blackbird. "If you have anything to say I hope you will speak to the point."

Blackbird, who sought always to maintain traditional Ojibwe values and ways of living, was on this occasion dressed in white man's clothes. He paused to look at the hundreds of people seated around him, took a deep breath, and, looking away from the commissioner, he spoke.

"My brother chiefs, headmen, young men, women and children. I have listened well to all the men and women and others who have spoken in our councils and shall now tell it to my father. I shall have one mouth to speak your will."

Blackbird spoke openly and honestly to his Ojibwe kin. He turned and directed his words to Commissioner Manypenny.

"My father. We salute you in the name of our Great Father, the president, whose representative you are. We want the Great Spirit now to bless us. The day is clear, and we hope our thoughts will be clear, too. My intention is to tell you what the owner of life has done for us."

Blackbird spoke of his spirituality, a spirituality that was important and sacred to the Ojibwe, even to those who had converted to the Christian faith. It was a dynamic that was ever present.

"He has provided for the life of us all. When the Creator made us, he provided for us here upon this earth in the running streams, in the woods and lakes which abound with fish and in the wild animals."

Blackbird gestured to the trees and lake and open skies that surrounded the assembly.

"We regard you as if men like a spirit. Perhaps it is because of your education, because you are so much wiser than us; but if we can trace our tradition right, the Great Spirit has not made the white man to cheat us. There is a difference of opinion as it regards the different people among us, as to which shall have the preeminence, but the Great Spirit made us to be happy before you discovered us."

Listening to Blackbird, Makwa understood that this was about much more than the payment owed to the traders. It was about the value of a native life and a native culture. Although Commissioner Manypenny showed himself willing and wanting to set aside land for the Ojibwe, he still looked down upon their culture and sought its assimilation for what he believed was better. Reverend Wheeler, too, who was a great friend and advocate of the Ojibwe—even he sought to erase their language and history and manner of living. Blackbird knew this, and he wasn't afraid to point it out. Here, in front of those who saw the Ojibwe in one of two forms, a spectacle or a savage. Now, as the final screw was being turned against the Ojibwe, Blackbird was making his plea.

"I will tell you about how it was with us before our payments, and before we sold any land. Our furs that we took we sold to our traders. We were then paid four martin skins for a dollar. Four bear skins and four beaver skins for a dollar, too. Can you wonder that we were poor? I say this to show you what our condition was before we had any payments. It was by our treaties that we learned the use of money. I see you white men that sit here how you are dressed. I see your watch chains and seals and your rich clothing."

Blackbird pointed specifically to an elaborate gold watch worn by Commissioner Manypenny.

"Now I will tell you how it was with our traders," he continued. "When they first came among us they were very poor, but by and by they became very fat and rich, and wear rich clothing and have their watches and gold chains such as I see you wear. But they got their things out of us. They were made rich at our expense. My father, you told us to bring our women here, too. Here they are, and now behold them in their poverty."

Several women stood. They were dressed in worn blankets and tattered garments. The crowd let out a gasp, but it was hard to tell if this was out of astonishment or some preconceived theatrical expression. In either case, it was sad to see the poor women among the wealth of the white spectators.

"My father, I am now coming to the point. We are here to protect our own interests. Our land which we got from our forefathers is ours and we must get what we can for it. Our traders step between us and our father to control our interests. One year ago, we shook hands with you to uphold us in our poverty. We are thankful to see you here to attend to our interest, and that we are permitted to express to you our wants. Last year you came here to treat for our lands we are now speaking about. We sold them because we were poor. We sold our land for our graves, that we might have a home, where the bones of our fathers are buried. We were not willing to sell the ashes of our relatives which are so dear to us. This was the reason why we sold our lands. It was not to pay debts over and over again, but to benefit the living, those of us who yet remain upon the earth, our young men and women and children. Behold them in their poverty and see how poor they look."

The crowd and the commissioner remained silent. Only the lake could be heard crashing against the shore and the breeze passing through the leaves.

"Let what I have said, my father, enter your head and heart, and let it enter the head of our Great Father, the president, that it may be as we have now said. We own no more land. We must hereafter provide for ourselves. We want to profit by all the provisions of the treaty we have now made. We want the whole annuity paid to us as stipulated in the treaty. I am now done. After you have spoken, perhaps there are others who would like to speak."

Blackbird bent to sit but then turned back toward the commissioner.

"This is the first time, my father, that I have appeared dressed in a coat and pants. I must confess I feel a little awkward."

With this comical statement, the entire assembly laughed and applauded. It was a lighthearted moment on an otherwise serious occasion. But as Makwa watched, he understood that it was much more than a joke. It was an expression of acceptance by Blackbird, trying to win the favor of the commissioner. But, thinking of Kechewaishke, he began to worry. *Where is Kechewaishke?* he thought. *He has never missed a council.*

The speeches continued, but to little effect. In the end, payment was made directly out of the annuity funds and into the hands of the traders.

Following the council, Makwa went in search of his great uncle. "Where is Kechewaishke?" he asked the elders. "Why was he not in council?"

The elders looked gravely at each other. "He has taken ill. Soon he will be on his way west to the spirit world."

Makwa was deeply affected. He had come to love and respect Kechewaishke more than anyone else. "Is he still among us? Where can I find him?"

The elders pointed to the old Catholic church which stood in the distance. Makwa turned and went there as quickly as he could.

"Inzhishenh!" he called out while entering the church. *Uncle!*

There, surrounded by caregivers, was Kechewaishke lying on a cot. The caregivers stepped aside as Kechewaishke raised his head and held out his hand. "Makwa," he said softly.

"I did not see you at council," Makwa said as he lowered himself to one knee. "Now I find you here pale and cold. Are you okay?"

Kechewaishke smiled. "I can see the spirit world in front of me, but I do not have fear or pain. I have lived well."

Tears began streaming down Makwa's face. "I have so much more to learn. You cannot go now."

Kechewaishke tightened his grasp on Makwa's hand. "I have done my part and fulfilled my role. I can do no more. But I can see that the world is still changing faster than when the leaves change color, quicker than when the lakes turn to ice. Soon our people will be forgotten. Our spirits will be erased."

"What do we do, Great Uncle? You can't leave us if we don't know what to do."

Kechewaishke coughed violently and beads of sweat rolled down his forehead. The caregiver leaned over and patted his head with a towel. After he had collected himself, Kechewaishke looked Makwa directly in the eyes. "You are a storyteller, Makwa. It is in your blood. Now you have the wisdom to write our story. Remember our history and tell it to our future generations. Tell them what happened at Sandy Lake. Tell them what happened to your father. Then go out and shout in all directions, telling all those who share our mother earth what happened to the Ojibwe. Tell them how we suffered and were wronged. Tell them how we were cheated and deceived."

His face wet with tears, Makwa held on to Kechewaishke with both hands. "I will, Great Uncle. I will."

"Tell them our story, Makwa. Don't let them tell it."

"Who?" Makwa asked desperately.

"Those who cannot see. Those who look back and see only themselves. Those who fail to understand the wisdom that comes from the mother earth or the brother animal. They are all around us now. Even if you do not know it. Even if you cannot recognize them."

Kechewaishke's voice was grating and slow. He barely had the strength to continue speaking. From under his robe he pulled out an ornate, red stone pipe along with his tobacco pouch. "Give this to Benjamin," he said, "I have no more use for it now."

"I will," Makwa said, his voice filled with emotion.

Kechewaishke fell into another fit of coughing, this one more violent than the one before. The caregivers crowded Kechewaishke as they tried to relieve his suffering. Makwa could only stand back and watch, his heart breaking.

Kechewaishke, the oldest and wisest Ojibwe, died a few days later on September 7, 1855.

Makwa remained on the island for several days while he joined the Ojibwe who grieved the death of Kechewaishke and celebrated his life.

"We are happy to grieve," said one Ojibwe while Kechewaishke was laid to rest in the Catholic cemetery. "To grieve is human. It connects us. We are grateful for the opportunity to grieve because it means we had the opportunity to love."

Surprisingly, Makwa could not find Benjamin. He longed to see his uncle and adopted father, so they might grieve together. He sought to give him Kechewaishke's pipe, but he could not be found.

Eventually, the tourists and spectators boarded their luxury steamers and returned to the hustle and bustle of their eastern cities. With the annuity payment complete, the Ojibwe also departed for their fall rice harvest. The island was quiet once more.

As Makwa made one last walk to the company store, he heard Benjamin speaking from around the corner.

"That land is rightfully mine," he heard Benjamin say. "It is spelled out in the treaty that it should be given to me for services rendered. I own the land at the tip of Lake Superior."

Benjamin spoke in a demanding tone that Makwa did not recognize. He sounded more like the traders at council than he did his uncle who took care of him. Peeking around the corner he saw that Benjamin was speaking to Joseph, Antoine, and Matthew Maydwaygwon, Kechewaishke's three sons. Makwa leaned against the corner of the building and listened.

"That land was sectioned into four corners, one for each of us," one of the sons said. "We are his sons, we should get something."

"I am his adopted son and I have done great things for this community. That is why the treaty states that the land should be given to me."

One of the sons answered back, abrasively. "You are the one who wrote the treaty. You are like the other greedy white men. You wrote it for yourself. And now you say you are his adopted son? Is that what you tell people?"

"I am his adopted son! I traveled to Washington at great financial peril to earn these reservations. I am the one who earned a meeting with the president. I am the one who made all this possible. I should be given the land. And if you don't give it to me, I will take legal action."

Calmly, the son answered. "You waited for our father's death to tell your lies. Your tongue is forked, your face is split. We pity you and all your people. Keep the land; it will only give you trouble."

The three men walked away. Standing still against the building,

Makwa was saddened and confused. Benjamin was telling lies. Benjamin was making up his own story.

"Why?" Makwa said as he turned the corner of the building.

Surprised, Benjamin quickly turned. "Makwa!" he said his face brightening.

"I heard. I heard your lies."

"What lies? I don't know what you mean."

"We never visited the Great Father. We were turned away, remember?"

Benjamin was silent and motionless.

"You said you were his adopted son. He loved you. He respected you. He even gave you an Ojibwe name, but there was never an adoption ceremony."

Benjamin pleaded. "Makwa, please. You don't understand. Sometimes we have to change the truth to get what we need. I have not hurt anyone. The people, they enjoy hearing about a meeting with the Great Father. They expect that I should be rewarded for my efforts. I'm just giving them the story they want to hear."

When Makwa heard the word 'story' he was reminded of Kechewaishke's final words to him. *Tell them your story.* But he was conflicted. Looking at Benjamin, he wasn't sure who he was anymore. He had seen all the good Benjamin had done for Kechewaishke and the La Pointe community, but now he was a different man.

"You've changed," Makwa said. "Why have you changed?"

"I have not changed," Benjamin pleaded. "I just ... I just accept the inevitability of it all."

"You have changed the story, too! You have changed the story to fit your purpose, haven't you?"

Benjamin slumped his shoulders and lowered his head, like a child caught in a lie. "Makwa," he said, "a story is only as good as the storyteller. I may have embellished here and there, but the truth is still there within. I wouldn't change the truth."

Makwa could feel his heart breaking. "It doesn't matter," Makwa said. "You are like the sun when it is behind the clouds. We can see the light, but we do not know where it comes from. You have told the story of my people from your eyes, and you have made it to benefit yourself. Haven't you?"

Benjamin opened his mouth, but no words came out.

"So much has been taken from us, but you cannot have our history; you cannot take our story. I will tell a new story. One that parts the clouds and shines so brilliantly that yours is forgotten."

Softly, Benjamin replied. "I have to consider myself, too, Makwa. I have Charlotte and the children to look after. I have my reputation. I wasn't trying to hurt you."

"You don't understand, you couldn't," Makwa said. "You come from a world that rewards greed and celebrates personal achievement. I know you tried your best, but I also know you cannot see what you are doing. Kechewaishke told me so."

"This story needs to be told," Benjamin said, his posture less defeated than before. "And I must be the one to tell it. Yours would never be heard. You must know that?"

Makwa sighed and looked toward the clouds, thinking of his father and his great uncle. "Maybe you're right. Maybe your story will be told and retold and will go down in history as the way it happened. But not forever. Not as long as the native voice survives. Eventually, the truth will shine through from behind the clouds. The Ojibwe will trade their nets and wigwams for pencils and paper. My people will tell their story, and someday, the world will be ready to receive it."

Benjamin looked regretfully at his nephew and adopted son. "Good bye, Makwa. Good luck." He reached out in sympathy but then pulled his hand back and walked away.

Makwa slumped over, alone and grief-stricken.

———

Returning to Red Cliff, the permanent reservation provided by the 1854 treaty, Makwa realized that, although Kechewaishke was nearly one hundred years old, he did not die of old age. No, Kechewaishke died of heartbreak. He had seen it all and he had always known the outcome. He merely wished to live long enough to make a difference, to turn aside one inevitability in favor of his people, his ancestors, his future generations. It took him many years, but that is what he did. He truly gave hope to his people and a legacy for the future. Then, when he had done all he could, his heart finally gave in to the sorrow he felt, the sadness for his people overrun by the callous march of time.

But Kechewaishke's final gift was to see beyond the tragedy—to see beyond the death at Sandy Lake or the loss of land through unfair treaties. Looking back, Makwa didn't know the role he played in someone else's story. He didn't know the power words could carry through time, working their way into the hearts and minds of everyone who followed. He didn't know that, once his culture and traditions had nearly been destroyed, his recollections, perspective, and interpretation of that destruction could also be taken and manipulated—just as swiftly and just as thoroughly. It is one thing to destroy a people; it is another take their memory of it.

Years later, Benjamin wrote his story about the Sandy Lake Tragedy and his trip to Washington and the treaty negotiation of 1854. He titled it *Early Life Among the Indians: Reminiscences from the Life of Benj. G. Armstrong*. It has been read and reread countless times over.

Makwa has yet to write his story. Someday, when the time is right, he will. Until then, the Sandy Lake Tragedy remains an unfinished history.

CHAPTER NOTES

CHAPTER 1
Chapter one is a fictional account of a possible meeting that took place between Benjamin Armstrong and Thomas Wentworth around the time Armstrong decided to record his recollections. It is not based on any particular research or findings.

CHAPTER 2
Chapter two relies almost entirely on the biographical sketch of Benjamin Armstrong depicted in his memoir, *Early Life Among the Indians: Reminiscences from the Life of Benj. G. Armstrong*. Although the facts of this chapter are rooted in Armstrong's reminiscences, parts have been fictionalized for the purposes of this narrative.

"Peter was a Canadian of mixed race..." Being of mixed racial heritage was not uncommon on the ever-changing frontier. But it was viewed quite differently than it is today. At the time, those of mixed races were known as half-breeds or half-bloods and they were seen as their own, often inferior, ethnic group. Generally, their backgrounds represented a mixture of native and European ancestry. This is because traders, both native and white, sought to establish kinship ties among their different cultures in order to boost their advantages in trade and business.

CHAPTER 3
Taken directly from a Resolution of the Minnesota Legislative Assembly approved on October 11, 1849.

CHAPTER 4
Giizhigoon is a fictional character created for the purposes of this novel. His name has been borrowed from a book titled, *The Captivity and Adventures of John Tanner* by John Tanner. Giizhigoon's story, though not a scholarly historical account, is a creative depiction of Ojibwe oral history based on the book, *History of the Ojibway Nation* by William Whipple Warren. The council, which was a real historical event, and much of what follows was based on the research and writing of Bruce White in his essay, "The Regional Context of the Removal Order of 1850," and found within the text, *Fish in the Lakes, Wild Rice, and Game in Abundance* by James M. McClurken.

"It was indeed a life of sacrifice and privation…" Harriet Wheeler kept a journal of her experiences over the years. In it, she often wrote about the many challenges of frontier living as a missionary. Her journal has been published and can be read in the book, *Woman in the Wilderness* by Nancy Bunge.

CHAPTER 5

Chapter five is based on a letter written by John Livermore to Alexander Ramsey, March 26, 1850, and a letter written by Orlando Brown to Alexander Ramsey, March 26, 1850. The meeting itself has been fictionalized.

CHAPTER 6

The information in chapter six comes from a variety of sources and cannot be distinguished without thorough citations. The information about Ojibwe population, geography, and clan system are based on William Warren's *History of the Ojibway Nation*. Characters such as Julius Austrian, Leonard Wheeler, and Blackbird are real historical figures. Much of the information surrounding secondary characters such as these has been sourced from a historical blog titled *Chequamegon History*, written and published by Leo Filipczak and Amorin Mello. The website, which can be found at: https://chequamegonhistory.wordpress.com/, is an excellent source of primary material accompanied by thoughtful and objective commentary.

CHAPTER 7

Chapter seven is based on a letter written by Clement Beaulieu to Charles Borup, April 25, 1850. The meeting itself has been fictionalized.

CHAPTER 8

Chapter eight offers a brief overlook of the political complexity of the 1850 Removal Order. For a better understanding of the political intricacies in the years and months leading up the order to remove, read chapter four, "Pressure to Remove," in Bruce White's *The Regional Context of the Removal Order of 1850*. Below, I have provided a brief summary.

The ongoing tension that was felt at La Pointe was the result of the Removal Order which was more complicated than can be explained here. It was not just made on a whim but occurred as a result of many years and varying circumstances, as well as the influence and persuasion of varying people. Its origins could be traced back to the year 1830 when President Andrew Jackson issued the Indian Removal Act. This legislation authorized American officials to negotiate with Indian tribes for their removal west of the Mississippi River. At the time, there was no practical reason to force the Indian tribes of Wisconsin to move and so the order was ignored by officials of the Lake Superior region. Rather, it had a much greater impact on those tribes living throughout the southern half of the United States. One notable outcome was the Cherokee Trail of Tears in 1835.

It was not until the late 1840s that removal became a real and possible outcome for the Lake Superior Ojibwe. By this time Manifest Destiny, the belief that all land from east to west was destined by God for American settlement, was in full-swing and there seemed little time to waste. First, by act of treaty, the Ho-Chunk (Winnebago) living in Wisconsin and Iowa had been removed and made to settle on a reservation near Crow Wing. Then, in August of 1847, Commissioner of Indian Affairs William Medill ordered that the agency at La Pointe be closed down and its functions moved west of the Mississippi River. This provided the people at La Pointe the first inclination that removal was imminent.

The next major step toward removal efforts occurred in September 1849. This was shortly after Minnesota became an official territory. Its governor, Alexander Ramsey, asked the territorial legislature to send a formal request to the president for the removal of the Ojibwe. The request was approved and eventually found its way to the desk of the president. On February 6, 1850, the resolution, which became known as the Removal Order of 1850, was signed into law as an Executive Order by President Zachary Taylor. It stated that the privileges of hunting, fishing, and gathering upon the ceded lands previously granted to the Ojibwe were revoked and that the Ojibwe were "required to remove to their unceded lands." It did not specify exactly where or exactly when. This was important because it left all decisions regarding removal in the hands of two men, Alexander Ramsey, the man who initiated it, and John Watrous, the man who carried it out. As the story reveals, these two men made all the difference.

"One day Loon asked Beaver for a favor..." This is not a traditional Ojibwe story. It has been created by the author to reflect the tradition of storytelling that the Ojibwe people and culture are known for.

"Memorial to the President and Congress of the United States..." There were many petitions circulated around the time of the Removal Order. The petition of Cyrus Mendenhall, as well as several others, has been digitized and is available through the Wisconsin Historical Society, *Turning Points in Wisconsin History*. They can be found at: http://content.wisconsinhistory.org/cdm/ref/collection/tp/id/62186.

CHAPTER 9

According to historian Bruce White, "On June 17, Ramsey set out to investigate locations for a new agency. Travelling on the *Governor Ramsey*, he went as far as Sauk Rapids. There he met John Watrous, Sherman Hall, a missionary from La Pointe, and William Warren, who acted as interpreter on the trip" (White, *The Regional Context*, 185). The dialogue is fictionalized and is based on a claim filed by the trader George Nettleton and a letter by John Livermore to Alexander Ramsey, May 20, 1850. The statement by Ramsey that, "you must convey them to Sandy Lake, and there time the payment in such a way as to interpose obstacles to a return to the country they left" is taken directly from a letter by Ramsey to Luke Lea, July 16, 1850.

CHAPTER 10

Information about Benjamin Armstrong's marriage is limited. As a reference for this narrative I used a blog titled "Chief Buffalo and Benjamin Armstrong," published by Travis Armstrong, an enrolled member of the Leech Lake Reservation Band of Ojibwe Indians of the Minnesota Chippewa Tribe. According to the website, "Government documents and published reports suggest that Benjamin Armstrong may have had two wives, the first being Caroline (Chief Buffalo's daughter) and after her death, Charlotte (Chief Buffalo's niece). But some observers suggest these were the same person. One version says Armstrong was first married to Caroline Buffalo (born 1830) and they had one child, George, born 1848. Caroline is said to have died shortly after George's birth. Armstrong was later married to Charlotte, or Charollette (born in 1835 or 1836 according to census records)." This information can be found at: www.chiefbuffalo.com/buffalo/Their_lives.html.

Information about Ma'iingan (The Wolf) Our Brother, was taken from the White Earth Land Recovery Project and can be found at: http://welrp.org/maiingan-the-wolf-our-brother.

There are various accounts of the Sandy Lake Tragedy, all of which report different numbers for the death toll. What is clear is that very many died in a short period of time. One journalist, writing in the *Minnesota Chronicle and Register* on December 17, stated, "I cannot describe the distress of this poor people, and should I, it could not be believed, for it is incredible."

"Tell him I blame him for the children we have lost..." This was a recorded speech of Flat Mouth and can be read at the Sandy Lake Historical Site. The source for this text was taken from *The Assassination of Hole-in-the-Day* by Anton Treuer. Anton Treuer, *The Assassination of Hole in the Day*, (St. Paul: Minnesota Historical Society, 2011), 102.

CHAPTER 11

The gathering at Ramsey's house is based on Ramsey's diary entry of December 25, 1850. The conversation is based on a letter written by John Watrous to Alexander Ramsey, December 10, 1850, and the newspaper articles referred to were published by the *Minnesota Chronicle and Register* on November 25, December 17, and December 23, and the *Minnesota Democrat* on December 17, 1850. The information about John Watrous' wife has been fictionalized.

CHAPTER 12

As estimated in a petition dated November 6, 1851, two-hundred thirty Ojibwe died on the way home from Sandy Lake. The petition can be found through the Wisconsin Historical Society at http://content.wisconsinhistory.org/cdm/ref/collection/tp/id/62186.

"I can make a wind ..." This story of moose hunting has been adapted from the narrative of John Tanner in his book, *The Captivity and Adventures of John Tanner.*

"Over the years I have tirelessly endured many hardships..." The hardships of missionary life as expressed by Reverend Sherman Hall were reported in an essay titled "Missions on Chequamegon Bay" by John Nelson Davidson.

"I still wish to save these people..." From a contemporary point of view, it is difficult to understand the minds of frontier missionaries. Nonetheless, there are many letters and journal entries available from this time period. In these letters the missionaries express their beliefs about native peoples and culture. Though arguable, it appears that missionaries to the Indians did more harm than good to native cultures. The notions expressed by Sherman Hall can be read in a blog post titled "Sandy Lake Letters: Sherman Hall to the Wheelers," published by *Chequamegon History.* This post can be found at: https://chequamegonhistory.wordpress.com/2013/07/11/ sandy-lake-letters-sherman-hall-to-the-wheelers/.

CHAPTER 13

On January 8, 1851, Hole-in-the-Day addressed a public meeting at the Presbyterian Church in St. Paul, interpreted by William Warren. The speech was reported by the *Minnesota Democrat* on January 21, 1851.

CHAPTER 14

The August 1851 council depicted in chapter fourteen was witnessed and recorded by Joseph Austrian, the younger brother of Julius Austrian, who had traveled to Mackinac from Germany just a year earlier. Austrian left a description of the council in his memoir which has been published by the historical blog *Chequamegon History* under the title "Memoirs of Doodooshaboo" and can be found here: https:// chequamegonhistory.wordpress.com/2014/05/03/memoirs-of-doodooshaaboo -joseph-austrians-time-at-la-pointe-1851-52-pt-2/.

"Suspend all actions regarding the removal..." In a letter to the Secretary of the Interior A.H.H. Stuart written on June 3, 1851, Commissioner of Indian Affairs Luke Lea recommended that the removal order be modified to permit "such portions of those bands as may desire to remain for the present in the country they now occupy." In response, in a letter written August 25, acting secretary W.A. Graham authorized Lea to suspend the removal of the Chippewa Indians. Lea then sent a telegram to La Pointe suspending removal which was received by William Boutwell on September 3, 1851. Writing to John Watrous, William Boutwell noted that he had received the request, but that "The purport of the order remains a secret & as the Inds. are ready to go I shall start them." According to historian Bruce White, Watrous' only evident reaction to the telegram was to use "the strategy of stating that the removal effort was an accomplished fact and that little was left to do. Since all actions were completed, there was nothing to cease doing." Bruce White, "The Regional Context

of the Removal Order of 1850," in *Fish in the Lakes, Wild Rice, and Game in Abundance*, compiled by James M. McClurken, (East Lansing, Michigan: Michigan State University Press, 2000), 208-212.

CHAPTER 15

Based on a letter written by Alexander Ramsey to John Watrous, August 14, 1851, and a letter written by John Watrous to Alexander Ramsey, August 24, 1851. The statement, "be of good cheer and conquer all in the way of removal," is taken directly from Ramsey's letter to Watrous. The meeting itself has been fictionalized.

CHAPTER 16

"The Ojibwe see it as a victory and are now headed to The Soo..." The Soo was a term used to reference the city of Sault Ste. Marie in Michigan.

"I saw it with my own eyes..." It is doubtful that Benjamin Armstrong was aware of the telegram suspending removal. However, according to a report by Leonard Wheeler, Sherman Hall did see the telegram "with his own eyes." White, *The Regional Context*, 232.

"I have done what is necessary..." According to Leonard Wheeler, in a letter to Selah Treat, Agent Watrous admitted that "he intended to do just as little for the Indians there as possible, his object being to get them beyond the Mississippi as soon as he could." White, *The Regional Context*, 232.

The December 1851 council with Governor Ramsey in St. Paul was not as brief as it is conveyed in this narrative. It does appear that Benjamin Armstrong and Oshoga were members of this delegation to St. Paul that arrived on December 16 carrying several letters and petitions. The delegation visited Ramsey again on December 24 and December 25 and were sent away with many goods and supplies. The delegation persuaded Ramsey to reissue the failed annuity payment. White, *The Regional Context*, 222–224.

CHAPTER 17

Chapter seventeen is based on historical correspondence as well various conclusions drawn by the historian Bruce White in pages 294–297 of *The Regional Context of the Removal Order of 1850*. The correspondence includes letters from Leonard Wheeler to Selah Treat, March 2, 1852; Alexander Ramsey to Luke Lea, December 26, 1851; John Watrous to Alexander Ramsey, December 22, 1851; and Alexander Ramsey to John Watrous, January 2, 1852. The meeting itself is fictionalized, but it is not unlikely that Watrous and Ramsey met in St. Paul around that time.

CHAPTER 18

The January 1852 payment, as described in chapter eighteen, was based on the eye witness account of William E. Van Tassell, the government blacksmith at Fond du Lac. He told his story during his testimony about the 1852 payment in September 1855. White, *The Regional Context*, 234-235.

"... *a trip to Washington was their only choice.*" In his memoir Armstrong wrote, "I saw that great trouble was brewing and if something was not quickly done, trouble of a serious nature would soon follow." Armstrong, *Early Life Among the Indians*, 16.

CHAPTER 19

Chapter nineteen is based on letters written by William Boutwell to Alexander Ramsey, March 13, 1852, and March 14, 1852. It is also based on the speculation of Bruce White found on page 237 of *The Regional Context of the Removal Order of 1850*, in which he suggests the letter of March 14 was written by John Watrous and signed by William Boutwell. The meeting has been fictionalized but is not unlikely according to the speculation.

CHAPTER 20

Details about the 1852 delegation have been taken almost exclusively from the memoir of Benjamin Armstrong. Those details have been modified to fit this narrative. It should also be noted that the accuracy of Benjamin Armstrong's account has been called into question. According to historian Bruce White, "Some details, including dates, in Armstrong's memories of events that had occurred 40 years before, appear to be mistaken." Ultimately, it is unclear whether or not the Ojibwe delegation actually met with President Fillmore. It should also be noted that a similar trip was made to Washington in late 1848 and early 1849. Known as the "Martell Delegation," it was led by John Baptiste Martell and accompanied by Benjamin Armstrong. The goal of the delegation, which included twelve Ojibwe, was to get the United States to cede back title to the lands surrounding the major Lake Superior villages. According to the historical blog *Chequamegon History* in a post titled "Reconstructing the 'Martell' Delegation Through Newspapers," the delegation was unsuccessful because "Congress and the media were so wrapped up in the national debate over slavery that they forgot all about the concerns of the Ojibwes of Lake Superior." The article also noted that "John Baptiste Martell must be remembered as a key figure in the struggle for a permanent Ojibwe homeland in Wisconsin and Michigan." Chequamegon History, "Reconstructing the 'Martell' Delegation Through Newspapers," Posted November 2, 2013, Accessed January 31, 2017, https://chequamegonhistory. wordpress.com/2013/11/02/reconstructing-the-martell-delegation-through-news papers/. White, *The Regional Context*, 245.

"*It was a warm April morning...*" According to Benjamin Armstrong, the delegation bound for Washington, D.C. departed La Pointe on April 5, 1852. Armstrong, *Early Life Among the Indians*, 16.

"The delegation consisted of just seven men..." Armstrong's memoir states, "Chiefs Buffalo and Oshoga, with four braves and myself made up the party." I was unable to ascertain the names of the four braves. For the purposes of this narrative I have included Blackbird and two other men whose names have been taken from the signing of the 1854 treaty. Makwa is a fictional character. Armstrong, *Early Life Among the Indians*, 16.

"This is the wisdom of the Seven Grandfathers..." The information about the Seven Grandfathers has been summarized from the website, "Anishnaabeg Bimaadiziwin: An Ojibwe People's Resource." Michele O'Brien, "7 Grandfather Teachings," *Anishnaabeg Bimaadiziwin: An Ojibwe People's Resource*, Accessed 10/18/2017, http://ojibweresources.weebly.com/ojibwe-teachings--the-7-grandfathers.html.

CHAPTER 21

Ramsey's remarks were taken directly from a letter by Alexander Ramsey to Luke Lea, March 24, 1852.

CHAPTER 22

Chapter twenty-two is a fictional interpretation of the 1852 La Pointe Ojibwe delegation to Washington. It is based almost entirely on the memoir of Benjamin Armstrong. He details the trip in chapters one and two of his book, *Early Life Among the Indians: Reminiscences from the Life of Benj. G. Armstrong*.

Benjamin's anxiety quickly melted as the man, a stockbroker by the name of Smith..." In his memoir, Armstrong referred to the man only as "the stockbroker." I have given him a name for the purpose of the narrative.

CHAPTER 23

Although the meeting itself is fictionalized, Watrous was known to be in Washington at that time and it is likely that Watrous and Lea met face to face. The conversation is based on several correspondence which includes John Watrous to Luke Lea, June 2, 1852; John Watrous to Luke Lea, June 7, 1852; and Luke Lea to John Watrous, June 29, 1852.

CHAPTER 24

Chapter twenty-four is a fictional interpretation of the 1852 La Pointe Ojibwe delegation to Washington. It is based almost entirely on the memoir of Benjamin Armstrong. He details the trip in chapters one and two of his book, *Early Life Among the Indians: Reminiscences from the Life of Benj. G. Armstrong*.

"Those charges went straight to Governor Ramsey..." Writing in his journal on May 7, 1852, Ramsey noted that John Watrous "loaned me *one thousand dollars without interest*" (emphasis in the original). According to historian Bruce White, "It should not be supposed that this single financial transaction can explain Ramsey's entire

conduct in his investigation of Watrous. However, it is part of a relationship between the two men which transcended their official connection. Beyond that, for Ramsey, the investigation into Watrous' behavior was very much a matter of politics, in which the welfare of the Ojibwe was a secondary concern." White, *The Regional Context*, 243.

"If the Ojibwe were cold and asked for my shirt..." In a letter written July 23, 1852, addressed to "their father at St Pauls," chiefs Buffalo and Oshoga wrote, "We knoe that it is not worth while for us asking enathing of the ajent because on ower return from Washington we ast him to give us a shirt to put on when we got in to New York and he would not giv us a shirt." White, *The Regional Context*, 254.

CHAPTER 25

Chapter twenty-five is based on a letter written by Leonard Wheeler to Selah Treat, March 2, 1852, and a letter written by Alexander Ramsey to John Watrous August 9, 1852. The meeting is fictionalized and not known to have occurred.

CHAPTER 26

The letter of July 23 by Chiefs Buffalo and Oshoga, can be found as written in *The Regional Context of the Removal Order of 1850* by Bruce White (pages 253–254). The response from Governor Ramsey can also be found there (page 258).

Benjamin Armstrong's termination and the departure of his family are fictionalized parts of this narrative. However, the importance of the male as a provider and the consequences of faltering in that role have been based on the reading of *The Captivity and Adventures of John Tanner* by John Tanner.

"The St. Paul Minnesotian has even reported it..." While the Ojibwe delegation was in Washington, so was Agent Watrous. While there he continued to press for removal of the Lake Superior Ojibwe, insisting that removal had already been mostly successful. The Commissioner of Indian Affairs, Luke Lea, agreed with Watrous' view of removal but turned the final policy decision over to the Superintendent of Indian Affairs, Alexander Ramsey. Apparently, Ramsey agreed with Watrous' views and supported his recommendations because on July 24, 1852, the St. Paul *Minnesotian* reported that "The Chippewa Agency is to be removed to Crow Wing." White, *The Regional Context*, 249–258.

"It was a small gathering, almost private..." This council is entirely fictitious, though it is true that Michel Cadotte was a well-known and respected trader, and that Mary Warren was living with the Wheelers at or around that time. It is also true that Watrous had friends within the political system that protected his interests. Fearing that Watrous, a Whig, would lose his position under a new Democratic administration, Henry Sibley wrote a letter to the new Secretary of Interior Robert McClelland saying that, "Mr. Watrous is a sound and consistent Democrat and would doubtless

have been removed by the late Whig administration, but for the fact that his activity and efficiency were so great, as to render it difficult for the Department to find a substitute in whom, as Indian agent, the same reliance could be placed" (White, *The Regional Context*, 263). For a more complete understanding of the political complexities involved in the charges against Watrous and his role as Indian agent, read chapter nine, "The Watrous Investigation" in *The Regional Context of the Removal Order of 1850* by Bruce White.

"In an open and public letter..." This letter was printed in the *Democrat* on December 10, 1850, under the title heading, "The Chippewa Removal Exposed."

CHAPTER 27

Based on a letter by Henry Sibley to the Secretary of the Interior Robert McClelland found in the *Watrous Appointment Papers*. The meeting itself has been fictionalized and is based on a petition in favor of Watrous written by Democratic members of the Wisconsin Senate.

CHAPTER 28

"Benjamin, who still aspired to have his own trading post and store..." At some point Benjamin Armstrong operated his own trading post at La Pointe. It is unclear when he obtained that post, though it was probably many years earlier. According to historian John Holzhueter in his book *Madeline Island and the Chequamegon Region,* Armstrong owned 1,100 acres of land on Madeline Island and was a direct competitor to Julius Austrian (Holzhueter, *Madeline Island,* 45). Giving him work with the trader Michel Cadotte is a completely fictional part of the narrative.

"The fourteen men who had gone on to Crow Wing..." According to Watrous' annuity role, fourteen people representing forty-five members of the La Pointe band were paid at the 1852 payment at Crow Wing. It is uncertain if Blackbird was among them, but the records are available at the Minnesota Historical Society in the Chippewa Annuity Rolls, M390, Reel 1, dated December 15, 1852. White, *The Regional Context,* 262.

"All that was found in that ruin..." Benjamin Armstrong recorded the burning of the Crow Wing agency storehouse in his memoir, though he mistakenly attributed the time as September 1851, when the event actually occurred in January 1853. Armstrong describes searching through the ash, but it is likely that he traveled there after learning that the storehouse burned down rather than before as it is written in this novel. The confrontation with the agent that follows and the interactions with Makwa have been fictionalized. White, *The Regional Context,* 262.

CHAPTER 29

Chapter twenty-nine is based on a letter written by William Johnston to George Manypenny, October 20, 1855. The meeting is completely fictionalized and unlikely to have occurred. In his letter, Johnston made the statement, "But since the money payments have commenced to the Indians, the present Indian Traders are not human; they grasp and cheat him of his all and mock at his degradation and silent despair."

CHAPTER 30

"A special agent has arrived..." Henry Gilbert arrived at La Pointe on October 9, 1853.

The 1853 payment at La Pointe and Benjamin Armstrong's adoption by Kechewaishke are described briefly in Armstrong's memoir. Armstrong, *Early Life Among the Indians*, 32–33.

"I'iw nma'ewinan, maaba asemaa, miinwaa n'ode'winaanin gda-bagidinimaagon..." This is the beginning of a prayer called the "Thank You Prayer." It can be found at: http://ojibwe.net/projects/prayers-teachings/miigwech-thank-you-prayer/.

CHAPTER 31

Based on a report written by Henry Gilbert to George Manypenny, October 31, 1853. Also based on various correspondence including Henry Gilbert to George Manypenny, December 14, 1853; Willis Gorman to Commissioner of Indian Affairs, October 8, 1853; Willis Gorman to Unknown, December 17, 1853; and Willis Gorman to Commissioner of Indian Affairs, February 6, 1854. The statement, "There has been more fraud and cheating in the Indian trade in this Territory than it has been my lot to see or know of anywhere else on this earth," was taken directly from a letter written by Gorman. The meeting has been fictionalized.

CHAPTER 32

Chapter thirty-two is based almost entirely on the memoir of Benjamin Armstrong.

A first-hand description of the smallpox epidemic was printed in the St. Paul *Democrat* on April 20, 1854. An excerpt from that article was published in a blog titled *River Road Ramblings* and can be found at: http://riverroadrambler.blogspot.com/2012/08/small-pox-among-chippewas.html.

"Manypenny was dignified in his appearance ..." George Manypenny shares responsibility for having the payment made at La Pointe, but his policy toward native peoples may not have been any less detrimental to the Ojibwe than that of his predecessors. He merely changed Indian policy from that of removal to that of assimilation. According to the historical blog *Chequamegon History*, "In Manypenny the Ojibwe got a 'Father' who would allow them to stay in their homelands, but they also got a zealous believer in the superiority of white culture who wanted to exterminate

Indian cultures as quickly as possible." Manypenny's views are expressed in detail in his book, *Our Indian Wards*, published in 1880. Furthermore, Manypenny's views are summarized by historian Charles Cleland under the heading "Manypenny's Reservation Policy" (page 79) within the book *Fish in the Lakes, Wild Rice, and Game in Abundance. Chequamegon History.* "Blackbird's Speech at the 1855 Payment," Published January 20, 2014, Accessed November 14, 2017, https://chequamegonhistory. wordpress.com/2014/01/20/blackbirds-speech-at-the-1855-payment/.

"They embraced once more in a moment of complete forgiveness . . ." According to Armstrong's memoir, Kechewaishke did take him to a point along the southwestern tip of Lake Superior so that he could pick out a parcel of land. However, the family reunion has been fictionalized for the purposes of this narrative.

"As Lynde stepped forward . . ." It seems unlikely that during the 1854 treaty negotiations the traders sought to intimidate the Ojibwe through the use of violence. To begin, they were greatly outnumbered, and the proceedings were attended by a number of high-standing U.S. government officials. It is more likely that the traders engaged in backdoor dealings to manipulate negotiations in their favor. However, while describing the treaty negotiations in his memoir, Benjamin Armstrong wrote, "The American Fur Company filed claims which, in the aggregate, amounted to two or three times this sum and were at the council heavily armed for the purpose of enforcing their claim by intimidation." Armstrong, *Early Life Among the Indians*, 42.

CHAPTER 33

Chapter thirty-three is based on the Indian Policy of George Manypenny and found on pages 80–81 of *Preliminary Report of the Ethnohistorical Basis of the Hunting, Fishing, and Gathering Rights of the Mille Lacs Chippewa* by Charles Cleland. It is also based on the Annual Report to the Commissioner of Indian Affairs in 1855 by George Manypenny. The conversation is fictionalized, but Manypenny and Gilbert are likely to have shared a camp at La Pointe around that time.

CHAPTER 34

Chapter thirty-four is based almost entirely on the memoir of Benjamin Armstrong.

"Have you heard of the new town site, Ashland? . . ." A history of Ashland was published by *Chequamegon History* and titled, "Early Recollections of Ashland," by Asaph Whittlesey. It can be found at: https://chequamegonhistory.wordpress.com/ asaph-whittlesey-incidents/.

CHAPTER 35

Chapter thirty-five is taken directly from the Preface of Armstrong's book, *Early Life Among the Indians*, which was dictated by Armstrong to Thomas Wentworth, the writer. The book was published in 1892. The conversation is fictionalized.

CHAPTER 36

The 1855 annuity payment at La Pointe was recorded by several witnesses. Blackbird's speech as shown here was recorded by Leonard Wheeler and shared in a letter to Richard M. Smith. Primary documents from the payment have been published by the historical blog *Chequamegon History* and can be found here: https://chequa megonhistory.wordpress.com/category/1855-annuity-payment/.

"Give this to Benjamin . . ." According to the Obituary of Kechewaishke written by Richard E. Morse, shortly before his death Kechewaishke offered his pipe and tobacco pouch to Commissioner of Indian Affairs George C. Manypenny and asked him to take it to Washington. Richard E. Morse, "The Chippewas of Lake Superior," in *Collections of the State Historical Society of Wisconsin*, Vol. 3, (Madison: Calkins & Webb, Printers, 1857), 366.

"What lies? I don't know what you mean . . ." The conflict between Benjamin and Makwa is purely fictionalized. Armstrong has been called "one of the most intriguing characters in the history of the Apostle Islands" and "the chronicler of Ojibwe history in the Apostle Island region." Although he has been regarded as a friend to the Ojibwe who worked hard on their behalf, historian Bruce White argues, "There is no doubt that Benjamin Armstrong was a shady character." According to White, Armstrong was not adopted by Chief Buffalo, but rather "crafted" the term to benefit himself which he did to "swindle Buffalo's children out of the land on September 17, 1855 for the sum of one dollar." The deceit shown by Armstrong in this novel is based on these claims and can be read in further detail in *An Ethnographic Study of Indigenous Contributions to the City of Duluth*, (Turnstone Historical Research, July 2015), http://www.duluthmn.gov/media/461501/Duluth-Ethnographic-Study-Final -July-2015.pdf. The quote characterizing Armstrong as an intriguing character can be found at: http://www.chiefbuffalo.com/buffalo/Home_Page.html.

BIBLIOGRAPHY

BOOKS

Armstrong, Benjamin Green. *Early Life Among the Indians: Reminiscences From the Life of Benj. G. Armstrong.* Dictated to and Written by Thomas P. Wentworth. Ashland, WI: A.W. Bowron, 1892.

Bunge, Nancy. *Woman in the Wilderness: Letters of Harriet Wood Wheeler, Missionary Wife, 1832–1892.* East Lansing, MI: Michigan State University Press, 2010.

Callahan, Kevin L. *An Introduction to Ojibway Culture and History.* Callahan, 1998.

Cleland, Charles E. "Preliminary Report on the Ethnohistorical Basis of the Hunting, Fishing, and Gathering Rights of the Mille Lacs Chippewa." In *Fish in the Lakes, Wild Rice, and Game in Abundance: Testimony on Behalf of Mille Lacs Ojibwe Hunting and Fishing Rights,* compiled by James M. McClurken, 1–140. East Lansing, MI: Michigan State University Press, 2000.

Davidson, John N. "Missions on Chequamegon Bay." In *Collections of the State Historical Society of Wisconsin,* Edited by Reuben G. Thwaites, 434–452. Vol. 12. Madison: State Historical Society of Wisconsin, 1892.

Erdrich, Louise. *Books and Islands in Ojibwe Country: Traveling in the Land of My Ancestors.* Washington, DC: National Geographic Society, 2003.

Gilman, Carolyn. *Where Two Worlds Meet: The Great Lakes Fur Trade.* Museum Exhibition Series No. 2. St. Paul: Minnesota Historical Society Press, 1982.

Holzhueter, John O. *Madeline Island and the Chequamegon Region.* Madison: State Historical Society of Wisconsin, 1974.

Kugel, Rebecca. *To Be the Main Leaders of Our People: A History of Minnesota Ojibwe Politics, 1825–1898.* East Lansing, MI: Michigan State University Press, 1998.

"Life and Public Services of Hon. Willis A. Gorman," (Compiled from Obituary Notices in the St. Paul Journals). *Collections of the Minnesota Historical Society.* Vol. 3, *1870–1880.* 314–332. St. Paul: Published by the Society, 1889.

Loew, Patty. *Indian Nations of Wisconsin: Histories of Endurance and Renewal.* Madison: Wisconsin Historical Society Press, 2001.

Manypenny, George Washington. *Our Indian Wards*. Cincinnati: Robert Clarke and Co., 1880.

"Mission to the Ojibwas." In *Forty-First Report of the American Board of Commissioners for Foreign Missions, 1850,* 193–196. Boston: Press of T.R. Marvin, 1850.

Morse, Richard M. "The Chippewas of Lake Superior." In *Collections of the State Historical Society of Wisconsin,* Edited by Lyman Copeland Draper, 338–369. Vol. 3. Madison: State Historical Society of Wisconsin, 1904.

"Ojibwas." In *Forty-Second Report of the American Board of Commissioners for Foreign Missions, 1851,* 157–159. Boston: Press of T.R. Marvin, 1851.

Paap, Howard D. *Red Cliff, Wisconsin: A History of an Ojibwe Community.* Vol. 1, *The Earliest Years: The Origin to 1854.* St. Cloud, MN: North Star Press, 2013.

Peacock, Thomas and Marlene Wisuri. *Ojibwe Waasa Inaabidaa: We Look In All Directions.* Afton, Minnesota: Afton Historical Society Press, 2002.

Schenck, Theresa M. *William W. Warren: The Life, Letters, and Times of an Ojibwe Leader.* Lincoln and London: University of Nebraska Press, 2007.

Tanner, John. *The Captivity and Adventures of John Tanner.* Prepared for the Press by Edwin James M.D. New York: G&C&H Carvill, 1830.

Thwaites, Reuben G. "The Story of Chequamegon Bay." In *Collections of the State Historical Society of Wisconsin,* edited by Reuben G. Thwaites, 397–425. Vol. 13. Madison: State Historical Society of Wisconsin, 1895.

"Treaty with the Chippewa, 1854." In *Indian Affairs: Laws and Treaties,* Vol. 2, *Treaties.* Compiled and Edited by Charles J. Kappler, 484–487. Washington, DC: Government Printing Press, 1903.

Treuer, Anton. *The Assassination of Hole in the Day.* St. Paul: Borealis Books, 2011.

Warren, William W. "History of the Ojibways Based Upon Traditions and Oral Statements." In *Collections of the Minnesota Historical Society.* Vol. 5, *History of the Ojibway Nation.* 21–394. St. Paul: Minnesota Historical Society, 1895.

White, Bruce M. "The Regional Context of the Removal Order of 1850." In *Fish in the Lakes, Wild Rice, and Game in Abundance: Testimony on Behalf of Mille Lacs Ojibwe Hunting and Fishing Rights,* compiled by James M. McClurken, 141–328. East Lansing, MI: Michigan State University Press, 2000.

JOURNALS

Clifton, James A. "Wisconsin Death March: Explaining the Extremes in Old Northwest Indian Removal." *Transactions of the Wisconsin Academy of Sciences, Arts, and Letters* 75 (1987): 1–39.

Danziger, Edmund J. "They Would Not Be Moved: The Chippewa Treaty of 1854." *Minnesota History* 43, no. 5 (Spring 1973): 175–185.

Gilman, Rhoda R. "Last Days of the Upper Mississippi Fur Trade." *Minnesota History* 42, no. 4 (Winter 1970): 123–140.

Paper, Jordan. "Clothed-in-Fur and Other Tales: An Introduction to an Ojibwa Worldview." *Studies in Religion/Sciences Religieuses* 13, no. 2 (1984): xviii—182.

Satz, Ronald N. and Carl N. Haywood, Ed. "Chippewa Treaty Rights of Wisconsin's Chippewa Indians in Historical Perspective." *Transactions of the Wisconsin Academy of Sciences, Arts, and Letters* 79, no. 1 (1991).

Treuer, Anton and David Treuer. "A Day in the Life of Ojibwe." *Minnesota History* 56, no. 4 (Winter 1998): 172–174.

White, Bruce M. "The Power of Whiteness, or the Life and Times of Joseph Rolette Jr." *Minnesota History* 56, no. 4 (Winter 1998): 178–179.

ONLINE RESOURCES

"An Ethnographic Study of Indigenous Contributions to the City of Duluth." *Turnstone Historical Research.* Published July 2015. http://www.duluthmn .gov/media/461501/Duluth-Ethnographic-Study-Final-July-2015.pdf.

Armstrong, Travis. *Chief Buffalo & Benjamin Armstrong* (Blog). http://www.chief buffalo.com/buffalo/Home_Page.html.

Breitenfeldt, Sara. *Leonard Wheeler and the Ojibwa.* http://www.academia.edu/ 254416/Leonard_Wheeler_and_the_Ojibawa.

Busch, Jane C. "People and Places: A Human History of the Apostle Islands: Historic Resource Study of Apostle Islands National Lake Shore." *National Park Service.* 2008. https://www.nps.gov/apis/learn/historyculture/upload/ historic%20resource%20study.pdf.

Chequamegon History (blog). http://www.chequamegonhistory.wordpress.com.

"Miigwech (Thank You) Prayer." *Ojibwe.net.* Accessed June 11, 2017. http://ojibwe .net/projects/prayers-teachings/miigwech-thank-you-prayer/.

Minnesota Humanities Center. "The Four Seasons of the Ojibwe." Accessed May 11, 2017. http://www.earthscope.org/assets/uploads/misc/Seven.The_Four_ Seasons.pdf.

"Naabaagoondiwin (Traditional Adoption)." *Indigenous—Coolest People on the Planet* (blog), Published November 19, 2015. https://coolest indigenous.wordpress.com/2015/11/19/naabaagoondiwin-traditional- adoption/ https://coolestindigenous.wordpress.com/2015/11/19/ naabaagoondiwin-traditional-adoption/.

O'Brien, Michele. "Ojibwe Teachings: 7 Grandfather Teachings." *Anishnaabeg Bimaadiziwin: An Ojibwe Peoples Resource.* Accessed August 15, 2017. https:// walkinginhermoccasins.org/wp-content/uploads/2018/02/Ojibwe-Teachings

-The-7-Grandfathers-Anishnaabeg-BimaadiziwinAn-Ojibwe-Peoples-Resource.pdf.

"Small Pox Among the St. Croix Chippewa." *River Road Ramblings* (blog), Published August 28, 2012. http://riverroadrambler.blogspot.com/2012/08/small-pox-among-chippewas.html.

"Traditional Ojibwe Adoption." *DeBahJiMon: A Publication of the Leech Lake Band of Ojibwe.* 12, no. 1 (July 2007). http://www.llojibwe.org/news/deb2007/debJuly07_web.pdf.

Treuer, Anton. "Ojibwe Lifeways." *Minnesota Department of Natural Resources.* Accessed May 11, 2017. http://files.dnr.state.mn.us/mcvmagazine/young_naturalists/young-naturalists-article/ojibwe/ojibwe.pdf.

White Earth Land Recovery Project. "Ma'iingan (The Wolf) Our Brother." Published December 22, 2012. http://welrp.org/maiingan-the-wolf-our-brother.

Wisconsin Historical Society. "Ojibwe Winter Spearfishing Decoy." Published January 19, 2006. https://www.wisconsinhistory.org/Records/Article/CS2758.

Wisconsin Historical Society. "United States Bureau of Indian Affairs Documents." http://content.wisconsinhistory.org/cdm/ref/collection/tp/id/62186.

MANUSCRIPT COLLECTIONS

Minnesota Historical Society, St. Paul

Letters Received by the Office of Indian Affairs, 1824–1880, M175
    Chippewa Agency, R149–168
    Chippewa Agency: Emigration, R168
    La Pointe Agency, R387–400
    Minnesota Superintendency, R428
    Sandy Lake Agency, R767
    Mackinac Agency, R402–415

Letters Sent, 1824–1882, M298
    U.S. Office of Indian Affairs, R49

Records of the Minnesota Superintendency of Indian Affairs, 1849–1856, M215

Acknowledgments

First and foremost, I'd like to thank John Haymond for his patience and wisdom. John could have easily overlooked me in pursuit of his many personal endeavors, but he has taken the time and energy to provide me with much needed feedback and support. For that I am indelibly grateful. I'd like to thank Cass Dalglish for her very kind, benevolent guidance and mentorship. Without her this would be another first-person narrative. Thanks to Boyd Koehler for his very careful and capable proofreading. He appropriately corrected more than I am willing to admit. Whatever errors remain are my own. Thank you to Ryan Scheife of Mayfly Design for his creative, prompt, professional work on the cover and interior design. Thank you to Rachel Anderson of RMA Publicity for her more than adequate representation. If I were left to publicize this work on my own, the book might never find a single reader. Finally, thank you to my father, Mark Mustful, for answering all my questions with compassion and patience.

CPSIA information can be obtained
at www.ICGtesting.com
Printed in the USA
LVHW032036081019
633405LV00003B/737/P